TOUCH'S USUAL

A Novel

CURTIS R. TRIMBLE

Archway Publishing books may be ordered through booksellers or by contacting:

Archway Publishing
1663 Liberty Drive
Bloomington, IN 47403
www.archwaypublishing.com
844-669-3957

ISBN: 978-1-6657-2163-9 (sc)
ISBN: 978-1-6657-2161-5 (hc)
ISBN: 978-1-6657-2162-2 (e)

Library of Congress Control Number: 2022906605

Print information available on the last page.

Archway Publishing rev. date: 04/27/2022

CHAPTER 1

Tanner "Touch" Thomas forked the last of his scrambled eggs, with bacon and cheese added, into his mouth and followed it up with a final sip of coffee. Breakfast and lunch daily at the Tiger's Den Café were routine for Touch since he'd returned several years ago to the town in which he had grown up: Cooper, Kentucky.

Famous, at least in his own mind, for the intensity of his morning workouts, Touch abided by nutritionists' theories on post-workout protein intake but remained old-school in how he went about consuming that protein. No shakes or bars—Touch opted for actual food. This morning's workout—Mondays, Wednesday, and Fridays were lift days, whereas Tuesdays, Thursdays, and Saturdays were cardio days, just like in high school and college—proved heavy on lifts targeting the quads, lats, and biceps. Touch was not quite as fit as in his college days, with youth decidedly in the rearview mirror and middle age passing quickly, but he still struck an imposing figure. A shade over six feet tall and just under two hundred pounds, just as Jimmy Dean sang about "Big Bad John" in another era, Touch was "kinda broad at the shoulder and narrow at the hip." The additional ten or twelve pounds Touch had added over the past twenty-plus years since college built out his biceps, quads, and glutes.

Touch Thomas followed up a storied high school athletic career— Mr. Football and State Most Valuable Wrestler, with an equally successful college career playing quarterback for the US Military Academy. Subsequent to graduating from West Point, Touch earned a Purple Heart and several other medals for meritorious service while in the army. Despite progressing toward middle age, veins ran like rivers through his arms, especially after a Monday work, making his uniform shirts tight through the arms and shoulders. Touch Thomas's ass, just like in high school, remained a marvel and a subject of admiration for many of the females in Cooper. As the sheriff of Walter County, Touch elicited side-glances as he walked to and from his office downtown, as well as occasional comments among the women working the downtown shops and counters about "bouncing quarters off his ass." Paying homage to leg day for three decades, Touch's legs carried the man through his three-mile morning runs with ease. The man still blew through miles at a seven-minute pace in spite of being built more like a sprinter—thick—than a marathoner.

"You good to go this morning, Touch, or you want me to fill up that coffee cup?" Reva, who ran the Tiger's Den, asked. Touch's usual breakfast and lunch spot was across the street and three doors down from the county courthouse and the sheriff's office.

"All good for this morning, Reva, thanks," Touch answered. "Time to get out and about and see what this day holds. Hopefully, it'll be a slow one. I need to work through the mountain of paperwork that somehow seems to magically grow without anyone wanting it to." Touch smiled slightly to himself as Reva walked away, the bassline of AC/DC's "Back in Black" running through his head. That song had defined the ends of his Monday workouts for as long as he had had workout playlists. While cassette tapes gave way to CDs, which faded into streaming services, Touch Thomas grasped onto a few things from back in the day and added new things as they motivated him. He'd added Live's "I Alone" in the early 1990s, "Take California" by the Propellerheads about 2000, Macklemore and Ryan Lewis's "Thrift Shop" in 2012, and Chance the Rapper's

"No Problem" a few years ago. More recently, he hadn't been able to resist adding Lizzo to his list. His buddy, Chris Hauser, Cooper's chief of police, had made fun of the sheriff adding Lizzo to a workout playlist for a month—until Hauser found himself singing along with it on his own one day.

Regaining the moment, Touch reflected on how long he'd known Reva. She had inherited the Tiger's Den from her father some twenty-eight years ago at the tender age of eighteen, after her father, Ronnie, had keeled over behind the counter from a heart attack at fifty. Ronnie had likely brought on his too-soon demise by consuming an overabundance of the plates of scrambled eggs, bacon, onions, and cheese that Touch also favored, but without the exercise. The café's name reflected the family's long-standing support for the local high school athletics teams' mascot, a blue and yellow tiger named Teddy. Ronnie and his father, from whom Ronnie had inherited the café as well, had engaged in a minor family squabble concerning the café's name. Prior to the "city" school, the "country" school, and the "Black" school all coming together as one in 1963, the town had known the Dennis family's diner as the Black Patch Café, a nod to the effect the dark tobacco grown in the region had on the local landscape. Reva's grandfather named the small lunch counter he'd opened in 1924 after the area's primary cash crop. Since expanded to a twelve-table floor with the same sized lunch counter, the Tiger's Den, with almost one hundred years of photos on its walls documenting the evolution of Cooper and its citizens, served breakfast and lunch from six in the morning until two in the afternoon.

Touch Thomas, a local legend for more than a few reasons, saw several of his younger selves staring back at him from those photos as he put his hat on his head and stepped to the Tiger's Den door. A twelve-year-old Tanner Thomas—a few years before his nickname found him in high school—stared back at him from a state championship Little League team photo. Tanner had been the star pitcher as well as the number three hitter, but with a pretty solid supporting cast. His dad, that team's coach, grinned at him as well. A few columns over and a couple of rows higher, a seventeen-year-old Touch beamed back at his forty-eight-year old self as the all-state quarterback of the Kentucky 2A State Championship football team for 1990. A few frames away, two other photos showed off what might be Touch's most impressive athletic achievements—for high school, at least—one of him from that same year's 1990 basketball team, which bowed out of competition in the regional final, and another of him with his hand raised as the 189-pound Kentucky State Wrestling Champion for 1991. No one could recollect an athlete even trying to play basketball and wrestle, sports played concurrently in the same season, at the same time, let alone doing both at more or less all-state levels. Touch had always had a lot of energy, though.

"I'll catch you later, Reva," Touch said as he stepped to the door. AC/DC's bass line had given way to Lizzo's "Good as Hell" with the hook ringing in his ears and confirming how the Walter County sheriff felt as he walked to his office.

"Good to see you again, Touch. No matter how busy it gets in here, you always calm me down. You have a good rest of your day," Reva shot back, the cowbell hanging above the Tiger's Den door to signal customers' comings and goings clanging as Touch exited the café.

From the Tiger's Den, Touch took a left, surveyed the light morning traffic around the courthouse square, and commenced walking to his office on the first floor of the Walter County Courthouse. About half the Walter County population of 15,400 lived in town in Cooper, and the other half inhabited the relatively sparsely populated 320 square miles that made up the county. He had spent more than a few years away from Cooper and Walter County, but Touch knew almost every nook, cranny, and ne'er-do-well in Cooper and the county. A couple of years after returning to Cooper, Touch had run for Walter County sheriff, winning by a record-setting margin. It didn't hurt that until ten years prior, his father, Dean Thomas, had been the county's longest-serving sheriff on record, never losing an election and running unopposed more often than not. The interim sheriff, Herk Schaeffer, had not fared nearly as well as Dean over his long and illustrious career, or as Touch in his much shorter tenure on the job.

"Mornin', Touch," Millie Davis, who ran the dry cleaner's on the southwest side of the square, greeted Touch as he ambled on the sidewalk past her, still smiling as Lizzo's lyrics ran through his mind. Among the few Black business owners in Cooper, Touch's family and the Davises shared a long family history. Millie's dad, Carl, had stopped years ago to help Dean change a flat tire. The two men had struck up a friendship that had lasted through the final decades of their lives, frequently passing each other on the street just as Millie and Touch had. When one of Millie's daughters, Carly, had endured some trouble with an abusive boyfriend several years ago, Touch had dislocated the man's elbow as he'd educated him on the necessity of treating a woman with respect.

"Hi, Millie! Looks like it's going to be another beautiful day if the heat doesn't rile up another thunderstorm. I appreciate you dropping those uniform shirts off at the office yesterday." As Touch moved closer to his office, Lizzo gave way to U2's "Beautiful Day." Unfortunately, that would be the last beautiful thing for the day.

"Sure thing, Touch. We'll see you around," Millie replied as she dawdled, waiting for Touch to turn and walk away. A grin spread across her face.

Touch walked to his office recollecting his confrontation with Carly Davis's boyfriend, Ben Boudreaux, years ago. With a video recorder–like recall of game situations and physical confrontations, Touch could still see himself in his mind's eye side-stepping Ben's punch, grabbing his wrist as it went by, and rotating it backward while punching Boudreaux's elbow with the open-handed heel of his hand. The feel of the humerus bone sliding out of its seat at the elbow sent a minor shudder up his spine. Some situations called for physical reactions, but the outcome of violence frequently left Touch nauseous. It was just one of those things.

Another forty paces, and Touch was to the door of the west side of the courthouse, just as Bono's fourth "Beautiful Day" rolled through his mind. He handled the pull as he'd done at least a thousand times before, swinging the door to the right just enough to ease through it without changing his gait but not so much as to clang it off its stop. Four more steps, and Touch was outside his office, admiring his name above the "Walter County Sheriff" title painted in script on the frosted glass. Touch had previously held higher ranking positions in much larger agencies and organizations before returning to Cooper, but he didn't take any more pride or command any less respect in those spots, at least for himself, than he did from being sheriff of Walter County.

After turning the doorknob, which already was unlocked by the department manager, Bonnie Bragg, Touch let himself in to the darkly paneled entryway. Ever a fan of whatever was on the local country station, WBVR, with its catchy "Slap of the Beaver Tail" tagline, Bonnie's radio played at low volume the late, great Keith Whitley's "I'm No Stranger to the Rain," which seemed out of place given the day's sunniness.

Bonnie said, "Whitley's voice was pure honey. Even his suicide can't ruin that for me."

Touch noted the contrast between the "Beautiful Day" running through his mind and Whitley's "No Stranger to the Rain" that Bonnie played. An omen, he thought, and unlikely to be a good one.

As he walked toward the knee-level swinging gate that separated the waiting area from the sheriff's department offices, Touch noticed the dark paneling and estimated that the office hadn't been remodeled in at least thirty years. He couldn't exactly remember whether it was before or after his last year of high school that his father agreed to allow the office to be "updated." Picturing the before and after states of the office in his mind, he knew why his father had been reluctant to agree to spending the money to redo the office: nothing much changed with it. The sole, noticeable impact that frustrated his father and led Dean Thomas to label the effort "a waste of taxpayer money" was that the office simply looked cleaner. The dark wood paneling, matching trim, and *Andy Griffith Show–*looking fence and gate between the lobby and desks remained a dark-stained hue while the walls were "updated" to a cream color as compared to the prior dingy white, darkened by the past era's preference for cigarette smoking. Nonetheless, Touch felt as at home in the sheriff's office as he had when he was an eight-year-old boy coming to visit his dad on a sultry summer day.

"Hey, Bonnie! Anything of note happening?" Touch asked, knowing that if it had, he would have known long ago because his Apple iPhone would have relayed the pertinent details.

Bonnie hummed the last bar of "I'm No Stranger" and answered, "No, Touch. Seems like everyone wore themselves out making trouble over at the lakes this weekend and got home without any energy left to make nuisances of themselves. No one even wrote a speeding ticket, a reckless driving, or a DWI. Strange."

The town of Cooper drew a few tourism dollars, and some trouble and related fines and court appearance fees, as a function of its location about ten miles from the northern edge of one of the largest human-made lakes in the world: Lake Barkley. Over any given weekend from March through October, as many as five thousand additional vehicles, mostly pickup trucks pulling boats, drove through Cooper on the way to Lake Barkley. Fortunately, very few visitors caused trouble Friday nights or Saturday mornings on their way to the lake. Leaving the lake Sunday afternoons and evenings, however, frequently proved to be a different story because alcohol-fueled auto mishaps clogged highways, or returning-home blues distracted drivers and resulted in speeding tickets and fender benders.

"Interesting: maybe folks have taken a turn for the better. What's the cell situation? Still have Mr. Jones in three, Mr. Benitez in five, and Ms. Turner on the other side in two?" Touch asked Bonnie. Long ago, the jail delineated male cells with odd numbers and female cells with even numbers. Jake Jones had yet to convince his uncle to bail him out on yet another low-level meth possession charge. Henrique "Hank" Benitez didn't know anyone who either could or would bail him out on another domestic violence charge. Layla Turner exhibited an almost addictive desire to pepper the entire western part of the state with bad checks. Touch knew Jones, Benitez, and Turner relatively well because each was a repeat offender. He considered none of them a significant threat to the quiet with which his day started. The lack of overnight disturbances proved noteworthy, however. "Bonnie, when's the last spring, summer, or fall weekend you can remember that ended without having a new jail resident?"

"Well, Touch, funny you should ask, because I had the same thought, went to the computer, and looked it up," answered Bonnie. "It's been a little over three years since we went a peak lake season weekend without a new customer. It was that peculiar September a few years ago, before you started and when that nitwit was interim sheriff, when half the state flooded. That same weekend, UK had that surprisingly good football team with an early season game at USC; I think it ended up being seventh ranked team at the eleventh ranked, or some such matchup that folks stayed home to watch. Wildcats laid a major egg, though, and managed to get its preseason all-conference quarterback's leg broken before halftime."

Touch recollected, "Now that you mention it, I remember that weekend. I actually stayed home too on account of the flooding and the football. Darn shame that game didn't turn out any better. This year's team might be that good, though, because it's the recruiting class what's-his-face, the coach they fired last year, managed to pull in on the heels of that team's anticipated success three years ago. I guess now would be a good time to catch up on some paperwork before I head out and survey that road construction site east of town and check in on Benitez's girlfriend, Mandy Herman. Anything else come immediately to mind, Bonnie, demanding my attention?"

"Just that massive pile of paperwork you've neglected to address over the past couple of weeks, Touch. If I were you, I'd keep my powder dry, so to speak, process that paperwork, and wait for whatever mess materializes. You know as well as I do that Cooper won't stay this quiet much longer. Plus, I think that heat will be joined with a lot more humidity later this afternoon. You know that makes some of us crazy."

"Paperwork it is, then."

Touch turned to enter his office as Keith Whitley's voice gave way to another "Slap of the Beaver Tail," and WBVR followed up "I'm No Stranger to the Rain" with a slightly newer, more upbeat song, "Boot Scootin' Boogie" by the world's all-time best-selling duo, Brooks and Dunn. Touch loved that song, but not as much as he loved Brooks and Dunn's "Brand New Man," which came off the same 1991 album.

CHAPTER 2

No sooner had Touch rounded his desk, boot-scootin' on his way to sit down, than his hip caught the edge of the top file of his paperwork pile, knocking half of the eight-inch stack onto the floor. Files and pages fanned out and scattered in an arc spanning a three-foot area between his desk and his filing cabinet.

"Son of a ..." uttered Touch, just loud enough for Bonnie to hear. She smirked: the sheriff's big ass frequently knocked stuff off his desk as he cut corners too closely.

Bonnie snickered and joshed, "Let me guess: your Cooper ode to the Leaning Tower of Paperwork Pisa tumbled to the floor as you and your honkey-tonk badonk-a-donk boot scooted around your desk? I told you last week that you'd better jump on that paperwork, or at least make that one gargantuan pile into two smaller piles. But nooo ... the great Touch Thomas can't be bothered to listen to little ol' Bonnie. You know that processing your paperwork offers an awesome recovery from all that exercising and running around you do that you should let your deputies do for you, right?"

"Thank you, Bonnie, goddess of paperwork and all things recovery," Touch snidely replied from his desk chair.

Although Bonnie had worked for the sheriff's department almost the entirety of the twenty years since she had left high school, she had managed to brush up against enough demons in her thirty-eight years to almost exchange all of her addictions for an addiction to recovery and self-help books, programs, therapists, and as of late podcasts. Bonnie had worked for Dean Thomas the final few years of his time as sheriff. Dean's death had sent Bonnie to no less than four recovery programs over the ensuing few years. Touch's arrival back in Cooper likely saved her from at least a passive suicide, if such a thing could be said to exist, and his winning the sheriff's election translated into a rebirth of sorts for Bonnie, even though at the time she still was more than a few years away from middle-aged. Always quick-witted, no one in Cooper or Walter County seemingly ever thought of Bonnie as attractive or not. She seemed to be one of those people that simply was, in that she never seemed to get to close to anyone, not even her parents or siblings, but always seemed on the edge of where the action was. Loyal to those that understood her, Bonnie taskmastered her time in the sheriff's office and then retired to her little house on the outskirts of town to fight her demons with the help of whatever aids she'd chosen at that point in time.

Touch knelt to scoop up the fallen files and papers, noticing notes from a cold case dating to 1977 peeking out of a folder. Handwritten on paper that yellowed through the years, his father's pen strokes still stuck out to him despite the fact that Touch hadn't seen anything written by his father in probably twenty years. He had been a cub deputy sheriff at the time, so the details of the 1977 murder of David Barnett had visited Dean's thoughts throughout his time in the Walter County Sheriff's Office. Only seventeen at the time of his death, Barnett was the only child of Dean's mentor and one of the most prominent attorneys in West Kentucky over the past forty years, Andrew Barnett. No motive ever surfaced for David's murder, and the combination of the sheriff's office and Kentucky State Police collected only a single piece of physical evidence, the slug that had killed him, and a freehand reconstruction of the murder scene. Why a harmless young man would be shot with a hunting rifle in June remained a mystery.

Touch picked up the associated papers from David Barnett's murder file and set it in his desk chair. He'd learned over the years to appease himself whenever possible and then go on about his less preoccupying tasks for the day. Otherwise, Touch's focus suffered until he could revisit whatever it was that churned in the back of his subconscious. The only things that ever seemed to allow him unfettered peace of mind were sports, exercise, and physical labor. All other times, Touch stewed on something: cold case details, upcoming trial proceedings, needed home improvement projects, yardwork, missed pass completion opportunities of the 1991 football season ... the list went on and on.

Touch picked up the scattered papers from his office floor, found their proper folders, and placed them in a second, shorter pile just as Bonnie had originally suggested. While staring at the two piles of paperwork, Touch alternately pondered on possible reasons for last weekend's dearth of trouble and the key details of David Barnett's case file. Obviously, no links existed between the two phenomena; over fifty years separated them. Nonetheless, Touch couldn't help himself from entertaining the concept of fate intervening to offer him the free time to sit at his desk, process his paperwork, and rekindle details of Barnett's case.

More immediately pressing, however, was a refresh of details from Henrique Benitez's domestic violence assault. The twentysomething son of one of the first Latin families to settle in Walter County in the mid-1990s, "Hank" Benitez had never been a "good" guy. The Benitezes followed the increase in meat-processing jobs in and around Walter County brought on by the move to industrial-scale farming in West Kentucky. The combination of relatively cheap land, aged farmers with no kids who wanted to stay in Walter County, and burgeoning worldwide demand for proteins made Cooper and Walter County among the most attractive locations for industrial-scale chicken and hog producers in the country. Hank's parents worked the system hard, coming up through the ranks of barn tenders to meat processors to supervisors until they'd socked enough money away to open a restaurant. Following a typical American dream playbook, Hank's parents did well as first-movers in satisfying the Thursday through Saturday night-out desires of the Latins that followed them to the area as well as the shifting tastes of the rest of the Cooper population. They'd done too well for Hank, though, and the kid turned out entitled and spoiled. Meth eventually found Hank, and while he and the system spent a few years getting it out of him, Hank had not yet figured out how to manage the disappointment that defined his existence and took his frustrations out on his longtime, live-in girlfriend, Mandy Herman. His abuse, usually applied with the back of his hand, recently gave way to Mandy enduring a closed fist. The abuse finally proved more than she was willing to bear. She reported it and had Hank jailed for it. Touch had a feeling that Hank was going away for a while this time.

Touch spent twelve minutes jotting notes on Benitez; twenty-seven minutes signing off on various requisition orders, invoices, and purchase orders for new and replacement equipment; and another thirty-five minutes documenting supporting details for an upcoming budget increase request from the Walter County Board of Commissioners to be presented at their upcoming meeting Thursday evening. That one hour and fourteen minutes resulted in his paperwork stack declining four inches in height, and Touch deciding to leave the other four inches for another time.

Before he left his office to check on Mandy Herman, Touch revisited David Barnett's file for a little more than fifteen minutes. The Barnett and Thomas families shared extensive history. Andrew Barnett, David's father and a prominent lawyer in the area, had befriended Dean Thomas, Touch's father, early in his career. The Barnett homicide marked the first homicide Dean Thomas had worked as a sheriff's deputy. Impressed with the young man's intelligence, compassion, and attention to detail on his son's case,

Andrew Barnett mentored the younger man early in his career. Touch was too young at the time to remember David or any details surrounding his death, but he knew the elder Barnett as his dad's best friend.

Touch read the coroner's report, noting their descriptions of the entry and exit wounds, conclusion on bullet trajectory, analysis of the slug (which appeared to be a .243), and the lack of any other meaningful physical characteristics, maladies, or imperfections. Dean Thomas's notes relayed that David Barnett had suffered an aversion to society that, as it read to Touch, likely would have placed him on the autism spectrum today, but that probably went undiagnosed and undiscussed in Cooper and Walter County in the era in which David grew up. From the back of the folder, Touch removed a taped-together and folded hand-drawn map of the immediate area, noting the relationships of where Dean found Barnett's body in the front yard of the house at which he'd been working, the gravel road that ran more or less east to west one hundred yards from the scene, and the wooded areas several hundred yards away to the east and to the west from where David died. Across the highway open pasture ran for about a quarter of a mile to another wooded area. The forested area behind the house likely was of little consequence given how close Dean and the state police had found Barnett in relation to the house, and the relative flatness of the contours that characterized the area around the house. Taking a moment to ruminate on these details, Touch also noted that David died only about ten minutes from Mandy and Hank's mobile home. Again, he thought, fate might be intervening in David Barnett's cold case.

"Bonnie, I'm heading out to Mandy Herman's trailer to check on her, get a formal statement to try and put Hank away for a while and get him some shrink help, and then swing by the site of our most haunting cold case," Touch hollered from his office. As he rounded his desk, he took a moment to order the now four-inch stack of paperwork and put a Lucite trophy paperweight on it. Touch also noted that he had failed to turn on his new, fancy laptop, which he'd last week connected to an also new and fancy monitor with a screen about twice the size of the Thomas family's first color TV set purchased by Dean about fifty years ago.

Touch exited his office into the reception and processing area of the Walter County Sheriff's Office. Bonnie asked for what seemed like the thousandth time, "Touch, you think we'll ever get to the bottom of David Barnett's murder? I mean, a new piece of physical evidence hasn't materialized in at least thirty years. More than half of the people who knew David have passed away, including several folks who would have been his age. About the only direct links left to the case are Charlie Sprague, who wasn't even home at the time of the shooting; David's father, who's about as old as Methuselah now; and, well, that's about it, right? Touch, don't you think it might be time to bury that folder with David Barnett and move on to another, more recent cold case that might offer a better chance of being solved? Is the Kentucky State Police investigator even alive, or at least not completely senile, at this point?"

Touch had asked himself the same question almost a thousand times. "Bonnie, you know the particulars in that case as well as I do, maybe better. Two things never change, though—the link to my father and the resulting lack of closure for me, him, and Mr. Barnett, who remains plenty sharp, old as Methuselah or not. You know my affinity for signs and hunches, and when I knocked the Barnett murder file in the floor earlier this morning, I got that tingly feeling like I get when a sign appears. It'll probably pass, leading to nothing, but then again, the murder scene just happens to be on the way to Mandy Herman's trailer—another sign, in my book. I promise I won't spend too much time on it. I'm already hungry and plan to be back at the Tiger's Den for lunch before Reva runs out of the special."

After exiting the courthouse, Touch turned toward the Tiger's Den and his reserved parking space in front of the courthouse building. Some years ago, Walter County had upgraded the sheriff's department from the long-tenured Crown Victorias that the vast majority of law enforcement offices nationwide drove to Chevy Tahoes. Touch spent a ton of time in both and remained a bigger fan of the Tahoe's elevated field of vision. He couldn't generate the same affinity for the beige-and-brown color scheme that, for whatever reason, seemed to define sheriffs' cars across the country. He would have preferred a royal blue and goldenrod motif like that of the state police; maybe creating some local-state line of delineation defined the reason for the sheriffs' unbecoming colors. Touch shrugged his shoulders at the thought, unpocketed his keys, and clicked the door lock open. After removing his hat, he slid agilely into the driver's seat, fired the ignition, shifted the Tahoe's transmission into drive, checked for oncoming traffic, and backed out of his spot to head for Mandy Herman's mobile home trailer in the northwest quadrant of Walter County. Without even thinking about it, Touch began to sing along to Bruce Hornsby and the Range's "Mandolin Rain" as it played on the local radio station, WPKY. It was a little mellow for Touch, who preferred music with a little more thump. The sadness of Hornsby's lyrics, like Keith Whitley's earlier in his office, foreshadowed the darkness that would plague much of the rest of Touch's day.

CHAPTER 3

Touch Thomas traced the same road out of Cooper that he'd traveled several thousand times over the thirty-plus years he'd had a driver's license. Years ago, when he had been in high school, Cooper had had about a half dozen stop lights, with principals of the road department opting for the less daunting stop sign. However, the proliferation of lake-drive leisure traffic over the years and the periodic pursuits of shortcuts through the town when an inevitable wreck on the main highway led to lengthy backups resulted in a doubling of traffic lights in the small city.

Touch cleared two stoplights and the balance of the town inside of seven minutes, leaving about another eight or ten minutes until he reached Mandy Herman's trailer. As he left town and accelerated through the fifty-five miles-per-hour speed limit on State Highway 139, he noted the fields he passed looked healthy, green and well-watered by the recent rains. The handful of houses he passed offered a cross-section of life in Walter County: a shotgun-style near-shack, a McMansion, a well-kept 1950s ranch style, and a two-story farmhouse in need of a new coat of paint. Touch thought much of the dilapidated and cheap-looking manufactured housing, like that in which Mandy Herman resided, thankfully remained largely tucked out of sight in Cooper and Walter County, relegated to less convenient locations in the hills and hollers serviced by smaller, frequently unpaved, gravel roads.

In addition to reflecting on the state of the local crops and which houses had received and which still needed new paint, Touch thought about the last time he had come out to talk with Mandy—probably at least six months ago now—as well as the last time he had visited David Barnett's murder scene. Although his family farm was out this direction from town as well, Touch had not chosen to visit it in several months. He enjoyed the quiet and solitude of the land and the history surrounding its lone barn, but nothing much there required his attention. Touch had leased the cropland associated with the property to a high school buddy since he'd inherited it. As most in the area knew, the sheriff owned the land, so he never had concerns about theft or vandalism. His buddy kept him up on the state of the place with periodic phone calls.

Touch signaled and made a left-hand turn onto the gravel road that led to Mandy's trailer. After another two minutes, he made another left into the short driveway and traveled the last twenty-five yards to the mobile home. As Touch killed the engine, Bruce Springsteen sang on WPKY the last words of "Glory Days," one of his all-time favorites: "In the wink of a young girl's eye, glory days, glory days." Exiting the Tahoe, homely dog half-heartedly greeted Touch with a weak bark and a perfunctory sniffing. A short knock on the thin wooden door of the trailer led to a quick glance out one of its three small plexiglass windows from Mandy. A second later, Mandy unlocked the door, opened it, and greeted Touch with a black eye, busted lip, and weak, "Hey, Touch."

While looking at her battered face, Touch reflected on how long he had known Mandy and the Hermans. She was probably twelve or fifteen years younger than Touch, but the years with Hank proved to be tough on Mandy, and she looked at least as old as Touch. Mandy's dad had never been consistently at odds with the law and had been visited only a time or two over the years by Dean Thomas. Maybe a visit for a missing farm implement from an adjacent property or a follow-up on another investigation—Touch had heard pieces of stories from his father years ago before he had left town. Since his return, though, Touch had no reason to visit the Hermans' other than in response to the prior beatings and related stories about Mandy and Hank. Touch hoped this might be the last time he had to worry about that situation. He was wrong.

Once a modestly attractive young woman, Mandy had softened in the years since she had met Hank. She added weight in the manner that people who ate as much as they wanted when they wanted did. Disregard for any more exercise than that required to shuffle merchandise around or work the register of the dollar store she managed reinforced Mandy's softening appearance. The interior of her trailer, however, was as tidy as any place Touch had visited recently.

"Hi, Mandy. I'm sorry to be here. I sure wish you'd help me find a way to keep Hank away so we can greet each other under more pleasant circumstances. No person, especially a kind-hearted and hardworking woman like you, should have to put up with this shit. It's more or less obvious from your face and from Hank's condition in the jail this morning what happened. Will you make a formal statement on the situation and commit to pressing charges on Hank this time?" Touch pushed.

"Touch, I'm tired of Hank and more tired of getting beat on. Early on he was all right, but hard times made him a hard man. I'll tell you the truth, though: I'm scared to death. Hank got into some stuff when things got tight, and I don't think he'll be able to get out. I'm not in it. I don't like it. I'm afraid those people will catch me up in it with Hank in jail. I got no idea what Hank will do. I know he's freaking out, though, 'cause he hates the idea of going to prison. We both know he's not the sharpest knife in the drawer. He may think he can beat these guys if he can get you or the staties to give him a deal. They're always at least a step ahead of Hank, though. They already did a drive-by visit and got that dog riled up for no reason. Touch, I'm scared of Hank and of these new guys."

Touch stared up at the trailer's ceiling and took a moment to digest Mandy's thoughts, his history with Hank, the likely "guys" to which Mandy referred, and past dealings with those guys. He wrung his hands, and muscles tightened from his thumbs through his forearms, biceps, triceps, and shoulders. The built-up tension in his arms exited via flexed fingers as he rolled his neck, and Touch breathed deeply.

"Mandy, would these guys to whom you're referring be linked to the meth, pills and seemingly all things bad, that started flowing into the county several months ago?" Touch asked. "How in the hell did Hank get himself mixed up with this group? These aren't the low-level, weekend weed crews Hank goofed off with in high school. I don't know if they're straight-up Dixie Mafia or what, but I can assure you what I've read and heard is no different than that scum of the Earth. Good Lord."

"I think we're speaking about the same group of fellas, Touch. Hank was at least smart enough to never meet them here or, as far as I know, bring any of that mess here. I know he had to be caught up in it somehow, though. Random gobs of money started to show up when those guys did. Next to none of it ever stayed around here. While it's tough to say much good about Hank, it at least looks like he managed not to steal from them. I gotta think that if he did, I probably wouldn't still be here because my trailer would be the most likely hiding place. The earlier visit, though, I'm guessing was a message that Hank and I should keep our traps shut. What can I do, though? Hank'll probably have to tell you everything if he doesn't want to go to jail for wailing on me. I want him to go to jail for wailing on me, though. I'm tired of it. I guess those guys would rather he not have to tell you anything he knows about whatever it is they're doing in order to avoid going to jail, right? So that probably means they'll eventually be after me to not press charges against Hank for walloping me. None of this looks any good for me, does it? Shit."

For the second time in five minutes, Touch stared at the ceiling of Mandy's mobile home, wrung his hands, felt his muscles tense, breathed deeply, and rolled his neck. He told Mandy, "I know it's not your fault. I've known you all your life, and you've never been anything by kind, thoughtful, and unlucky. This might be the unluckiest you've ever been, though. Hank, although he's not even here, has managed to ruin what started out as a wonderful, low-work day. If he wasn't in line for the ass-kicking of his life already, I'd give it to him just out of principle. How he could be so damned dumb, selfish, and shortsighted is beyond me. He could have simply taken over his parents' restaurant or even opened another location in Terryville and done just fine. No, like he's always done, he tries to take the easy way out. Mandy, for you to avoid utter disaster, I recommend that you slap me right now so I can lock you up for assaulting an officer. It'll keep you safe while I try to speak with the US Attorney's office in Paducah and get some information and guidance on which direction this thing could go. One second, though; throw your things together for a couple nights, then swat me. You got five minutes. You can call the rest of your family on the way and let them know to be on the lookout for any of those warning drive-bys and the like. I don't know this group of drug runners very well—yet."

Before she shuffled off to put together an overnight bag, Mandy paused and asked Touch, "You really think they could try and scare my family?"

"Again, Mandy, I don't know these guys, and I'd guess they don't know me either. Typically, though, there's not a lot of feeling out time when jail becomes involved. Obviously, if they linked up with Hank, these guys aren't the brightest bulbs in the socket, or they would have moved along to one of Walter County's shrewder and better skilled ne'er-do-wells, right?"

Mandy bustled past Touch, grabbed a plastic dog food bowl, filled it with food, shouldered her overnight bag, and headed out the door. Touch rose from Mandy's aged couch, glanced around the trailer, and followed her out the door. After setting down the dogfood bowl, Mandy turned toward the trailer's stairs and gently whacked Touch across his face with a force more like that used to swat a mosquito than to inflict pain.

"Geez, Mandy, I give you a free shot, and that's the best you can do?" teased Touch.

"Touch, I know Hank and I put you in a dangerous position. I appreciate you doing this for me. I only hope it works," Mandy said as she walked toward Touch's Tahoe.

Touch let Mandy ride in the front. Allowing a "prisoner" to ride in the passenger seat violated sheriff's department policies, but Touch also wrote those policies and figured he could interpret them as he saw fit.

After firing the ignition, the Tahoe's radio, most of the time tuned to WPKY (the twenty-four-hour news station out of Nashville) or WBVR, squawked. Touch turned down the volume and spoke quickly to Bonnie on the short-wave. When he turned the volume back up on the radio, it played an ad for the local Sonic drive-in before the opening chords and drumbeat of AC/DC's "Dirty Deeds Done Dirt Cheap" filled the air. While a certain mismatch for the somber prevailing mood about Mandy's current situation, the lyrics offered a little "bargainer's hope" that if a job needed doing, someone, somewhere, would get it done—for a price.

"Mandy, it may not be the smartest thing, but I'm going to make a side trip on the way back to town. Something's been on my mind most of the morning, and if I don't make this stop, I may not get it off my mind in spite of you and Hank massively complicating my once peaceful morning."

After putting the Tahoe in reverse and executing a three-point turn in Mandy's parking area, Touch reversed the path down the gravel road he had taken to get to Mandy's trailer. Once he reached the blacktop, he took a right rather than the left that would have taken him back to town.

Sensing Mandy's tension, Touch asked, "You ever hear of a murder that happened forty-some years ago over at Sprague's farm? I know now may not be the most comfortable time for you to discuss old murders with me, but hearing the backstory might help get your mind off your current situation. My father never solved the case, and as a result, it's now plagued my family for over forty years. The young man murdered was the old lawyer Mr. Barnett's son. He was only seventeen years old when he was shot. No one really talked about it then—David Barnett was autistic, I think—but it was my understanding he could work by himself really well. David simply couldn't be around people other than his mom and dad. Asocial is probably how folks refer to it now.

"To hear my father tell it, David was a whiz with all things mechanical: he could take apart anything and put it back together from rote memory. My father said it was like David Barnett saw things when they were disassembled, as though all the parts were labeled with the instructions on where and how they fit back into the whole, but nothing was ever written anywhere. Mr. Barnett and my dad used to try to trick him when he was putting a mower or a kitchen appliance back together by snatching one of the bolts or screws. David always knew which one of the parts he was missing, though. He was mowing Sprague's yard and was shot dead; the John Deere riding lawn mower he was on kept mowing right into the side of Charlie Sprague's house, and it appeared the motor kept running until it ran out of gas.

"I keep a cold case file or two on my desk just in case something new or unthought of shakes loose. When I knocked over the big stack of files on my desk earlier this morning, David Barnett's fell on top. Taking it as a sign, I decided it might be a good time to revisit the scene. I usually check it out a time or two a year, but I haven't been out to Charlie Sprague's in months. He's not getting any younger, and with him likely goes the final direct link to David Barnett other than his father, who's also no spring chicken. It'd be a weight off my soul if I could somehow solve this case, just like putting this Hank mess behind you probably would lift a huge burden for you."

Touch drove a few miles, retracing a route he'd traveled many times, and took a left onto a poorly kept gravel road that was washed out by rains weeks ago. Touch's Tahoe creaked and moaned while bumping over the pothole-riddled peaks and valleys of the graveled road. A few minutes later, Touch took another left into Sprague's farmstead and drove a hundred yards toward a 1950s-era, ranch-style red brick house with a tidy red barn another hundred yards behind it. He stopped, stepped out of the Tahoe, and took a 360-degree survey of the surrounding area. Then he cut the engine, and the radio's broadcast cut out right in the middle of Wilson Pickett's "Call My Name, I'll Be There." Mandy shrugged her shoulders and exited the Tahoe opposite Touch.

CHAPTER 4

David Barnett loved to mow grass. The mower created immaculate lines delineating cut grass from uncut grass. Up, right-hand turn, another perfect row mowed at a ninety-degree angle to the prior row, right-hand turn back toward his starting point, also in a perfect line, a third right-hand turn and another perfectly mowed row, and one last, squared right-hand turn brought David back alongside his first swath of perfectly mowed grass on his still new and shiny 1976 John Deere 100 Lawn Tractor. Though he didn't know why, the adjacent green and yellow colors of John Deere always agreed with David far more so than the red and gray of Massey Ferguson, Ford's blue and white, or the whatever-and-white color scheme that Sears offered for its various riding lawn mower models.

Details mattered to David Barnett. Order mattered to David Barnett.

It was always David, never Dave, Dave-O, Davey, or any other diminutive. David always politely corrected people who shortened or augmented his name, but only once. Anything other than David more than once, and he simply walked away.

Everything in David's life had a place or was discarded. Items found out of place were quickly relocated to where they belonged. Otherwise, David remained preoccupied at best, or depending on an unknown variable, physically aggressive at worst. As a result, the mechanical world generally appealed to David. Nuts magically seemed to find matching bolts in young David's hands, and an older David exhibited a preternatural ability to take things apart with an apparent encyclopedic memory of how to perfectly put them back together again.

He was a good-looking boy who was growing into a handsome man, but social interaction nevertheless proved awkward for David Barnett. He failed to understand the value of small talk and thus chose not to engage in it if at all possible.

"Hey, David, how's it going?" or a similar greeting from a friend of the family or a neighbor would leave a younger David dumbfounded as he puzzled with what the "it" to which the person referred might be, as well as the direction in which "it" could be going. In the generally kinder and gentler era of the early 1970s in which David spent his adolescent and teenage years, classmates might pleasantly tease David with such otherwise inert or thoughtless phrases and pleasantries just to see the puzzled look on his face or hear the all-too-logical response from David: "How's what going where?" To the question "How are you today, David?" a young David may have replied all too honestly, "I'm sad I ate an apple for breakfast," or, "I'm happy my dog licked my face when we got home from church." As David got older, he shied away from speaking and instead mimicked the pleasant wave so often used by his father as a greeting, even if the ducking of his head in combination with the rapid motion of his arm made for an awkward exchange with people who didn't know David well. However, David knew all of his lawn mowing customers really well, and they in turn knew David and his social awkwardness. David's father lined up all his son's mowing jobs, confident that David's attention to detail, strict adherence to plans and schedules, and cheap rates would meet well with the accommodating personalities of understanding friends and neighbors. Over the last seven years, David had gained only three new clients—children of family friends who acquired their own yards—and lost only two clients, elderly folks who had passed away.

David knew his riding 1976 John Deere 100 Lawn Tractor held 1.25 gallons of gasoline and a quart of oil. He knew the little tractor had four forward gears as well as the ability to reverse included in its Peerless transmission. David remembered that the mowing deck choices for the tractor included thirty-eight-inch and forty-six-inch options. John Deere affixed the seven-horsepower engine, manufactured by Kohler, to the bright green-and-yellow body of the mower at its Horicon, Wisconsin, manufacturing facility. David knew Wisconsin was a state, just like Kentucky, but he had no idea where it was and little interest in where it or Horicon were in relation to each other or to his little area of familiarity in Kentucky. The order and stability of maps might have appealed to David, but the variability generally incurred while traveling sent David's mind into a tailspin.

Andrew Barnett, David's father, purchased the John Deere 100 for $830 for his son several months earlier, well before the start of the 1977 mowing season, which in West Kentucky ended up delayed until mid-April due to a blizzard that dumped eight inches of snow on Cooper in early March. Andrew remembered David's nervousness in mid-February concerning the potential for a late spring and a possible delayed start to the mowing season, especially after Punxsutawney Phil, that persnickety Pennsylvania groundhog, again forecasted a late-ending winter. Only a couple weeks earlier on Sunday, February 2, Phil had stuck his nose out and seen his shadow, and the entire United States hunkered down for another six weeks of winter weather.

David was a mechanical savant in a part of the world ill-equipped to deal with "special" people and at a time well before the intricacies of autism would begin to be mentioned, let alone discussed or understood. Therefore, he occupied himself through the winter months with a combination of intense lawn mower maintenance, repairs on other small engines for family friends and neighbors, and assemblies of myriad models: cars, airplanes, boats. David's mathematical abilities and manual dexterity likely rivaled those of the world's finest engineers and surgeons in 1977, but dependence on order and the development of only relatively simple social skills significantly distinguished him from the other side of the social spectrum.

By June 1977, when a high-caliber .243 slug entered David's upper back on the left side, piercing his heart on its way out of his chest and into the dirt some thirty feet away, David was well into his summer lawn-mowing routine. The spring snowstorm well out of his mind, David Barnett enjoyed a carefree existence with a well-established routine, according to his father. He used his dad's Ford F-100 half-ton pickup to haul his mower from job to job. As an attentive and cautious driver, David well understood the interaction of the clutch and three-on-the column transmission.

If any of David Barnett's customers had a complaint, it was more than likely that David mowed their yards according to the same pattern every time. Charlie Sprague never complained, and David used the same square pattern to cut his grass that he'd used the prior few years. When Charlie Sprague arrived home late that June afternoon, he knew something was wrong immediately because the pattern on which his grass was cut was amiss. His eyes followed the out-of-place diagonal swath cut through the middle of an unmowed portion of his yard through the shade of a crabapple tree near his house to discover David Barnett's John Deere mower abutting his house several feet to the right of the master bedroom window. Charlie Sprague parked his 1972 Buick LeSabre, cut the engine in the middle of Merle Haggard's hit "Branded Man" playing on the radio, quickly opened the driver's door, and ran toward David and the tractor. Sprague found David slumped over the tractor's steering wheel, blood having soaked his right workboot as well as the tractor's pedal and mowing deck on that side. Charlie Sprague raised his right hand to cover his mouth, and with his left hand, he slid his hat off his forehead. He took several moments to survey the scene, looking toward the trees and the horizon in front of him and to the left of the house. He turned toward the road and beyond his driveway, to the treed area behind him and opposite the direction David had been mowing. Touching nothing, Charlie Sprague walked back to his Buick, shut the driver's side door he had neglected to close earlier, and proceeded inside his house to call the Walter County Sheriff's Office.

CHAPTER 5

Forty-three years later, not much had changed with Charlie Sprague's farmstead. The red brick house remained much the same as it was when first constructed, just a few years before David Barnett's death. Charlie Sprague, now approaching ninety years old, remained the chatty and high-energy character he'd entered life as, which was strange for a farmer because that occupation frequently required many hours of physical labor toiling alone. Upon hearing someone pull into his driveway, Charlie made his way to his side door and outside, as eager as ever to meet whoever came to speak with him.

"Sheriff, I can definitely tell how much this case troubles you," Mandy said. "I can't really follow all that you're saying, though, because I'm freaking out about Hank and those guys from earlier."

"I'm sorry, Mandy. I don't mean to burden you any more than you already are. I just thought you might have heard your parents, or maybe a neighbor, say something about David Barnett over the years," Touch replied.

Awaiting Mr. Sprague's arrival to them, Mandy said, "Do you know who lived around here forty or fifty years ago? Seems to me, given the Barnett case details you've rattled off, that whoever shot David might have been off in those trees to the west, sort of the direction where the sun's shining now. I know my dad and his brothers used to hunt on other folks' leases—with their permission, of course."

Touch said, "The Michaels lived to the east, on the other side of that set of trees about half a mile. Charlie Sprague owns the land across the road for quite a bit, as well as behind the barn for at least a quarter mile. Just like now, Sprague says he always had at least one dog around the house that sort of made the near-house hunting prospects poor. To the west, though, I don't know that I've ever seen any notes on who owned or spent any time on that land in the file. I don't think there's even been a house there since Sprague started farming here. That being said, living and hunting don't necessarily always go hand in hand. Checking on land ownership or inquiring about hunting leases and who might have hunted where in 1977 might be the new lead this case needs. Now, until I know, I'll spend the rest of the day wondering why I never thought of that."

Touch greeted the old man as he ambled alongside Mandy. "Charlie Sprague, you appear to be getting along pretty well! Good to see you; I appreciate you coming out to greet us. Do you remember Mandy Herman? She lives a few miles down the highway on the other side. Charlie, Mandy and I were just chatting about who used to live around here. I'm sorry that I don't come out here just to chat with you and pass the time. It's definitely not you—it's me. By this point, though, you know good and well why I come around. Mandy's too young to know anything other than the town's tale about David Barnett, if that, but she brought up a point I hadn't thought of or seen anything about before. Did anyone ever lease or hunt on that piece of land to the west over there?"

Charlie Sprague thought for a moment. He glanced to the west as Mandy and Touch looked that direction. "I don't remember anyone ever asking about hunting over there. I haven't thought about that in decades, although David Barnett seems to creep into my thoughts daily. Other than my wife's passing, seeing that boy dead on that tractor at my house was the worst thing in my life. I know his death broke Andrew's heart. How that man ever got back to work, let alone became the attorney he did after a tragedy like that, still amazes me. Andrew and I went to school here together, been friends over seventy years. I'm gonna have to think on that question, though. Lots of people cycled through in the past forty-some years. I'll give you a call at the sheriff's office if anything comes to mind."

"Thanks, Charlie. Rather than call, why don't you stop by the office next time you're in town? It'd be nice to see you about something other than this murder. Maybe we can grab lunch at the Tiger's Den and see Reva Dennis, Ronnie's daughter?" Touch asked.

"I know Reva, Touch," Charlie Sprague replied. "I don't eat out much, but I see her at church. Wouldn't mind seeing you there too."

"Mandy, we'd best be on our way, now. A day of nothing to do turned into a day with too much to do. I've got to get you situated, get on the phone to the US Attorney's office in Paducah, and check my computer, visit the county clerk's office, and chat with Andrew Barnett regarding any prior discussions on land ownership, hunting leases, and who might have been over in those trees to the west in 1977."

Upon leaving Sprague's farm and heading back to Cooper, Touch was too preoccupied to notice the Saturn beater that waited for his Tahoe to pass on the gravel road leading to Mandy's trailer. Mandy, having rarely passed by the turn-off for her house from this direction, noted the car—the same sun-bleached Saturn that had driven by her mobile home just before Touch arrived.

"Touch, I'm pretty sure that car back there on my road was the same one that came by my place before you got there. Your side trip got my mind off things while we were there, but those guys are definitely on my mind again now. What do you think's gonna happen?" Mandy inquired.

Taking a moment to segment his thoughts, Touch answered, "I'm guessing that you're going to have to endure more than a little intimidation until we can start to get this you-and-Hank thing taken care of through the US Attorney's office or something else. You and Hank may be a danger to each other, but I don't think you're a danger to society. These Dixie Mafia guys, or whatever they are, almost certainly are a danger to society. You need to be prepared to give a statement, convince Hank to give a statement, agree to testify regarding those statements, and probably move somewhere else for a while. This isn't gonna be easy. I'm sorry about that."

Mandy pondered the particulars of her situation. She'd lived in Walter County her entire life, as had all of her family. Briefly, after high school, she'd thought about moving to Paducah, getting a roommate and an apartment, and getting a night-shift job in order to go to the community college. Mandy opted for the dollar store and Cooper instead. Having only ever heard of "witness protection" on the occasional movie or crime drama TV series, she allowed her mind to wonder what relocating to a big city like LA or Chicago might be like. They had dollar stores there, which she knew from conversations with her regional managers over the years. Exiting the Tahoe with Touch in front of the sheriff's office brought Mandy back to her darkening reality.

"Hey, Bonnie, Mandy here blew up my slow day. Can you get the paperwork started on booking her for assaulting an officer? I'll explain it all later," Touch promised. "Mandy, take a left, head down that hallway, find cell eight, and pull the door shut behind you. Don't take it personally, but I'm going to put you in a corner cell as far away from anyone else as I can get you."

Then Touch turned to Bonnie. "I'm going over to the Tiger's Den after I make a phone call. Please contact one of our off-duty deputies and have them come in and babysit things for the rest of the afternoon," he instructed as he headed to his office to call the US Attorney's Paducah office.

"Hi, this is Jim Jusczwicz in the US Attorney's Paducah, Kentucky, office. How may I help you today?" was the greeting Touch received in response to his call.

"Hey, Jim, this is Touch Thomas, Walter County Sheriff. To whom do I need to speak with concerning some Dixie Mafia, or some similar group, and their movement in my county, as well as possible witness protection or relocation for a low-level thug idiot and his oft-battered girlfriend?" Touch asked the surprisingly pleasant and chipper man.

"One minute, Sheriff Thomas, and I'll put you through to US Attorney Richardson's office in Louisville."

Touch waited for them to pick up his call. He fingered an oblong button to turn on his shiny new laptop computer and run through some emails while he waited. Touch opened Outlook, noted he had sixty-two new and unread emails, paid them no mind, and clicked to open a link to a property records search application added to his desktop a few months ago, right after he got the laptop. No sooner did the app's interface pull up than Richardson picked up Touch's call.

"Touch Thomas, Shel Richardson, US Attorney for your part of the world: West Kentucky. What can you do for me today? Jim in Paducah conveyed to me that you've got what you think might be Dixie Mafia involvement in Walter County?"

"Here's the short-and-sweet of it, Mr. Richardson: I've got a battered girlfriend whom I've known her whole life, beat up by an imbecile from a hardworking Latin family that owns and runs a local Tex-Mex restaurant. It sounds and now looks like he got involved in a Dixie Mafia drug operation. Although really preliminarily on my part, it appears like he's going to have to turn state's evidence on these Mafia guys in order to avoid at least a couple years' prison sentence on a repeat-offender assault charge. I've got the man and the woman locked up here. The man, because he's an asshole and deserves it. The woman, for her own protection. What's my next step? Is this worthwhile for you in Louisville, or am I misassessing this situation?"

Richardson answered, "Touch, I appreciate the call, as

always. I think you're barking up the right tree here. I can in no way, shape, or form commit to any protection or relocation at this point in time without any concrete information, but if you can get verifiable information from the imbecile regarding his Dixie Mafia connections, I think we can commit to helping move this couple to safer confines. No way we're giving them carte blanche, "ID'd an international arms dealer" treatment, but we can help each of them find an apartment and an hourly job in a city far away. These Dixie Mafia SOBs have started slinging meth like sliders, opting for a price war in order to gain market share, and bodies are piling up on both sides of the equation—drug taking and drug dealing. Take their statements; push them for details, including names, as high up the food chain as you can get; and fax or scan those statements to me."

"Will do, Mr. Richardson. Providing the imbecile's sobered up enough to make a coherent statement and understand the gravity of his situation, I'll have these statements to you by the end of the day. I picked up the woman an hour or so ago, and it looks to me like the intimidation has already started. We're not a very big sheriff's department in Walter County, as you probably know, but I'd rather not have any Dixie Mafia jokers messing with prisoners or witnesses if I can avoid it. Are you aware of these clowns moving up the family tree to try to get at folks, or do they view themselves as above and beyond that level of underhandedness?" Touch asked.

"I've not heard of anything going beyond the clear and present," Richardson said, "but the escalations in things over the past few months sort of opens the door for anything. They appear to have recruited some newbies who don't play by the same set of rules as the Dixie Mafia captains we hear and read about farther south in the larger cities of Tennessee, Georgia, and Alabama."

"Thanks, Mr. Richardson," concluded Touch as he returned the phone receiver to its cradle. After rising from his desk chair and looking again at his stack of paperwork, Touch headed out of his office and over to the Tiger's Den for lunch.

"Bonnie, I'll be back in about forty-five minutes to fill you in on everything. You got a deputy coming in to monitor things?" Touch asked Bonnie.

"Sure thing. I got Mike Menser coming in; he should be in here in about twenty minutes. He was due to come in late this afternoon for the evening shift anyway. Have a good lunch," Bonnie said as Touch opened and walked through the sheriff's office door.

CHAPTER 6

Touch yet again, retraced his steps from earlier in the day. He dismissed a recurring thought that his life boiled down to a never-ending cycle. Instead, he reflected on how returning to the Tiger's Den seemingly always put a smile on his face, no matter how dark his mood. Something about the Tiger's Den comforted Touch: pictures on the wall, Reva's pleasantness, food, memories of being there with his father, or some combination of those things set Touch at ease regardless of what else was on his mind.

"Hey, Touch," Reva hollered from the back of the café, where she was wiping down a table. "Don't know if you saw it as you walked out this morning, but today's special ranks among your favorites, I believe: fried pork tenderloin sandwich, cole slaw, and fried potatoes. If that's not enough, I've got a few slices of pecan pie, and maybe a couple of lemon meringue left as well."

"Oh, good Lord, Reva, that just made my day right there! Special all the way, with a slice of lemon meringue, should just about make up for what turned into a mess of a morning. Can I have a bucket full of sweet tea with that too, please?" Touch asked.

"Already started pouring it! I'll have that plate out to you in just a few minutes. Johnny's been on the spot today at the fryer. That man just doesn't seem to age! Seemed like you were anticipating a slow morning when you left a few hours ago. What transpired to mess that up for you?"

"Well, I'd love to offload that two tons of crap onto someone, but you wouldn't top my list. You're way too sweet, kind, and busy doing your own thing to have to put up with this trouble. Truthfully, I don't know if anyone that knows about it would be safe either, at this point. Every once in a while, our small town encounters some big-city problems, and I'd really like to nip this one in the bud before it oozes any further into Cooper," Touch said. "Cooper's always had a minor drug problem since soldiers returning from World War I. No one knew much about it because that episode passed pretty quickly, as I understand it. A similar situation arose following World War II and the return of the injured soldiers, but as with much of the country, the weed and pills phenomena of the seventies somehow plagued Cooper less than other areas, at least according to my dad. The latest meth mess, though, threatens to mushroom beyond a relatively small number of wayward souls. A couple, or at least I hope it's only a couple, regional networks—I wouldn't call them gangs yet—learned some economics and started a price war that may vastly expand demand. The offset, I'm speculating, is that heads literally will start to roll if losers aren't soon declared. Only so long that these jokers will lose money to grow their markets is my experience," Touch concluded.

"I appreciate that, Touch," Reva said. "While I may not be as qualified at commiserating as some of our local bartenders, I've gained quite a bit of experience at it over the years. The old-timers tell me that my dad was among the best as well. Of course, he managed through that seventies period you mentioned and probably was as active in the community during that time as anyone. I'm sure you see the other folks cycle in and out of here as much as anyone, but my food's pretty popular with the lawyers and the judge as well. Our fry guys and other help haven't always been as dependable as Johnny either, occasionally falling into drug use." She turned to the kitchen. "Johnny, do me a favor and throw a couple extra taters on this plate, would you? Touch sounds like he's had a morning. A little more starch to soak up some of that angst might do him some good. Plus, I think he's been overexercising again. Looks like his muscles may be bulgier than they were a few months ago!"

"Sure thing, Reva. While facing this wall and working the fryer and stove, I don't see too many bulging muscles other than the two or three in my forearms," said Johnny. He pulled a couple of fried potatoes from the batch waiting on an adjacent plate and threw a small replacement handful into the fry basket. "Tell Touch I say hi too. Never will forget that touchdown he scored against Mayfield his junior year; still puts a smile on my face that Cooper finally beat them a few times when he played. He and his dad also helped my family out more than I care to mention over the years. Good people."

Reva set Touch's sandwich in front of him. "Johnny says hi," she said. "Says he always gets a smile on his face thinking about that TD to beat Mayfield your junior year. Also said he's still appreciative of you and your father helping his family out over the years."

"Reva, that tenderloin looks as awesome as always! I'm gonna let it sit just a little while so I don't burn my mouth like I usually do when I get in a hurry with it. I'll enjoy some of this cole slaw while I wait, though." Touch swallowed the first bite and asked, "How long have you known Johnny? He grew up on the northwest side of the county before he got out of school and moved into town, right?"

Reva took a moment to think. "Yeah, I think you're right. Johnny's mom and dad had a small farm years ago out there, not too far from Creswell. I think his mom had to sell it after his father passed. That was years ago, and Johnny's dad was still pretty young. Just one of those heart attacks that used to hit people before doctors started testing and screening folks like that for early signs. Let me get these people at the register and some more tea, Touch. I'll drop by in a few minutes with your pie." She headed behind the counter to the cash register.

Touch returned to his food, forked a few fried potatoes into his mouth, chewed, and added a couple shakes of salt and pepper to the balance of the still sizeable pile on his plate. He made a mental note to chat up Johnny before he left the Tiger's Den. Touch wanted to know whether Johnny might have known anyone who regularly hunted in the part of the county in which he grew up. If not, then maybe Johnny would remember who owned the parcels of land around Mr. Sprague's farm when David Barnett was shot. Mandy's comment started a new thread of thought in Barnett's murder for Touch: possibly an errant shot from a careless hunter found David. Given the almost certainty that David Barnett posed a threat to no one about anything of importance, something accidental seemed the most plausible explanation. Still, clarity would aid everyone with achieving closure after all this time, most notably closure for Touch himself.

Touch finished his sandwich, served with dill pickle slices and mustard as it had been for thirty-some years, and the last of the fried potatoes. Reva returned with a slice of lemon meringue pie. Seemingly, she had saved the slice with the highest meringue peaks for him. It probably wasn't actually the case, but Touch liked to think so. "Thanks, Reva!" he said.

Always torn between devouring the pie in three or four quick bites and slowly savoring the sweet meringue mixed with the tart lemon in more measured forkfuls, Touch split the difference as he usually did. He started slowly and savoringly, only to gulp the final monstrous bite in one tastebud-overwhelming, little kid shoveling move. Watching from the edge of the counter, Reva, shook her head with a sly grin and walked back toward the cooks' station.

Touch wiped his mouth with a paper napkin, scooted his wooden chair back from the table, and placed the napkin next to the pie dish. He stood and started to move toward the counter as well. "Hey, Reva, that was excellent as always. Do you mind if I have a quick word with Johnny?"

Addressing Johnny, Touch asked, "You got a quick minute for a couple questions, please?"

Reva said she'd be glad to take over for Johnny for a minute because the lunch rush largely had cleared out. Johnny agreed, and he and Touch walked out the Tiger Den's backdoor and into the alley behind the restaurant.

"Thanks, Johnny," Touch said, and he commenced his questioning by setting up the situation. "I was out to Mr. Sprague's farm earlier this morning. You remember David Barnett's murder from years ago? It's haunted my dad and, now me, for decades at this point. Maybe you didn't know, but Mr. Barnett and my father were friends all my dad's life. The inability to give his best friend closure on the death of his son, a boy my father loved like another son, haunted him until he died. Anyway, I usually have a cold case or two I keep on my desk to revisit the facts when a spare moment materializes or to reset a line of thinking. This time, that cold case ended up being David's. I managed to knock the file in the floor this morning, as a matter of fact; my hand-eye coordination must be going."

"Shit, Touch, your hand-eye'd have to go a long way downhill before it reached the level of most men's," Johnny joked.

"I don't know, Johnny," Touch demurred. "Anyway, I had another issue that took me out to that side of the county this morning. So, I decided to stop by Charlie Sprague's farm and survey the scene again, probably the hundredth time I've been there over the years. My companion for that trip, who also grew up on that side of town, said folks used to lease and hunt in the woods around Sprague's way back when. You grew up in that part of the county too, right? You remember anyone of note that used to lease or hunt around there in the mid to late 70s?" Touch asked.

"Oh, Touch, you're going back a ways there. Gimme a second and let me walk through time. I didn't play as much ball as you by a longshot, but I been hit in the head more than a few times, and things don't appear as quickly and as clearly as they once did … Let's see. I would have been twelve to fourteen around that time. I did a fair bit of exploring and hunting in that area. You're right: I grew up on my parents' farm there outside of that Creswell community, until my father had the heart attack a couple years later that forced my mom to sell that farm and move to a rental here in town. Luckily, I never ran into anyone then—Black boys running around the woods in the 1970s wasn't the safest thing to do—but I did hear of some of the well-to-dos from town leasing out there for hunting in the fall and early winter. Maybe the Welches that owned the bank, or the Shakopfs, or however you pronounce it, that had that service station on the south side of town and that auto parts store just outside of downtown back then?"

Touch thought for a moment, looked off at the horizon to his left, turned back toward Johnny, and offered his hand to the man. "Thanks, Johnny. I'm sorry to take you away from your work. How're your kids and grandkids? How many of them are there, now?"

Johnny grinned at the thought of his grandkids, something his father never got to experience, and replied, "My pleasure, Touch. My family always appreciated your dad helping us out. My kids, Tonya and Herc, are doing fine—good jobs, good spouses, all's good that I can tell. Each of them has a boy and a girl, so four grandkids total, with ages pretty close together from eight to thirteen. Running around to all the kids sporting events and school activities keeps us entertained and busy. I'm thankful to Reva for running such a nice place and paying me so well that I get the time and the means to share life with them. Obviously, doin' so puts a smile on my face! You be good, Touch, and let me know if I can help you some more," Johnny offered as he turned and headed back to his cook's station.

Touch paused a moment longer in the alley to organize his thoughts, reach in his pocket for a couple bills with which to pay his lunch check, turned toward the Den's back door, and followed

Johnny back into the restaurant to pay his bill. "Thanks again, Reva," Touch said as he laid the money on the counter near the register and exited the café, ringing the bell above the door for the third and fourth times of the day.

CHAPTER 7

The afternoon turned out to be as hot as the forecasts predicted. As the sun beat down on the sidewalk and Touch walked back to his office, the closing words of John Prine's "Illegal Smile" played in his head:

> Won't you please tell the man I didn't kill anyone—
> No, I'm just tryin' to have me some fun—Well done,
> hot dog bun, my sister's a nun.

Touch sure as hell hoped that he'd not have to kill anyone. His move back to Cooper entirely centered on not having to kill anyone ever again. As he entered the Walter County Courthouse for the second time that day, he walked through his afternoon to-do list:

1. Get on his computer and check the property records for the area surrounding Charlie Sprague's farm
2. Check in with Mr. Barnett on his recent line of thinking and conversation with Johnny
3. Fill Bonnie in on the Hank and Mandy developments
4. Talk with Hank
5. Get Mandy to write down her statement
6. Update Chris Hauser, Cooper's chief of police, on Dixie Mafia activities

Bonnie sat at her desk as Touch entered the sheriff's office. He decided to take advantage of her presence and cross number three off his mental list. "Hey, Bonnie, would you follow me into my office, please? I'll update you on what's happened this morning."

"Sure thing, Touch, I'll be right there."

Touch reached out to click on his laptop as he sat down at his desk. No sooner had the computer booted up and the screen blinked through to the sheriff's department chevron that served as Touch's screensaver than Bonnie walked through his office door and closed it behind her. "What's up, Touch?" she asked as she seated herself across from Touch.

"Bonnie, Mandy and Hank put themselves in a world of shit, I'm afraid," Touch started. "According to Mandy, Hank's gotten in with a group that I'm guessing is Dixie Mafia, running meth and pills in Walter County. I've got a call in to the US Attorney in Louisville trying to get Mandy, if not both Mandy and Hank, relocation assistance. I'm reading between the lines here, but as quickly as my phone call got transferred from Paducah to Louisville, I'm guessing that the US Attorney's office recorded increased drug or Dixie Mafia activities in this part of the state, if not the whole state. Anyway, I'd expect some trouble, which is why I asked you to call in Mike Menser. Also, I'm working a hunting lease angle that Johnny over at the Tiger's Den mentioned to me on the David Barnett murder. May be nothing, but we've had almost fifty years of nothing at this point."

"Thanks, Touch. I appreciate you keeping me in the loop. It helps the deputies stay alert to know something unusual's going on, even if they don't know exactly what it is," Bonnie replied as she got up to return to the reception area.

Touch rose with a notepad in hand. "I'm going to get Mandy to put everything she can remember down in writing: days, dates, names, cars, money amounts, anything. While she's doing that, I'm gonna drag Hank to another interview room and have him tell me everything he knows before I make him write it down. I want to be able to corroborate what he says and drag out whatever he doesn't want to tell me."

After taking another notepad and two blue pens out of his filing cabinet, Touch stepped beyond his desk, exited his office, and headed toward the even numbered cells. Several steps later, he rapped his knuckles on the bars of cell eight and greeted Mandy Herman. "Hey, Mandy, did Bonnie manage to scare up some lunch for you?"

"She sure did, Touch. I appreciate the cold can of Coke, sandwich, apple, and bag of Funyuns she brought me," Mandy replied.

"Good, I'm happy to hear it. I need you to take this notepad and pen and write down absolutely everything you can about this Hank and Dixie Mafia situation. No matter how trivial you might think the detail is, please write it down: days of the week; dates; car colors, makes, and models; names and appearances. Whatever you can think of, please write it down. I'm going to talk to Hank first and then have him do the same thing. I won't tell him about a single thing you write down. I'm also not going to mention that you're even in here. I want him to think he's bearing the burden of this all himself."

After leaving Mandy to her writing, Touch walked back toward the odd-numbered cells, found Hank asleep in cell five, and roused him by banging his metal cased flashlight on the cell's bars. "Hank, wakey, wakey. Time for you to talk to me. On your feet, let's move," said Touch.

"What, no lunch? I thought you ran a tight ship here at the Walter County Sheriff's Office," Hank said.

"We do run a tight ship, Hank, and I don't want you throwing up on our spic-and-span floor as a result of that hangover you're nursing," replied Touch. "I need you moving, though, because I've got a shit-ton of stuff to do now because of you. Let's go before I grab a handful of hair and start dragging—you're about to piss me off."

Hank exited the cell, turned to the right, and took a couple shuffling steps, awaiting directions from Touch.

"Take a left at the end there and enter the first office on the left, please," directed Touch.

Hank took a seat behind a small table. Touch followed him in and seated himself opposite Hank at the table. Touch set his notepad and pen on the table and brought Hank up to speed on what he knew about the domestic assault of Mandy. After finishing the description of Mandy's injuries to her lip, jaw, and eye, Touch shared that this time, it looked like Mandy had grown tired of Hank's abuse and bullshit and that he probably was looking at a couple years in the state pen next door in Franklin. Touch let Hank stew on that for a few minutes while he left to grab a paper cup of water for each of them.

Upon returning, Touch dialed up the heat on Hank. "The US Attorney also shared with me that he's hearing about increased meth and pill activity in and around Walter County. You wouldn't know anything about that, would you, Hank? While I'd hate it for Mandy, this could be worth a 'give a little, get a little' tradeoff providing you've got some useful details on the Dixie Mafia or whatever organization it is that's moving drugs through here. Tell you what: I'll give you a couple more minutes to drink your water and organize your thoughts while I look over a couple things on my computer, okay?"

Touch exited the room again and headed back to his office and his laptop, figuring that the longer he gave Hank to calculate what he and the US Attorney might know would work in their favor. He clicked over to the property search app on his computer, tapped in Charlie Sprague's address, and started methodically highlighting the surrounding parcels, noting current and prior ownership on a notepad on his desk. Nothing of note immediately stuck out to Touch as he recorded details on six properties, but he thought the names might jog Mr. Barnett's, Johnny's, or Charlie Sprague's memories as to what might have happened around there in 1976 or 1977. Touch also thought he might check with the state fish and wildlife officer, not knowing whether folks tagged deer they shot in the 1970s. Again, one never could tell what might jog someone's memory or who might remember what. After about seven minutes on the computer, Touch rose from his desk chair and headed back to question Hank.

"Hank, anything you have to say in your defense with respect to assaulting your girlfriend? By the looks of you, whatever damage you suffered appears to be self-inflicted and involving a bottle. Nonetheless, it's the proper question to ask," Touch said.

Staring at the ceiling Hank said, "No, I've got nothing to say against Mandy at all. This is all my fault, as it's pretty much been the past fifteen years. I'm sure you've heard all the hollow repents before, so I'll save you from mine. You think I might be looking at a couple years for this, though?"

"Just speculation on my part, Hank. You haven't really done anything, though, to positively distinguish yourself in the community. A little drug use in the past, but that's just between me and you. I think if you can share some intimate Dixie Mafia details, though, the US Attorney might be able to assist on a relocation package, at least for a little while. Nothing special, mind, you, but then again, it ain't like you had anything special around here after you thumbed your nose at your parents' restaurant."

Hank lowered his chin to look Touch level in the eye. "Touch, those boys mean business. Talking to you about them may end me. May end Mandy. They don't seem to give a damn about anything other than money. I took a beating a few weeks ago, and I was just late delivering money, not even stealing any of it."

"Well, Hank, the way I see it, they can either get to you inside or outside. At least outside, you've got more room to run and hide," Touch said. "Tell you what: I'll give you a little more time to think on it while I give the chief of police a call and fill him in on things, okay?" Touch rose again from his seat and headed out the door of the interrogation room for his office.

After grabbing his desk phone as he rounded his desk, careful not to disturb his file pile again, Touch dialed the number for his old buddy Chris Hauser, Cooper's chief of police. Hauser, who was a couple year's younger than Touch, had been his go-to receiver on the football field and sparring partner on the wrestling mat. Whereas Touch had left Cooper for college, Hauser had remained around the town all his life, attending the small state school about forty-five minutes southwest of Cooper.

After an attendant picked up on the second ring and patched Touch through, Hauser greeted his old friend. "Touch Thomas, what the hell's the matter now?"

"Chris, we're gonna have a Dixie Mafia problem. I don't know when or how big, but I think it's coming. That dumbass Hank Benitez managed to get mixed up with them and assault his girlfriend Mandy Herman again, and I've now got both of them locked up. Hank is in for assault, and Mandy is in for her own protection. I just wanted to give you a heads-up because I saw a spotter when I went to check on Mandy earlier this morning. I assume we can team up on this as we have in the past?"

Hauser replied, "Thanks, Touch, and you can always count on me. Just let me know when and how you want to play it, and we'll do it like we've always done it."

Touch replaced the phone in its cradle and headed back to finish interrogating Hank. It turned out he didn't need to do anymore interrogating, though. When Touch reentered the interrogation room, Hank was busy scribbling every last detail he could recollect on his Dixie Mafia dealings with the pen and pad of paper Touch had left in the room. Thirty minutes later, Touch possessed six pages of handwritten notes from Mandy and Hank as to their dealings and observations with at least a half dozen Dixie Mafia named members, an equal number of cars described, and a few dates of meetings.

Smiling to himself, Touch escorted Hank back to his cell. Hank doing the right thing and providing this much information and detail should take a lot, if not all, of the heat off Mandy. It likely made things hotter for Hank, but that numbskull had brought it on himself. As Touch opened the cell and saw Hank into it, he assured Hank as much as he could. "For the first time in a long time, I think you did the right thing here. I'm going to try to return that solid by doing you one as well, but no guarantee I'll be able to pull it off. Sit tight for a while, and I'll try to get back to you tomorrow on which directions I see these things going, okay? I want you to focus on what productive things you're going to do once you get through this, whether that be three days or three years from now. Once, you were a good dude. You've got lots of time to be one again, I think."

CHAPTER 8

Touch settled in at his desk, pleased with the degree and depth of info provided by Mandy and Hank. He phoned Shel Richardson in the Louisville US Attorney's office, anxious to get Mandy moving toward a safer location soon.

"Mr. Richardson, please. This is Sheriff Tanner Thomas in Walter County," Touch said to the attendant answering the phone.

"Sorry, Sheriff Thomas, but Mr. Richardson likely won't be available until end of day. Shall I have him call you back, or would you like to call later this afternoon?" the pleasant, young-sounding man answered.

"Yes, have Mr. Richardson give me a call ASAP. I've got some Dixie Mafia info I think he'll find interesting and valuable. I'd like to get an arrangement we discussed earlier rolling as soon as your office can do so. Thank you." Touch hung up. "Damn," he cursed to himself, anxious to maintain his recent momentum. He rose from his desk and headed back to converse with Mandy and then Hank.

Shaking his head at Bonnie as he walked toward Mandy's cell, Touch considered his afternoon to-do list. Doubling back to speak with Bonnie, Touch asked, "Would you please call Andrew Barnett and see if he can meet me later this evening? Whatever venue he prefers; he always pays and might as well choose."

"Got it, Touch," Bonnie replied as she picked up her phone's receiver dialed Mr. Barnett's number from memory.

Touch about-faced and continued toward Mandy's cell. "Hey Mandy, thank you for writing all that down: I think it'll end up helping you a lot," he said. "Maybe it'll set your mind at ease, but Hank did the same thing. My guess is that his doing so will refocus whatever harm might've come your way onto him. I'm going to continue being careful, though, and I've got a call in to the US Attorney to try to expedite this process. I expect he'll call me back before the end of the day: Bonnie's on the lookout for his call too. I'm going to have another chat with Hank as well. You as comfortable as you can be? If you need anything, just ask Bonnie. I'll have her come check on you periodically, okay?" Touch then turned and walked back toward the male cell block.

He approached Hank's cell and signaled for him to step to the bars. "Hank, I've got a call in to the US Attorney, and I'll share your information with him when he returns it. I think you doing this will shelter Mandy from any Dixie Mafia blowback, but that means it'll likely be all on you. I'll have a couple deputies watching out for your mom and dad. Anyone else we need to have eyes on?"

"Thanks, Touch," replied Hank. "I really got no one else."

Touch nodded and walked back toward his office.

Bonnie was just hanging up the phone and relayed, "Andrew Barnett said tonight at 7:30, at the country club. Do they allow you in uniform in the country club, or do you have to put on actual clothes, Touch?"

"Thanks, Bonnie. I think I'll just pull on one of my 'uniform' polo shirts in a nice, fetching tan color with a mostly clean pair of our dark work slacks. That'll do for sitting and eating, won't it?" Touch sniped back at Bonnie as he ducked back into his office.

No sooner had Touch reseated himself at his desk than a small, squirrelly looking fellow entered the sheriff's office. Sporting a Confederate Flag neck tattoo along with more skin graffiti on his arms and fingers, the man generated a toothy grin about as wide as he was tall. "Excuse me, ma'am, but I wanted to check on a couple prisoners you might have: Hank Benitez and Mandy Herman. Would it be possible to visit with either or both of them, please?" the man asked.

Touch decided it best to let things appear "normal" and allowed Bonnie to handle the situation as she usually would.

"Providing that they want to speak with you, Deputy Menser here can escort them to one of our visiting rooms. I didn't get your name, though, sir. We've got a procedure for signing in and such for prisoners visited in the sheriff's office," Bonnie informed him.

"Yes, ma'am. My name is Dougie Delaney. I'll just wait over here, if that's okay. Thanks," Delaney said as he backstepped toward the four guest chairs that occupied the corner of the space directly across from Touch's office.

Bonnie took note of his name, punched some keys on her computer, took some more notes, carried the notepad on which she wrote it into Touch's office, and closed the door behind her. She said, "I'm sure you heard all of that, but a fellow named Dougie Delaney with a piss-poor Confederate Flag neck tat and sleeves is out there to speak with Mandy and Hank. What should I do?"

"Pretty bold on the part of the Dixie Mafia to send a lackey into the sheriff's office to forward messages to a couple of prisoners, huh? I think we let him speak to them, consistent with our information-gathering exercises. But make sure everything stays safe, right? Ask him for his driver's license and social security number, run a few checks to buy us some time, and send in Mike Menser, please," Touch instructed Bonnie.

Roused by the entrance of Dougie Delaney, Mike Menser now sat straight up in his desk chair. Responding to Bonnie waving him toward Touch's office, Menser rose from his chair and headed into Touch's office, pulling the door closed behind him.

"Mr. Delaney," Bonnie addressed the small man, "could I please see your driver's license and collect your social security number? I just need to run a couple quick background checks."

Mike Menser settled into one of Touch's guest chairs. Touch commenced to giving instructions. "Mike, that Dixie Mafia bastard out there is going to chat with two of our prisoners, Mandy and Hank, separately in a couple of our interrogation rooms. We're going to play it normal with you posted outside those rooms' doors, okay? This'll only be a 'message' meeting, and it's entirely expected, but we'll see if we can pick up anything else of value from it. At this point, I'm guessing that neither the Dixie Mafia, and certainly not Mr. Delaney, know that both Hank and Mandy rolled over like a dog in soft grass on their drug involvement in Walter County. So, if you'll collect the man's license from Bonnie on your way out, search him well, and direct him to an interview room, we can get this underway. Just seat him and go get Mandy first. I'll chat with her after she and Delaney talk, and then you can go get Hank and escort him in to speak with Mr. Delaney."

"Got it, Touch. Just play it normal but be on point for any weirdness. I'll get him settled and get Mandy," Mike Menser said as he rose out of the chair and headed toward the door.

After grabbing Dougie Delaney's driver's license as he moved past Bonnie's desk, Menser addressed the man. "Mr. Delaney, I need to search you before I allow you speak with Ms. Herman or Mr. Benitez. If you'll empty the contents of your pockets into this basket, I'd appreciate it."

"Understandable, Deputy. I got some car keys, fingernail clippers, a cellphone, my wallet, and some lint," Delaney said.

"Thanks, Mr. Delaney. Stand still, please, while I frisk you," Menser said. "Turn around, please," he said after frisking Delaney's front. "You appear clear, Mr. Delaney. If you'll follow me, I'll get you settled into one of our interview rooms."

At six feet four inches and 240 pounds, Menser dwarfed Delaney. Shortly after getting the man settled, informing Mandy of the situation, and bringing her in to talk to Delaney, Menser posted himself outside the room. About ten minutes, later a quick rap of the knuckles on the office door alerted Menser that the meeting was over. He opened the door, instructed Delaney to stay seated and to wait for Mr. Benitez, escorted Mandy in to chat with Touch, and headed toward the male cell block and Hank. While Mandy exhibited little discomfort speaking with Delaney, likely because she had never laid eyes on the man before today, Hank was decidedly less comfortable as Menser escorted him into the room with Delaney.

While sitting at his desk and looking at Mandy, Touch didn't mince words, "What did Mr. Delaney want?"

"He let me know that he and the Dixie Mafia knew who I was, where I lived, who my relatives were, and that Hank was my long-term boyfriend. Pretty much what you said would happen, but I didn't expect them to do it in person in the sheriff's office. Did you?"

Touch stayed seated and looked up at her as he answered her question. "No, Mandy, I didn't expect them to be that direct. I'm not aware of any Dixie Mafia activity to speak of in our county previously, though. I think it'll play to our advantage because everyone now knows that everyone else knows. Increasingly, though, I think this focuses the heat on Hank, which probably stays good for you providing we can convince folks you've had all the Hank Benitez you need for this lifetime."

Mandy walked over to Touch's office window and stared out of it. Touch stepped out of his office and signaled to Bonnie to escort Mandy back to her cell while he awaited Menser walking Hank to his office once Delaney finished threatening him. Touch thought it strange that a gang would send who had to be their tiniest member to convey threats. Although he'd never actually done it before, Touch was pretty certain that should he want to, he could grab Delaney by the neck and the waistline of his pants, pick him up over his head, and break his back over his knee like snapping a dry twig. Touch's abs and biceps tightened at the thought of violence, which made him mildly anxious.

When Mandy indicated she was ready, Bonnie walked with her back to the women's cells. Touch waited another few minutes, and soon Menser escorted Hank into Touch's office. Hank resided in the jail for a reason, so Menser was decidedly more alert with Hank than with Mandy. Hank's uneasiness was obvious to Touch, and the sheriff indicated for him to have a seat in one of his guest chairs. He nodded to Menser that he could go, and Touch heard Menser escorting Mr. Delaney out of the office.

"Playing out about the way we thought, Hank?" Touch inquired.

"Yeah, Touch. I fucked up six ways from Sunday on this one," confided Hank. "Delaney threatened to put an end to me and burn down my parents' restaurant and house, though not in so many words."

"Did they mention anything to you about Mandy?" asked Touch.

"Nope, nothing concerning Mandy," answered Hank. "Why?"

"No particular reason, Hank. Just looking out for her, is all. I could see that if the Mafia concluded you still had feelings for her or didn't understand the situation, they might try to get to you through her. It sounds like they may have concluded she's had enough of you, though—which, by the way, is the case." Touch rose from his chair and indicated to Hank it was time to return to his cell.

After resettling Hank in his cell, Touch returned to his office and made some notes on Mr. Delaney's visit to share with Richardson when he called. Touch reached out to his laptop, clicked through to Google, searched "Dixie Mafia Kentucky," and read for several minutes until Richardson interrupted his research with a phone call.

"Sheriff Thomas," Touch answered the phone.

"Shel Richardson," the US Attorney announced to Touch. "Sheriff, what's changed with your situation?"

"Mr. Richardson, I've got six pages of written statements and details each from Mandy Herman and, somewhat surprisingly, from

Hank Benitez. It might take a little extrapolation and interpolation, but the conclusions I make from their information are that the Dixie Mafia plans to use Lake Barkley and its relatively looser policing to move significant amounts of heroin and pills through Tennessee into Kentucky, Illinois, Indiana, and Ohio, if not further. Apparently, Walter County's intersection with the lake, a handful of decent highways, and an interstate make it an ideal location to set up a distribution hub.

"Furthermore, Mr. Richardson, Dixie Mafia sent a representative, Dougie Delaney, to my office to chat with Mandy and Hank just a few minutes ago. Pretty bold move, in my book. We ran him through the system and came back with nothing, but he's so damned small that he may have simply slipped through everyone's fingers before now. What're the chances you can get a US Marshal over here tonight to escort Ms. Herman somewhere safer and more comfortable? I think she may be off the hook with Mr. Benitez slated to take the bulk of any heat, now, but she's been through enough, and I'd rather be safe than sorry," Touch concluded.

Shel Richardson thought for a moment before replying. "Sheriff, I'm going to send a car and a marshal your way ASAP. I don't see any reason to dangle bait beyond Mr. Benitez. He doesn't sound like he'd be such a great loss anyway, if things went sideways. I recommend you decide how you want to proceed with Mr. Benitez given his help in this affair, but I can't offer him anything because it sounds as though Ms. Herman provided enough detail to corroborate facts and observations previously recorded by my office," Richardson said as he hung up on Sheriff Thomas.

CHAPTER 9

Dougie Delaney left the Walter County Sheriff's Office. The day crossed over into midafternoon: peak heat for West Kentucky's summer, compounded with intense humidity created by Lake Barkley and all of the rivers and tributaries that flowed into and out of it. Touch sat back in his office chair, recounted the items on his to-do list, and took a little solace in the fact that he'd checked each of those items off the list with a few hours still left in his day. The trade-off was that he'd created an evening to-do list as well: meet with Andrew Barnett and meet a US Marshal. Hopefully that was all, though.

For what seemed like the hundredth time that day, Touch walked out of his office to chat with Bonnie. "Bonnie, we're going to have a visitor later tonight to escort Ms. Herman out of here. Who do we have on duty tonight that can help her out?"

"Mike here's going to be on through at least midnight, right Mike?" Bonnie answered.

"Sure thing, guys. Whatever y'all need," Mike chimed in.

Touch thought for a minute and then said, "How about a quick huddle in my office, then?"

Mike Menser was years younger than Touch, but the sheriff's legacy ran so deep and wide in Cooper and Walter County that he cracked a wide smile at the thought. "Wow, I didn't think I'd ever get to be in a Touch Thomas huddle: wait until I tell my dad!" Menser quipped as he rose and started walking toward Touch's office.

"Mike, I've been in a Touch huddle about a hundred times. Let me just say he's not the player he once was," said Bonnie.

"Hardy, har-har, folks. Mike, I appreciate the nod; Bonnie, fuck off." After closing the door behind him, Touch continued, "Later tonight, a US Marshal will be here to pick Mandy up and get her to a safer location. Hank stood up, believe it or not, and I hope that will take all the heat off Mandy. Regardless, I think it'll do her a world of good to get out of here and get a restart, so to speak. So, the US Attorney's office agreed to sponsor a relocation for her. Hank will remain here until we see which way this Dixie Mafia situation goes, for his own protection as well as for beating up Mandy again. If we can get this Mafia situation diffused over the next few weeks and Hank behaves himself, I think we might be able to reintroduce him to society without sending him up the river in the system. Not that he doesn't deserve it, but we know he's got family support and could be a decent guy. We'll just have to see, though."

Mike said, "Should Bonnie and I run over to Mandy's place and put some things together for her, or let the marshal or whoever help her out?"

"With Delaney's visit, I'm skeptical of doing anything around Mandy's place," Touch replied. "Bonnie, let me check with Mandy and see if there's anything pressing she might need. If there is, can you take care of it for us, please?"

Bonnie assured Touch that she could do it. Nothing else came to mind that they needed to address, and Mike and Bonnie returned to the outer office as Touch went to update Mandy on her planned nighttime departure with the Marshall. Mandy asked Touch to have Bonnie throw together a couple changes of clothes and some toiletries from her trailer.

"Mike, would you mind running Bonnie out to Mandy's place to grab some clothes and toiletries, please?" Touch asked. "Let's go to her trailer in a roundabout way, just in case Mr. Delaney or another of his Mafia associates is lurking around waiting to see if something happens."

"You got it, Touch," Mike affirmed. "Bonnie, let me know when you want to go. I'll move my car from the front and take a little drive beforehand, and then I'll meet you in the back and out of sight, okay?"

Bonnie thought a second. "Thanks, Mike. Let's got in about an hour; it'll be the last thing I do today. Just run out there, grab some stuff, come back here, drop it off, and head out for the evening."

All of that sounded fine to Touch. He pivoted back to David Barnett's case, hoping to cover one more of his bases in his revisiting of its details. Touch reopened the file and searched the documents for the Kentucky State Police investigator's name. Upon finding it, Touch dialed KSP's main number to inquire whether the officer was still alive and, if so, how he might be contacted. The attendant answering the call said that the officer remained alive but had endured Alzheimer's and its deleterious effects on his memory. Touch took his inquiry another step further and asked if he might be granted access to the officer's files, and he learned that most of KSP's files prior to 1979 were lost to a fire in an off-site storage facility.

Increasingly, it looked like Andrew Barnett represented the last living link to his son's murder.

Following up on a prior thought, Touch called Jamie Trask, Walter County's Fish and Wildlife Department representative. "Hey, Jamie, this is Touch Thomas. How's your day going?"

"Not bad, Touch. To what do I owe the pleasure of your call?" Jamie, one of the few female Fish and Wildlife officers in the state, replied.

"Does Fish and Wildlife keep historical records of deer tags, and if so, how far back do those records go?"

After a pause, Trask answered, "Yeah, Touch, I think I've got a few boxes of old tags in the corner of the office basement. Specifically, what are you looking for?"

"I keep a cold case or two laying around to jog a thought every once in a while. I don't know if you ever heard of the David Barnett murder out in the northwest part of the county, but that case always bugged my dad, and now it bugs me. I'm looking for anyone that tagged a deer and reported it while hunting around Charlie Sprague's farm in the mid-1970s—1976, 1977. Any chance such a thing exists?" Touch asked hopefully. "The homicide I'm investigating occurred in June. I'm just trying to see if someone might have leased adjacent land for deer hunting. If so, maybe they were out there taking down a stand, or hunting groundhogs or crows or some other varmint."

"Whoa, Touch, that's going back a ways, huh? I don't even know exactly how many of my predecessors that would be to get back to the officer in the mid-1970s. I was planning to do a drive by those watersheds south of town this afternoon, but let me check on this before I go and get back to you. Sound okay?"

"Thanks, Jamie. That sounds like about all I could ask for. Johnny over at Reva's got me thinking on this line of thought. Surprisingly, I saw no mention of it in the file. The KSP guy who worked the homicide has Alzheimer's, and their pre-'79 files were burned in a fire. So, Barnett's case is as much at a dead-end as it ever has been. I'm talking with Andrew Barnett tonight. I certainly don't want to get his hopes up for anything fifty years later, but feeding him a little new information could jar something loose on his end as well."

Touch glanced at his watch: it was just before 4:00 o'clock in the afternoon. Taking his conversation with Johnny another step further, Touch decided to walk over to the Walker County Bank and see if Mr. Welch, its chairman emeritus, might be visiting his office in the bank.

After coming out of the courthouse, Touch realized how much his time in the office and car had sheltered him from the ridiculous heat and humidity of the afternoon. He vowed to spend tomorrow afternoon out on patrol with his windows down if there was any way he could do so. No one else risked breaking a sweat, and as a result, the sidewalks leading to the bank from the courthouse were vacant. Touch waved at a couple cars he recognized, but little was happening in Cooper this afternoon. Seven minutes later, Touch arrived at the bank to discover that Mr. Welch had failed to come in today. Instead, the teller divulged that Mr. Welch was at the Cooper County Club playing a round of golf with Edmund Shakopf. Touch mentally recorded the four coincidences as another sign that something positive was developing in David Barnett's case: dinner with Andrew Barnett at the Country Club where Welch and Shakopf, the two names that came to mind for Johnny as maybe hunting near Charlie Sprague's house, played golf together this afternoon at the Country Club. Given the Welch and Shakopf family histories, he was fairly certain he'd catch the two elderly men at the bar lying about their golf scores before he had to join Barnett for dinner.

Touch broke into a full sweat on his walk back to his office from the bank. As he turned the final corner toward the courthouse, he caught sight of Bonnie and Mike Menser driving off in the direction opposite of Mandy's trailer. Looking to the left of the courthouse, in front of Davis's dry cleaners, Touch also noticed what looked to be a very hot and sweaty Dougie Delaney sitting behind the wheel of a decade-old Crown Victoria. Touch smiled to himself because it appeared Menser and Bonnie had left without it registering to Delaney. Touch passed through the courthouse and sheriff's office doors and into the reception area. Two of his night duty deputies were chewing the fat and checking the status of the cells. Touch asked them both to step into his office.

"Fellas, we've got a US Marshal coming to pick up Ms. Herman later this evening. Whoever's on phone detail, I need you to let me know when the marshal calls with an update on his arrival time. I've got a meeting at the country club, but I should be done well before nine, which is when I anticipate the marshal arriving. We've got a little weirdness going on with the Dixie Mafia, so be on the lookout."

As the deputies left his office, Touch noticed the light blinking on his phone signifying new messages. After entering his voicemail and keying in his passcode, he learned that Jamie Trask had returned his call. Edmund Shakopf had recorded a deer with Fish and Wildlife killed by his son, Laceon, in January 1977. No specific location other than Walter County was recorded on the tags back then.

Touch bade his deputies a good night and left his office. He got in his Tahoe and headed home. He wanted to shower and change clothes to leave plenty of time to get to the country club and talk with Welch and Shakopf after their golf game and before meeting Andrew Barnett.

CHAPTER 10

Touch pulled into the Cooper Country Club parking lot with Jimi Hendrix's "All Along the Watchtower" playing over the Tahoe's speakers. Touch looked clean and crisp in Walter County Sheriff Department's finest polo, and he parked and approached the golf course attendant to find out on what hole Welch and Shakopf might be playing. Touch estimated he had an extra half hour before the two finished their game.

"Sheriff Thomas, what can I do for you today?" the club-drop attendant inquired.

"Do you happen to know what hole Welch and Shakopf might be on?" Touch asked.

"Yessir, the girl running the drink cart just passed by them on sixteen. She added that she thought they'd dropped at least three extra balls each, just for fun," the attendant said.

"Thanks. How about Mr. Barnett? Have you seen him by chance?"

"Mr. Barnett's hitting a few balls on the driving range around back, sir," the attendant answered.

Touch started off to the left of the main clubhouse, hoping to catch Andrew Barnett on the driving range and quiz him on Welch and Shakopf before catching up with them at the country club bar.

Upon coming to the back of the clubhouse, Touch saw Barnett about six stalls away from him on the driving range.

Touch watched Barnett address the ball and swing, and then he followed the trajectory of the ball on two shots as he walked toward the man. Touch thought back on the number of times he'd played golf with his father and Barnett over the past forty years or so. Although stiffer and, as a result, less fluid, Barnett's swing remained much the same as it had when Touch had first seen the man golf. After drawing even with Barnett's golf bag, Touch pulled out the man's five iron from the bag and headed over to the adjacent stall of the driving range.

"Andrew, how're they flying for you today?" Touch asked as he scooted a ball from the pile the attendants kept near the stalls into position, assumed his stance, and addressed the ball.

Andrew Barnett turned around in time to see Touch pull his five iron into a full backswing, shift his weight forward from his back foot to his front foot as his hands led the club through a near-perfect semicircular arc, and finally strike the ball with the head of the club. With a modest fade from right to left, Touch's ball traveled about 210 yards on the fly, rolled another few yards, and came to rest between flags marking the 200- and 250-yard distances from the driving range stalls.

Shaking his head at the shot, Andrew Barnett smiled to himself and reflected on how the man had acquired his nickname. "Touch, I see you can still live up to your nickname. Still haven't taken the game back up after your dad died?" Barnett asked.

"No, Mr. Barnett, the thought of it just didn't seem enjoyable without him around," Touch shared. "Some of my fondest memories, though, are of playing with you and him. I see from your swing that your game remains sharp. You look a little stiff, but then again, you're also old," Touch joked. "Mr. Barnett, how well do you know Jerry Welch and Edmund Shakopf?"

Barnett looked up from his practice ball. "Let's see, Touch," he said as he rewound his dealings with Welch and Shakopf over the past sixty or so years. "We crossed paths socially over the years, if for no other reason than we shared time at this club. Businesswise, I've banked at Welch's bank for the entirety of my adult career. As you probably know, though, I'm a well-to-do but not a wealthy man. Being a country lawyer and then a judge makes for a very comfortable living, but not for generational wealth. Even if it did, I wouldn't have chosen to use my community bank for dealings of that nature, I don't think. As for Shakopf, I've filled my cars up at his pumps and had them repaired in his garages for forever. It was not necessarily for Edmund's expertise, but because he always employed the best mechanics in town. Both men probably gave as much as they took from the community. I can't say I'm a fan of the way they raised their children, though. Spoiled comes to mind as a short description of those kids; grandkids are even worse in my view."

"Yeah, I've had a handful of interactions with the grandkids, and I concur," Touch said. "The second generation's five years or so older than me; I remember my dad having a few issues. Did the Welches or Shakopfs hunt together or hunt anywhere near Mr. Sprague's farm that you know of? For that matter, do you remember either my old man or the state police mentioning anything about hunting leases in the context of David's murder?"

Andrew Barnett adjusted his stance, reserving himself to the probability that he'd likely struck his last golf ball for the day. "Ah, Touch, I wondered what was on your mind when Bonnie called my office earlier today. Back on the cold case, are we? I appreciate it, but I don't know that there's a stone left to turn over.

"As for the hunting queries, I don't recollect either your dad or the KSP mentioning anything about that. Of course, it entered everyone's mind given the caliber of the slug recovered. Sprague wasn't aware of who did what or where they did it around there way back then. He really hadn't lived there that long when David was shot. That being said, I know that the Welch and the Shakopf boys ran around together back then. The dads and the boys were thick as thieves, golfing out here, dining together, and that sort of thing. I certainly wouldn't be surprised if the boys or the dads hunted together. I don't know for sure, though."

Touch thanked Barnett for his help, let him know he planned to chat with Welch and Shakopf when they came off the golf course, and then confirmed that the two remained on track for dinner at the club in an hour or so. Touch concluded their preliminary talk by inviting the old man to join him, Welch, and Shakopf at the club's bar once he'd cleaned up from hitting his practice balls. Touch turned, returned Barnett's five iron to his golf bag, and proceeded toward the eighteenth hole to wait for Welch and Shakopf.

CHAPTER 11

While looking back toward the golf course, over the eighteenth green and down the fairway, Touch caught sight of Welch and Shakopf, the former waiting on the latter to hit his approach shot from about 150 yards away and the left side of the fairway. Shakopf's swing looked like that of most octogenarians Touch had seen: a sort of half backswing followed by a sharp downward motion and a sort of high "olé" finish. Touch couldn't argue with the result, though. Shakopf's ball arced high, dropped toward the putting green in line with the pin, and scotched up about ten feet downhill from the marker. Welch, who still put his ball on the putting green, would have a more difficult putt: downhill about eighteen feet with a left-to-right break.

Seven minutes later, Welch and Shakopf, having completed two and three putts, respectively, placed their putters back in their golf bags and pulled their cart up to the attendant's shack. They were greeted by Touch after asking the attendant to clean their clubs and leave their bags at the pickup area near the club's exit. "Gentleman, can I join you for a drink at the bar? I'd like to run down a couple of old facts, if I could share a few minutes of your time," Touch said.

"Tanner Thomas, we'd be honored to buy local law enforcement a drink," replied Jerry Welch with typical community banker aplomb.

Edmund Shakopf, ever the conversationalist, joined in. "Touch,

I'm interested in why you'd want to waste time with a couple washed-up old fogeys like us. Over the past fifteen years, I don't know that anyone under the age of sixty has wanted to speak to me who didn't want money. I don't owe you money, do I?"

"No, Mr. Shakopf, I don't think you owe me or the county any money. I'm just looking for a little information from way back when." Touch alluded to his chosen topic, and the three ambled toward the club's bar, which overlooked the eighteenth green on one side with the practice green bracketing the other side. Touch could see Andrew Barnett taking some putting practice through the opposite-side windows of the bar as he, Welch, and Shakopf entered the building and walked toward the bartender.

After sidling up to the bar, which he'd probably done a couple thousand times over the past sixty years, Welch greeted Sarah Smith, Cooper Country Club's long-serving bartender. "Smiling Sarah, I'll have my usual, and I'd guess Shakopf will as well, but I admit I don't know Sheriff Thomas' drink of choice. Touch, what'll you have?"

"Thanks, Mr. Welch," Touch started. "Sarah, I'll have a Knob Creek on the rocks, please."

Sarah commenced preparing a dry Ketel One martini for Jerry Welch, drafting a Budweiser beer for Edmund Shakopf, and pouring a Knob Creek bourbon over ice for Touch. Several seconds later, she turned around and placed each man's drink in front of them on cardboard coasters with the club's insignia emblazoned on them. Jerry Welch asked Sarah to place the cocktails on his tab and toasted "Good health" to his companions.

"So, Touch, what can we do for you?" Welch asked. "While we would welcome a social call from you, I doubt you've got the time for such pleasantries these days."

Touch thanked Welch for the bourbon, took a sip and enjoyed it, and explained his purpose. He noted his affinity for cold cases, underscored the importance of solving the murder of David Barnett, and reviewed his visit to Charlie Sprague's farm earlier in the day.

"Gentleman, did you or either of your boys ever have a hunting lease or hunt out toward Mr. Sprague's farm?" Touch inquired. "A former resident of that area recollected that either or both of you might have hunted out there at one time. I had Fish and Wildlife check their tag records—can't say I wasn't surprised that they still had them—and Jamie Trask, the current officer, informed me, Mr. Shakopf, that your son, Laceon, tagged a deer early in 1977. Can you tell me where he shot that deer? I know that's going back a ways and that you might have to talk to him about it, but I'd like to know.

"Mr. Welch feel free to chime in if you remember anything from that period. At this point, you fellows represent among the last links to that period. Kentucky State Police's files from that era burned in an off-site storage facility fire some years ago. The investigator's battling Alzheimer's. One way or another, this case finally is winding down."

Andrew Barnett sauntered up to the bar just as Touch finished chatting with Welch and Shakopf. "Jerry, Edmund, good to see you guys. Hope Touch hasn't been too rough on you. He had Bonnie call and soften me up earlier today. Touch, what's on your mind today?"

Touch said, "Well, Mr. Barnett, I'm just running down what's got to be one of the last leads in David's death. A resident of that area of the county back then mentioned the idea of leased hunting land to me. To my knowledge, which involves all the files, notes, and discussions Mr. Barnett, my dad, and I had over forty-plus years, no one ran down the possibility of a hunting accident. Following up on this line of questioning, a source recollected the possibility that Mr. Welch and Mr. Shakopf leased hunting rights near Mr. Sprague's farm sometime in the 1970s. Further, I birddogged with Fish and Wildlife that Mr. Shakopf tagged a deer in 1977, but those tags didn't include where the hunter took the deer back then. I just asked Mr. Welch and Mr. Shakopf if they could give the situation a little thought and get back to me with any information that might help. The last question that I think might shine a little more light on the situation is, if you did have a hunting lease around Sprague's spread, did you or anyone you allowed to hunt on it shoot with a .243?"

"Jerry, Edmund, you both have your sons and have had them for a long time. Someone took mine from me when he was only seventeen. If you can help Touch find me closure on David's death, I would be eternally grateful. Just a little info one way or the other could go a long way. It's been over forty years, so not much left that can be done at this point," Andrew Barnett pleaded.

Edmund Shakopf sipped his cocktail, listening respectfully to Touch and Andrew Barnett. Jerry Welch diddled with the cocktail skewer, contemplating consumption of the last olive Sarah had served with his martini. Welch spoke first. "Touch, Andrew, I'm going to have to look back on what I leased from whom. Many years we leased pieces of land in different parts of the county, sort of following news flow as to where the deer seemed to be running the thickest. As for the rifle, the answer is similar: we owned quite a few guns over the years. Trading them and then collecting them became a hobby of mine. As I'm sure you know, Touch, the .243 was about the most popular hunting rifle in the country before hunting went designer in the 1990s. Guys, I'll check my records and talk to Will, and I promise I'll get back to you. I'm sure Edmund will do the same. I know you talked to us together because you know we and our sons hunted a lot with each other over the years."

Satisfied that the two elderly men, pillars of the Cooper community for all of Touch Thomas's life, would do as they said, Touch and Andrew Barnett wished them good evening and walked toward the hostess stand of the club's dining room. The hostess seated Barnett and Touch at the lawyer's usual table at the back of the dining room in a corner with views of the first and eighteenth tees. As they had done many times before, the two men shared stories of Barnett and Dean Thomas's favorite times together, Barnett's memories of Touch's athletic endeavors, and stories of Touch's times away from Cooper. Touch had been like a surrogate son for

Barnett after David had died. Dean Thomas, proud of his son's achievements, proved more than capable and happy to share the joy of his son's accomplishments with his oldest friend. When Dean passed away, Andrew Barnett returned his friend's favor by offering Touch a father's wisdom and guidance. The possibility of finally putting David to rest offered comfort for both Andrew Barnett and Tanner Thomas.

CHAPTER 12

Touch awoke at 5:30 a.m. feeling only half rested the morning after questioning Welch and Shakopf and having dinner with Andrew Barnett. He had dropped by the sheriff's office to see Mandy Herman off, a process that appeared to progress unimpeded. Nothing overnight disturbed him, but he couldn't shake the feeling of being fed half-truths and platitudes the prior evening. As Touch laced up his On Cloudflow running shoes for his usual Tuesday morning three-mile route from his house, around the high school, and back, he recounted his dreams of the prior night. A particular sequence flashed Will Welch hunting as a young man, but Touch could not place any of the other relevant details: place, time, rifle, partners. As he left his house and found his usual early morning gait, he vowed to dig a little deeper and question Will Welch, Laceon Shakopf, and maybe Sam Stevens, the longtime publisher of the *Cooper Courier*.

About twenty-three minutes later, Touch arrived right back where he had started, entered his house, showered, pulled on another set of hideous uniform pants and a short-sleeve shirt in tan and brown, and headed over to the Tiger's Den for breakfast and his morning chat with Reva. More often than not, like yesterday, Reva's food and chats provided the highlights of his days.

Touch parked in his spot at the sheriff's office and strode down the sidewalk to the Tiger's Den, waving to Millie Davis at the dry cleaner's across the street. To the left of the dry cleaner's, Touch noticed another beater car with an out-of-place, grimy-looking fellow in it. As he entered the Tiger's Den, he grabbed a table with a clear view of the car and its inhabitant, and he greeted Reva and Johnny. Seated with his cup of coffee, a tall glass of ice water, and his usual order on the cooktop, Touch caught up on a little local gossip with his usual breakfast companions: the Babe Ruth baseball team had dropped both games of a double-header to Harperville yesterday, the district attorney was chomping at the bit to try a high school teacher accused of improper contact with an underage coed, and rumor had it one of the local banks was in line for a big hit on an out-of-town real estate loan that had gone bad. As Touch's breakfast arrived, the man from the beater across the street rang the Tiger's Den doorbell and stepped through the threshold. It wasn't Dougie Delaney, but the man appeared to be Dougie's larger, more tattooed, and more muscled cousin. Touch got the feeling that this morning's Tiger's Den visit wouldn't be the highlight of his day.

Nonetheless, the food was excellent, especially after his run. Touch polished off the last of his eggs, scooping them onto his fork with a corner of buttered toast. He chased that with his last swallow of coffee and then drained his glass of ice water. After rising and making his way to the counter to pay, Touch noticed that Johnny was in between orders with an empty stove. "Johnny, you got a minute to have a quick chat with me out back?"

"Sure thing, Touch. Follow me," Johnny replied.

Touch stepped behind the counter and followed Johnny through the back door of the café. "Johnny, you ever remember Will Welch or Laceon Shakopf hanging out around the north part of the county when you lived out there?"

Johnny got a thoughtful look on his face. "Touch, I gave that time some thought yesterday when things slowed down. I can't remember anything specific about who did what or where they might have done it out there. I asked my wife and the other folks I speak to at church about that time and area. Nothing seemed to shake loose."

Touch thanked Johnny for his time and turned to head back into the Tiger's Den. As Touch walked past the cooktop, the man from the beater had Reva by the arm. A water glass spilled and broke on the floor behind the cash register. Seeing someone with hands on Reva triggered an animal response in Touch. In a step and a leftward power shuffle, Touch cleared the counter. The man unhanded Reva, hearing someone moving strong and fast to his right. Touch, sensing a backhand right coming from the man, countered with a circular right forearm to the man's elbow. Pivoting to close the distance and reinforce the power behind his forearm block, Touch grabbed the waistband of the man's pants and hiked them up as he swept his feet out from under him. Clearly and crisply, Touch dropped the man on his face and brought his wrist halfway up his back with his left hand while pulling a set of handcuffs off his service belt with his right hand.

Touch said, "Sorry, fellow, but some folks around here are untouchable, and Reva Dennis is one of those people," Touch explained to the man. "I'm guessing this was an ill-thought-out setup of some sort to get thrown into my jail so you can tune up or maybe cancel Hank Benitez. Not gonna happen. Reva, you okay?"

"Yeah, Touch, no problem. I don't know what his problem is. He just came in, knocked a glass of ice water out of my hand, and got aggressive," Reva said.

Touch fished the man's wallet out of his right-hand back pants pocket; the wallet was chained to a belt loop. His name was Ricky Drummond, and nothing about the name rang a bell. His driver's license gave an address in a small town in Eastern Kentucky.

"Ricky, I believe I'm going to walk you back out to your car, and we're going to have a quick little chat," Touch informed the man as he hefted him to his feet by his right bicep. The two walked across the street toward Davis's Dry Cleaners and Drummond's piece of shit car. "All right, Ricky, I'm going to take these cuffs off you. I want you to seat yourself in your car with your hands on the steering wheel. You do anything other than that, and I'll drag you out of your car by your hair, cuff you again facedown, and escort you to the city police station, where you can meet my buddy, Chief of Police Chris Hauser.

"From the address on your driver's license, the appearance of your car, and a few of your tattoos, which match a couple on my new friend Dougie Delaney, I'm guessing the two of you are somehow affiliated. If so, I want you to tell your boss that whatever you're up to in Cooper and Walter County isn't welcome and isn't going to work. I know you guys intimidated Hank Benitez: we've got multiple, around-the-clock watches on his parents' house and restaurant. The US Attorney liked a great deal what Mandy Herman had to say about the Dixie Mafia and its plans to move pills and meth across the lake. She's already shipped out, but I'm guessing you guys know that too. The more y'all screw around over here, the more I learn about you. I suggest y'all move on somewhere else. Or better yet, just go legitimate. I can find you a job this afternoon with one of our local shops; I bet you're really good at deliveries, huh? Either way, neither you nor any of your Dixie Mafia brothers are messing with Hank or any of the other Benitezes."

Drummond responded, "Sheriff, I don't think you've got much of a handle on what's about to go down around here. Once the people I work for decide to go, they don't stop. Product demand just grows, and things adjust around it. I'm sure you've compared notes with your partners in Pikeville and Monticello, maybe even the Tennessee towns south of there. Associating with Hank was a mistake, but we've got longer-standing associates much higher up in Cooper. Hank was just a street-level mover like me, nothing more. I'll pass your word on, though."

"I see you again, locked up you will be," Touch said as he turned to walk back to the Tiger's Den. "Reva, I believe I forgot to pay my bill. If you see that fellow in here again, give me a call immediately."

Touch paid his bill, rang the doorbell of the Tiger's Den for fourth time that morning as he exited the café, and turned to make his way to his office. As he walked down the sidewalk, Queen's "Another One Bites the Dust" played in his head. It was not even nine o'clock yet, and Touch had already encountered the Dixie Mafia. Tuesday felt like it'd be as difficult a day as Monday had been.

CHAPTER 13

"Good morning, Touch," Bonnie greeted the sheriff as he entered his office.

"Hey, Bonnie," Touch returned the greeting. "Can you destroy whatever Mandy Herman paperwork we had, if any, please? Also, can you find me a phone number for Will Welch and for Laceon Shakopf? I'm going to give Sam a call over at the paper."

Touch flipped through the Rolodex on his desk. Upon finding Sam Spencer's number, he lifted the receiver on his phone and dialed the number. Whoever answered the phone at the paper let Touch know that Stevens usually didn't make it to the office before 10:00 a.m. Touch asked them to let Stevens know that the Sheriff would be over at ten to chat and returned the phone receiver to its cradle.

"Touch," Bonnie hollered from the reception area, "I emailed you Will Welch's and Laceon Shakopf's phone numbers. I didn't find any paperwork on Mandy Herman."

Touch called both men and left messages for them, asking for a return call and letting them know he would stop by for a visit if he hadn't heard back from them by midafternoon. Touch crossed a few items off his to-do list early this morning, but he didn't feel like he'd accomplished much.

Still running a bit of an adrenaline high from his Ricky Drummond encounter, Touch decided it would be productive to take a moment and make some notes on the two things dominating his thoughts: David Barnett's murder and the Dixie Mafia moving drugs through his county. Ten minutes later, Touch had buzzword lists for both situations on separate pads of paper: "Hunting, leases, .243, Welch, Shakopf, motive, accident" for the Barnett case and "Hank, meth, pills, Dixie Mafia, lake, money, distribution, users, overdose" for the Dixie Mafia situation. Touch felt his outstanding calls and prior night conversations were all he could do for the time being on the David Barnett case. His list revealed a couple loose ends on the Dixie Mafia situation, though: distribution, users, and overdose. Touch thought "users" and "overdose" called for a hospital visit to chat with the folks manning the emergency room. Walter County deputies responded to their share of drug-related calls, but Touch had yet to realize or search for any sort of pattern in those calls. Similarly, he thought another conversation with his buddy Chris could shed more light on the county's drug situation.

Touch decided a walk over to the Cooper Police Station sounded like a good idea. On his way out of the office, he checked with Bonnie on overnight and early morning developments: "Bonnie, anything interesting happen around here last night or this morning?"

"No, Touch, nothing. None of the deputies mentioned anything out of the ordinary. No additions to the prisoners' docket. The three we had yesterday are fed and appear in as good a shape as they were yesterday evening," Bonnie replied.

"Stay vigilant, Bonnie," Touch instructed. "Reva and I had a run-in with another Dixie Mafia clown earlier this morning at the Den. Fella by the name of Ricky Drummond from East Kentucky put his hands on Reva, and I almost lost it. Dropped him, dragged him back out to his car, and had a conversation. Taller, grimier, more muscled looking version of Dougie Delaney. If you see him, let me know ASAP because I issued him a warning on which I intend to follow through should it go unheeded."

Touch exited his office, turning right toward the south side of the courthouse. Cooper's municipal police station, which was about one hundred years newer and, as a result, just as large as the courthouse that housed the Walter County Sheriff's Office, stood a couple blocks southeast of the courthouse. Even if Chris Hauser wasn't at this desk, Touch figured he could glean the information he needed from some of the officers manning the counter and desks in the station. Despite long-standing differences, the people in town and the folks in the country went about their business and lived their lives, Cooper and Walter County shared similar crime trends. The city simply encountered more of the crimes due to its larger and denser population than did the county. Hauser and Touch typically grabbed breakfast together on a monthly cadence to compare notes, but more often than not their "business breakfasts" devolved into more a reliving of the old days and less a systematic review of what each other saw from their respective jurisdictions. Hence, Touch's pursuit of an impromptu meeting.

"Hi," Touch greeted the officer manning the front counter of the Cooper Police Station. "Is Chief Hauser in?"

"Hey, Sheriff," the officer returned Touch's greeting. "I'll check and see if Chief Hauser is at his desk. Gimme one minute, please."

Touch waited at the station's front counter humming Hank Williams Jr.'s "All My Rowdy Friends" quietly. Touch didn't agree with a number of Bocephus's late middle-age comments and positions, but he still liked the singer-songwriter's ability to capture the trials and tribulations of getting older. No sooner did Touch get to his favorite part of the song, the one with the "cooked the pig in the ground and got some beer on ice," than Chris Hauser stepped out of his office and walked toward the counter. The sight of Hauser reinforced the smile on Touch's face from humming Williams's song.

"Touch, what brings you over to the poorer side of town this morning?" said Chief Hauser.

"Poorer, my ass, Chris. Your office is the size of the entire sheriff's department!" Touch said. "Who says crime doesn't pay?"

"Why don't we duck into my office before we get ourselves in trouble?" Hauser asked.

Touch followed Hauser back to his office. "Chris, what can you tell me about recent drug trends in the city—up, down, flat?"

Hauser thought on the question for a moment and moved the mouse of his computer to awaken it. "I want to say we've seen an uptick in meth-related arrests, as well as confiscations of larger amounts of pills: Vicodin, Percocet, and the other hydrocodone-derivative pain pills. Thankfully, the fentanyl-laced stuff doesn't seem to have arrived here ... yet. I don't know that the numbers support those hunches. Let me check the recent drug-related offenses to be sure."

Hauser navigated his computer to recent drug-related case files while Touch played out the events of the last thirty-six hours or so, as well as his thoughts on possible implications for Cooper and Walter County. "I've now had two Dixie Mafia encounters in less than twenty-four hours: one, a borderline midget stepped right into the sheriff's office in a blatant intimidation attempt, and two, a larger and uglier henchman tried to get thrown into the county jail by laying hands on Reva at the Tiger's Den. Hank Benitez remains behind bars in my jail and is the target of that intimidation. The US Attorney shipped off Hank's girlfriend to greener pastures for a while, at least. Both Hank and Mandy Herman, his now ex-girlfriend, corroborated that the Dixie Mafia plans to use Lake Barkley as a primary means of undetected north-south transportation in order to move more meth and pills at least, if not also heroin, into West Kentucky, Southern Illinois, Indiana, and points farther north. I don't know enough about the players, though, to tell who's bankrolling this move into the area."

Hauser clicked through a few screens and typed several search terms into his office's file manager program as Touch spoke. When Touch paused, Hauser provided the results of his searches. "I was pretty close to right, Touch, as usual: modest increases in meth and pills confiscated. Logically, it looks like overdose activity also rose. I'm sure we can validate that with the EMTs and the hospital's ER. As for potential dealers, we have yet to discover amounts consistent with anything other than low-level dealing and sharing. Care to take a quick drive over to the ER with me? Not a bad idea to show our faces there every once in a while, huh?"

"Fine idea, Chris," Touch agreed. "Any interest in dropping by Sam Stevens's office on the way back? The *Cooper Courier* may not have *New York Times* or *Washington Post* investigative reporting capabilities, but they seem to do a solid job linking things together and don't scare perps or victims quite to the degree that uniformed folks do."

Hauser looked over at Touch with a raised eyebrow as the two exited the police station and worked their way toward Hauser's cruiser in his reserved parking spot. "I've heard worse ideas, but I admit it feels strange for the cops to be going to the reporters for the story," Hauser admitted.

"Maybe there's not even a story yet, Chris," Touch posited. "Something here doesn't feel right, and I don't sense it's a small wrong either. I'd rather gather more info from more sources than try to piecemeal a bunch of unrelated tidbits that maybe someone's already started to link together. As usual, we don't have to tell anyone anything we don't want to tell them. Might as well get a few free gumshoes on it, though, don't you think? How many true detectives does Cooper have, anyway?"

"True detectives, Touch?" Hauser repeated. "I'd argue we have zero true detectives. What the city of Cooper has is one over-the-hill former patrol officer more interested in free coffee and donuts than in stemming crime in Cooper, and one wet-behind-the-ears recent college graduate intent on moving up to the city attorney's office ASAP by taking law school classes at night. Now, mercifully, the lack of much in the way of detective skills may be a direct result of a lack of serious crime, but everyone would probably be more comfortable if the two detectives Cooper has would take their jobs a little more seriously."

As Hauser and Touch navigated through Cooper's relatively light midmorning traffic on the approximately twelve-minute drive to the hospital, Touch was surprised to discover the radio in Chris Hauser's police cruiser tuned to the same country station, WBVR, to which Touch frequently (and Bonnie always) listened. As the DJ concluded their quick synopsis of the lack of traffic situation around Bowling Green, the home of WBVR, the station segued into the Chicks' "Travelin' Soldier," a somber account of the quick-love connection between a young, shipping-out soldier and a café waitress. Thinking of a potential meaning of the song in the context of his current frame of mind, Touch mentioned to Hauser how quickly some things could escalate—the love of a young couple and a city's drug problem. No sooner had he mentioned that than "Travelin' Soldier" concluded and gave way to Toby Keith's "A Little Less Talk and a Lot More Action."

"What the hell is this DJ's problem this morning?" Hauser asked. "Not only is messaging between 'Travelin' Soldier' and 'A Little Less Talk' completely bass-ackwards, but following up the Chicks with Toby Keith is just plain wrong even if their George Bush–related dustup happened damned near twenty years ago."

Touch smirked a little and then affirmed Hauser's stance. "Yeah, I remember that mess. Everyone would have been so much better off if Toby and the Chicks had cowritten a song about destroying weapons of mass destruction and launched it at a benefit concert for wounded soldiers. Finger pointing almost always screws both sides over. I hear the Chicks rebranded, though. I've not heard much about Toby lately."

Both Hauser and Touch were singing Keith's refrain as they entered the hospital ER parking lot. They parked, exited the cruiser, and walked into the ER. Both men were mildly pleased to see not much going on Tuesday at midmorning. As they stepped toward the triage nurse at the check-in counter, they addressed the nurse at the same time. "Hi."

"Gentlemen, to what do I owe the pleasure of the sheriff and the chief visiting our ER this morning?" the ER nurse, Lenny Curry, asked.

"Lenny, we were hoping to chat with you a bit about observations you might have on drug activity in the city and county over the past month or so. Anything different in your mind?" Hauser inquired.

About fifteen years younger than Touch and Chris Hauser, Lenny Curry had left Cooper for college and returned to the town's hospital about eight years ago after a couple years as a nurse in one of Louisville's trauma centers. Lenny had been the lead ER nurse for the past few years.

"Strange you should ask, because I've noticed an uptick in opioid pill overdoses the past couple of weeks. Thankfully, we don't have many—two or three a month going to five or six—so it's difficult to say for sure, but overall drug-related patient flow feels like it's higher than it was a while back. It's certainly nowhere near the increase we saw several years ago as heroin gave way to much cheaper, fentanyl-laced stuff. I think the massive reduction in pill availability from the "factories" probably took a lot of availability off the streets, but again, there are not a lot of cases from which to draw conclusions. It certainly feels like prescriptions are far more difficult to come by and patient education substantially improved regarding pain meds and related potential addictions. Can I ask why you guys are asking?"

Touch responded, "Thanks, Lenny. We're following up some increased activity and possible encroachment from the Dixie Mafia. Anything come to mind that might relate to that group?"

"I can't say that I know much of anything about Dixie Mafia versus any other tattooed white folks who make their ways into the ER. Certainly years ago we saw their presence in Louisville, but nothing anywhere close to that around here. People got some crazy mess on themselves nowadays; you wouldn't believe some of the stories I hear about why an otherwise normal person decides to get themselves stamped. Plenty of Black folks tatted up as well for equally strange reasons. Myself, I prefer to keep my money in my pocket and hang my art on my walls."

Hauser concluded the conversation. "Thanks, Lenny. If anything else interesting—other than opinions on tattoos—comes to mind, you know where to find Touch and me and how to get hold of us. Have a good one."

Touch and Chris Hauser loaded themselves back into Hauser's cruiser. Blanco Brown's "The Git Up" greeted them on WBVR. It was a feel-good song, and both men modestly bobbed their heads to the song's catchy beat, which was followed by a flurry of commercials. Touch and Hauser soon pulled into the *Courier's* parking lot, conveniently located only five minutes away from the hospital, before another song came on the radio.

Hauser held the newspaper office's door open for Touch, and the two entered a small reception area. "Hi," Touch said to the receptionist, who was stuffing what appeared to be account statements into envelopes. "Is Sam Stevens in?"

"Hey, Touch Thomas and Chris Hauser. Are y'all looking for Policeman's Ball donations or something? Kind of strange to see the two of you together at the news offices," the receptionist said.

"Now that you mention it, Rhonda, we wouldn't mind the paper stepping up to the plate with a fat donation to help out Walter County law enforcement's youth programs," countered Hauser. "What we're really here for, though, is to pick Sam's brain about any increased drug activity she or your reporters might have noticed over the past month or so. Is she in?"

In the case of Sam Stevens, Sam was short for Samantha. Now approaching sixty and aging like a fine wine, Sam Stevens had inherited the publisher role of the *Cooper Courier* from her father upon the man's ten-years-too-late retirement several years ago. Long the source of news and the primary advertising medium in Cooper, the Stevens family had launched the *Courier* about 170 years ago, 50 or so years after the founding of the city.

"Gentlemen, take a seat, please, and let me see if Ms. Stevens can see you," the receptionist instructed the two men. Shortly after disappearing into Stevens's office, the receptionist returned. "Give her about five minutes to finish up what she's doing, and then feel free to knock and enter."

Touch and Hauser thumbed through the recent papers and a magazine or two they picked up from the coffee table and end table of the seating area while they waited the allotted five minutes. Nothing of note struck either of them from perusing the periodicals—mostly items they'd seen or heard about over the past ten days or so. After noting the passage of time on the wall clock directly in front of them, Touch finished glossing over a *Kentucky Living* article on Bourbon Trail bed and breakfast inns while Chris Hauser left half read a piece in the *Louisville Courier-Journal* on Pat Kelly, the manager of the minor league Louisville Bats, the Cincinnati Reds AAA affiliate.

Rising from their chairs, Touch and Hauser walked the few steps towards Stevens's office, rapped lightly on the door, waited a few seconds, and entered the office. Hauser went first, followed by Touch. "Sam, thanks for seeing us this morning," Touch said as he and Hauser entered the office.

"My pleasure, Touch. Hi, Chief Hauser," Sam Stevens said. "I'm mildly honored, and maybe a little frightened, that you came to see me together."

"No reason to be frightened, Sam, I assure you," Touch said. "As you're well aware, Chris and I go way back. We just used this morning as an opportunity to catch up on a few mutual interests as we look to educate ourselves on a potential development in the city and county. Anything you can tell us about increased drug-related activities you or your reporters may have picked up on recently?" Touch asked.

Stevens pushed back from her desk, looked up to the ceiling, and thought for a moment before she answered Touch. She drummed her fingers on her desk as she leveled her eyes on the sheriff and the chief. "Touch, Chris, we've been working on an investigative piece for a few weeks now. One of our more seasoned reporters, not to give away too much, got a tip about more drugs flowing into the western part of the state from an interview they conducted over at the state prison on a completely different matter. We've not gotten very far, though, because the money seems to run really quietly. Also, from what we can tell at this point, drug flows are slow but steady. Whoever's behind it appears intent on establishing process and system, knowing personalities and backgrounds, and not making a big splash early.

"We've had two staff people digging on this for about a month. At first, we allocated the lead reporter a week to run down other leads after initial mention in the prison. Nothing blatantly obvious jumped out, but it was clear from speaking with folks at the hospital and monitoring the calls from both of your offices that something changed. I want both of you to know that we don't have enough yet to share with you other than that it appears something changed. Although it's not usually the way things are done, I'd appreciate the opportunity to at least work in parallel on this, if not in partnership. What do you say?"

Touch and Hauser looked at each other and shrugged. Touch said, "Sam, I think we can agree to work together on this—a sort of covert community task force, if you will. Your personnel have to know and be comfortable with the fact that this situation likely comes with elevated risk as soon as we start poking around with them. How about Chris and I leave you a couple cards, and you have your people contact us about setting up an initial meeting?"

Both men reached into the shirt pockets, separated out a few business cards from their stacks, and passed them to Stevens. As the two men did so, they rose from their chairs, offered their thanks, and shook the older woman's hand.

Sometimes Cooper offered residents a "small town" feel; other times the small city seemed like a larger place than it actually was. In this regard, Touch got the feeling that Cooper offered the best of both worlds and expressed as much to Chris Hauser as the two men made their way out of the newspaper's offices and back to Hauser's cruiser.

"Chris, I don't think we could have pulled that meeting off if Sam Stevens didn't know me or you. I also don't think we'd have even tried it if we didn't have the history we do. Do you? In a larger place, we'd each be too worried about saving face or owning the case. In a smaller town, the newspaper wouldn't have the resources to even think about initiating an investigative piece like this, let alone allocate resources to track down sources the reporter didn't already know. Just maybe, we could be in a sweet spot to nip this thing in the bud before it gets any bigger."

Hauser took a minute to start the car and tune the radio to WPKY; he'd had enough country for one morning. As The Marshall Tucker Band's "Can't You See" now blared from the radio, Hauser offered his two cents. "I hear you, partner. It'd be nice to be lucky and cut this snake off at the head before it starts to slither."

Neither Hauser nor Touch had an idea how large this snake already was or how far it had started to slither.

CHAPTER 14

Touch and Hauser took advantage of what seemed to be a slow morning for everyone else to drop by the Tiger's Den for lunch. Reva, unfazed from the earlier excitement, greeted both men with a smile and a recitation of the special: turkey club sandwich with sides of roasted carrots and french fries. Two sweet teas were served to the two men, shortly followed by two specials. Johnny came out from behind his cooktop to greet Hauser and Touch. Johnny had known Chris Hauser his entire life, with a few cousins in common.

Touch and Hauser exited the café forty minutes later after catching up on the local sports scene, talented youngsters worthy of keeping an eye on, and hatching out a handful of scenarios on how the Dixie Mafia drug case might progress. They parted ways, and as Touch walked down the sidewalk toward his office, he ran through Cooper's and Walter County's sources of wealth and cash flow.

Most of the "old money" in Cooper fled the town for larger cities and opportunities to make even more money in the 1970s as small-town manufacturing gave way to international competition. Few of the legacy families, like Sam Stevens' family, remained in Cooper. The city housed several manufacturing facilities that collectively employed several thousand people: a washing machine assembly plant owned by a Korean conglomerate, an assembler of car seats for GM's Cobalt sedan, and a chemical plant that, Touch thought, made plastic pellets that got shipped all over the world and reformed into milk jugs or water bottles or some other consumer product containers. A handful of the money center banks saw fit to maintain at least one branch in Cooper, competing with the half dozen or so county and regional banks with offices in the city. The Welch Family's Walter County Bank, after numerous consolidations over the past twenty years, now stood as the only bank actually headquartered in Cooper. It launched and maintained branches in most of Western Kentucky's major towns and county seats. Car dealers made fine money decades ago, providing donations that funded scoreboards for Cooper and Walter County sports teams for as long as Touch could remember. However, the second and now third generations of those dealership families had long since consumed much of the original owners' wealth; they now solidly occupied upper-middle-class existences. Similarly, the agricultural players in the county held on to their acreage too long and, as a result, levered up and added debt into eras of much lower commodity prices. High-profile bankruptcies in the Farm Aid–era of 1980s Middle America left several families permanently separated. Those bankruptcies likely drove better negotiating terms for the Welches to continue consolidating banks in the area. Nothing else came immediately to mind for Touch as he entered the sheriff's office.

"Touch, Will Welch and Laceon Shakopf returned your phone calls from this morning," Bonnie said.

"Thanks, Bonnie. Either of them have anything worthwhile to say, or just that they returned my call?" asked Touch as he made his way back to the men's cell block.

"Just returning your call, Touch. Both said they'd be around after lunch. Neither Welch nor Shakopf left a cell number."

Touch mentally recorded the info as he rounded a corner on his way to check with Hank Benitez. "Hank, you feeling better today after a productive night's sleep and no booze?"

"Hey, Sheriff Thomas. Yeah, I feel a world better today. No smarter, but plenty better, thanks. Any update on my situation?"

"Yeah, I think you may be in as large a world of shit, as we feared. Some Dixie Mafia moron put his hands on Reva at the Tiger's Den earlier this morning. I had a discussion with him. Although he didn't say so directly, I think he was just pushing my buttons and trying to get thrown in here with you. That should make you plenty uncomfortable. Can you remember any indications as to who backed the Dixie Mafia's move into Cooper and Walter County? Chief Hauser and I had a conversation with someone that would lead one to believe that this new drug pipeline started at least two months ago. I can understand the move to use the lake to deal drugs, but I don't necessarily know who'd fund a loss-leading push into the county just to unseat the existing distributors. Moreover, I don't know why they would invite in the Dixie Mafia as muscle for that move. I can't imagine either of those initiatives is a cheap one."

"Sorry, Sheriff, but I always had at least one go-between I'd never seen before. I was just a bagman, more or less, for those Mafia fellas. I know a few of the low-level sellers from my user days; that's all I was good for. I thought I might be able to do more and move up, but I never got any buy-in for anything beyond simple drops and introductions. That's kinda what led to the fallout with Mandy: she thought I oughta get out altogether. Sorta too much risk, too little reward kinda thing," Hank revealed. "Mandy never wanted anything to do with it in the first place, honest."

"Who was it from the mafia that you dealt with, Hank? Always the same person, or always a different person?"

"Always a different person, Sheriff, like they never wanted the same person to see me one time to the next. Usually, trust makes it a more profitable relationship—a know-your-seller type thing—but they didn't seem to care about that at this point."

Touch thought for a moment. "All right, Hank, I appreciate you being straight with me. I'm going to see about getting you out of here. I don't know how safe things are going to be, though, given this morning's event."

"I appreciate it, Sheriff Thomas. I think it'd be best for everyone if I put Cooper in my rearview mirror for a while, if not forever. I know I should be going to prison. At this point, it might be safer than not going, but like I said, I really know nothing."

"One last thing, Hank. Where did you usually meet up with these fellas?"

Hank looked up at the ceiling of his cell and replied, "Always somewhere around the lake. Usually at one of the gas stations or convenience stores, so as to blend into traffic and not look out of place."

Touch wandered back to his office from Hank's cell. The balance of the cells was vacant because Jones's and Turner's relatives had seen fit to float bail after the two had spent a weekend in jail. Touch figured it'd be that way for the rest of the week because it was too damned hot to commit much in the way of meaningful crime until the lake scene returned to regular Thursday night through Sunday evening.

Touch pondered calling back Will Welch and Laceon Shakopf to set up individual meetings with them this evening or tomorrow morning. He reflected on how long he'd know each man and their families. Touch thought fleetingly about it while speaking with their fathers at the country club, but he still thought of the two old men as known entities—typical old, retired men. The younger generation, which was ten years or so older than Touch, were not so well-known. The world tilted, so to speak, through the sixties, seventies, and eighties as Will and Laceon came of age; it became smaller.

The Welch family merged into the Walter County Bank founding family two generations ago. Jerry Welch's father, Harold, married Mavis Carpenter, daughter of the bank's founder Peter. Peter Carpenter gave everything he had to save Walter County Bank from bankruptcy through the Great Depression. Harold Welch led the bank through the postwar years and into the 1970s before yielding the reins to Jerry. To Touch's knowledge, Walter County Bank never ventured outside its comfort zone: small business, consumer, and mortgage loans with a smattering of agricultural loans and syndicated economic development bonds related to Cooper's manufacturing base. It was a community bank through and through, and Touch guessed that the bank always was too tightly held by the family to be on the acquisition list for the larger firms that had snapped up every other local bank in Cooper over the last twenty years. In fact, Walter County Bank saw fit to bid against those larger institutions in picking up several once prime franchises in other West Kentucky towns.

The banker's touch, however, ended with Jerry Welch. Will Welch was given every opportunity to assume control of the bank, but he balked at each of those chances. Incapable of just playing follow the leader, Will Welch fulfilled the untitled role of chief community relations officer for Walter County Bank. A nephew of Jerry Welch, Davis Welch, rose through the lending ranks to become president of the bank about ten years ago. From all indications and prior discussions, none of this concerned Jerry or Will. It appeared almost as though both knew that leadership of the family bank likely would not be in Will's future, nor would Jerry or Will care much about it. The Welches appeared to live well within their means: nice but not flashy houses, country club memberships, vacations to attractive locations, and top-end but domestic automobiles.

Edmund Shakopf, despite an unlikely long-standing friendship with Jerry Welch, was cut from different cloth. Shakopf rose to success with nothing given to him, excepting a small business loan from Walter County Bank decades ago with which he purchased the filling station for which he'd worked the previous five years. A graduate of Walter County High School, Shakopf had worked at his southside filling station from the age of sixteen. When the original owner tired of showing up every morning at 7:00 and staying until

7:00 in the evening, Edmund saw an opportunity. With an agreement from his boss to cosign his bank loan, Edmund Shakopf took over the station. Over the years, Shakopf built a network of service stations, heavily buying into the convenience store expansion of the seventies and eighties. By the time he turned day-to-day operations over to his son Laceon, his empire spanned the entire western region of Kentucky. Shakopf so impressed Welch with his business acumen that he had invited the man to join Walter County Bank's board of directors thirty years ago.

Outside of Welch's and Shakopf's budding business relationship, the two men's sons also struck up a friendship in middle school. Neither at the top of their class nor chosen first for pickup sports teams, Will and Laceon basked in each other's mediocrity through middle school and high school, just old-school buddies cruising Cooper, fishing, and hunting. As typical boys growing into young men through the late seventies and into the eighties in small-town USA, the two boys never got into any major trouble. They lacked the bodies and thus the confidence to be bullies. Never the sharpest tacks in the board, Will and Laceon proved to be of the go-along-to-get-along class of kids.

Touch knew from conversations with his father that both of the Welches, Jerry and Will, fought bouts of drinking too much over the years. As far as he knew, though, nothing more problematic than that ever arose. To his knowledge, neither Edmund nor Laceon Shakopf ever had any run-ins with law enforcement. A quick search of Kentucky's criminal records database confirmed the same: no records for any of the Welches or Shakopfs. Nevertheless, Touch got another of his feelings. Things were too neat. Whether due to causation or correlation, the same names kept popping up from unrelated questions and events.

Resigning himself to the fact that no other way existed to figure out the mystery of David Barnett's death other than to keep doing the work, Touch picked up his phone and set up a late afternoon meeting with Will Welch at the country club bar. He followed up with a call to Laceon Shakopf, agreeing to stop by his house later that evening. With a few hours until his Will Welch meeting, Touch decided to see if he could visit Mandy Herman's parents.

CHAPTER 15

"Hey, Bonnie," Touch said as he left his office and walked through the reception area. "I'm running out to the Hermans' place northwest of town to inform them of Mandy's status. I've got an afternoon chat with Will Welch scheduled at the country club and doubt that I'll be back before that. I'll speak with Laceon Shakopf later this evening, too. Call me on the radio if anything interesting happens."

Touch fired his Tahoe's ignition and noticed the gas tank sat below a quarter tank. After exiting town on his way to the Hermans, Touch stopped at one of Shakopf's service stations—maybe the third or fourth Edmund had launched in his buildout. Over the years, Touch had probably stopped at the station for gas, a drink, or a snack several hundred times. As with most facets of everyday life, he'd never considered the typical traffic flow in and out of the place. Well located at a major intersection of the state highway that led out of town to the northwest and the primary drag that ran to downtown Cooper, cars and people beehived the place as they drove to and from the pumps and walked in and out of the convenience store doors.

After climbing back into his service Tahoe, Touch thought the place must be a cash cow, yet he never recollected it ever being robbed. Years ago, when the regional and definitely the local economy found itself in the shitter, Cooper's gas stations and convenience stores encountered a rash of holdups. Reflecting, back, Touch didn't remember this particular location ever getting hit despite the fact that it ranked among the busiest spots in town. The activity level may have deterred stickups, but rarely did such logic enter the minds of those holding up places. Going where the money was almost always outweighed the fears of getting seen or being caught.

While he drove the Tahoe out of Cooper and into Walter County and still noodled on the holdup idea, Robert Earl Keen's "The Road Goes on Forever," a song that never got the radio play it deserved, popped into Touch's head. It was about a couple of small-town loser-lovers that go on a hold-up spree with the guy taking the rap for the girl. Touch again thought that things may not be as they'd always seemed. He ruminated on the idea and the song for the rest of the fifteen minutes it took to drive to the Hermans'. Along the way, Touch passed the turnoff for Charlie Sprague's farm and David Barnett's murder site. He thought he'd take the opportunity to visit it again while he was on this side of town.

After pulling up to the Herman's house, Touch remembered the last time he'd come out here: another assault on Mandy by Hank several years ago. Dean Thomas had visited Bob Herman, Mandy's father, a time or two many years ago before Bob matured into the decent father and husband he'd now been for almost forty years. Both Bob and Maggie Herman, Mandy's mother, were home. Both had retired a couple years ago, Bob from a manufacturing job and Maggie from an office job with the school system, and they spent most days at home. Maggie puttered around the garden while Bob mostly tinkered with an assortment of small engines he took in to repair for friends and neighbors. Both were outside when Touch pulled up.

"Bob, Maggie," Touch opened, "how's retired life treating you?"

"Hey, Sheriff Thomas. We're doing okay," Bob replied. "What brings you out our way?"

"I'm sure you've heard through the grapevine one way or another that Mandy ran into some trouble with that no-good Hank a few days ago," Touch shared. "Do you mind if we take a seat over here at your picnic table? Hank got into some stuff he shouldn't have again, with some people he certainly should've steered clear of. Mandy didn't have anything directly to do with it—more along for a bad ride is how I'd describe it. Nonetheless, she came into some knowledge that I think will prove useful for us because we're trying to run down the folks Hank associated with. As a result, the US Attorney agreed to move Mandy to a safe location for a while, at least until this situation is in hand. Maybe it'll be permanent, depending on how everything shakes out. She's fine, and she'll continue to be fine, but she likely won't be contacting you for at least a few weeks. I promise you that if I hear anything, I'll come out for a visit."

Bob looked at Maggie. The two had become accustomed to Mandy encountering trouble through no efforts of her own. For whatever reason, difficulties seemed to find her. Through school, it usually related to being around the wrong people at the wrong time too, just like with Hank. Mandy was a good person but a terrible character judge—too trusting too early.

Maggie was the first to speak. "Touch, should we be concerned for our safety?"

Touch could tell from Bob's eyes that he'd had the same thought. Touch looked directly at the couple. "I don't think so, Maggie. The two of you don't know what Hank was involved in, do you? Plus, the information Mandy provided isn't directly linked to an individual in so much as it is to a larger organization. We've already endured some attempted intimidation, but I really can't see what scaring the two of you could accomplish now that the cat's out of the bag. I recommend remaining aware of your surroundings and situations, like older folks always should. My department and Chief Hauser's city police force are moving fast on this thing.

"While I'm here, let me pick your two brains on another issue, if I may. As you may or may not know, the murder of David Barnett years ago at Charlie Sprague's farm has bothered me and my dad for years. Not only was David's death never solved, but also the case largely has been cold for decades, with no new information offered or leads generated. While picking up Mandy at her house a couple days ago, we stopped by Sprague's house. I'm prone to do that every time I'm on this side of town, and I plan on doing it again after I leave the two of you. Anyway, Mandy mentioned that she thought someone maybe leased the land around Sprague's house to deer hunt. I know the Michaels lived to the east and probably never allowed anyone to hunt on their farm. Do you know if anyone leased the land west of Sprague's to hunt?"

Maggie Herman looked to her husband as he answered. "Well, Touch, that's going back quite a few years. I've actually hunted around Sprague's place in the past ten years or so. You know, that patch of woods is dense before it opens up to Charlie's spread across the road from his house. It's tough to get a decent shot, but it works well for stand hunting because you can hear the animals moving. Geez, over the years, though … let's see. Who even owned it thirty-plus years ago? I don't remember. I'm pretty certain that Edmund Shakopf, who owns all the gas stations, leased hunting ground out here off and on for years. I don't know that he specifically leased that tract, though, Sheriff Thomas. A handful of other names come to mind, but not another name as consistently as Mr. Shakopf's."

Touch's head rose from looking at the ground underneath the picnic table to looking Bob Herman in the eyes. "Thanks, Bob. I've got Edmund searching his records to see if he ever leased that piece to hunt on or not. Ever hear of Jerry Welch spending any time out this way?"

"Can't say that I have. I don't exactly run in the same social circles as the Walter County Bank president, though, Sheriff." Herman chuckled.

"Understood, Bob. Maggie, I appreciate your time. I'm sure Mandy'll be fine and in touch in a few weeks. Like I said, though, if anything suspicious happens, call me ASAP, please," Touch said as he arose from his bench seat. "One other thing: would you mind going over and grabbing Mandy's dog and caring for her? I hate the idea of that poor thing being alone waiting on her to return."

Bob Herman nodded his head as he replied, "Certainly, Touch. It'll be good for us to have an attachment to her while she's gone. Thanks."

Touch returned to the Tahoe and maneuvered it back toward the highway and Charlie Sprague's farm. Predictably, nothing had changed over the past two days since Touch had last visited the place. Touch checked his watch: it was just after two in the afternoon. Plenty of time to talk a walk over to the plot of land to the west of Sprague's farm. Eight minutes later, Touch was looking back toward his Tahoe and the spot in Sprague's front yard on which he previously stood. He guessed it wasn't too far off of where David Barnett had been on his lawn tractor when he had been shot. As Bob Herman said, the trees were thick with bushy undergrowth near the edges of the tract, where competition for sunshine was less than in the interior of the tract.

Touch never exhibited much interest in deer or squirrel or bird hunting, but he knew a great deal from prior professional experience about tracking, optimal shot setups, and bullet flight dynamics and trajectories. The dense underbrush likely had not changed much since 1977, but the mature trees offered excellent shot lines into the wide-open pasture that led up to Charlie Sprague's house. While looking up at the treeline, Touch imagined a hunter perched above the underbrush, sighting in a big buck making its way across the pasture. Touch made his way deeper into the wooded area, wanting to look at the larger trees and get an idea of light play. He thought the shadows might be similar to the those at Barnett's death given the time of day and the month of the year. However, the canopy was so dense that Touch had to take his sunglasses off to gain any detail from looking at the larger trees.

Upon exiting the woods and walking back to the Tahoe, Touch felt sure that whoever shot David Barnett did so from an out-of-season hunting stand in the wooded area to the west of Charlie Sprague's farm. Hunting from a stand in June made no sense, though—nothing of interest that one would hunt from a stand was in season then. As Touch climbed into his Tahoe, he concluded he may have learned some things, but he remained no less frustrated by the details of David Barnett's case.

CHAPTER 16

Touch drove back to Cooper and had about an hour to spare before his Will Welch meeting at the country club. After the third consecutive radio commercial on WPKY, Touch reached down and turned off the radio. Touch struggled with what to do with Hank after meeting with the Hermans.

Hank was a dumbass. Assaulting women was completely wrong and should never happen. When he was sober, though, Hank proved to be a decent guy. High or drunk, though, Hank was a danger to himself and others, more the former than the latter, especially now that Mandy safely was elsewhere. Touch possessed little confidence that running Hank through the penitentiary system would benefit the man or society in any way. Touch turned the situation over in his mind, understanding the system had evolved to pass the buck for exactly this type of case.

Touch settled on a deal he thought might serve Hank and the Cooper community well. He realized he was sheriff and not judge. Touch wielded a great deal of power in Cooper and Walter County, however, by virtue of reputation, accomplishment, and the trust those qualities earned him from his constituents and community. In the last election he had run unopposed, and according to Reva's regulars, no one in the county seriously considered running against him. Nevertheless, Touch avoided the contempt for his community of voters that might creep into the minds of others, and he frequently stressed on what defined the best move for the community. In this instance, Touch thought releasing Hank on his own recognizance, provided that he agreed to cut the grass and perform an additional four hours per week of service at the Cooper women's shelter until otherwise notified, might prove more rehabilitative and therapeutic than a prison term. It went without saying that the dumbass had to remain employed, clean, and sober to avoid indictment and a likely prison sentence. Touch thought he'd swing by the sheriff's office to present the deal to Hank and let the man think on it a night before agreeing to it.

After pulling into his parking spot, Touch stepped out of the Tahoe and surveyed the east side of the courthouse and the surrounding area. It was another powerfully hot, humid early summer day without much going on in downtown Cooper. Touch saw Bonnie doing her nails at her desk, so not a lot was going on in Walter County's Sheriff's Department either.

"Hey, Bonnie," said Touch. "I'm gonna have a quick talk with Hank Benitez and then head over to the country club for a chat with Will Welch. I take it from your nail work that nothing much's going on around here."

Bonnie replied, "Correct, Touch: nothing much going on around here. It's been quiet all day after your rough start to the morning. Too damned hot for much mischief."

Touch rounded the corner and strode a couple paces to Hank's cell. "Hank, I've been thinking on you the last few hours. I still want to kick the living shit out of you for raising a hand to Mandy. She should've kicked you in the balls and beaten your ass with an iron skillet; I'd have just laughed about it. All that's beside the point, though. You're a dumbass, but not necessarily a bad guy. I don't think prison time will do you much good. Likely, it'll just prey on your dumbassness and get you into more trouble. I fear you'd exit prison horizontally, not vertically. So what I propose is a three-pronged

Hank improvement program: One, get your shit together and get a job. Your parents' restaurant, another restaurant, whatever—you've got to do something productive. Two, remain clean and sober at all times, no questions or excuses. And three, cut the grass and give the Cooper women's shelter four more hours per week of volunteer time—lifting heavy stuff, painting, cooking, cleaning, whatever the staff asks of you with no questions asked. I'll get periodic reports from the women's center and check in with you every week or so. No one ever says a word about this, period. You think on it overnight, and we'll talk about it in the morning, okay?" Touch closed the offer and walked back to his office.

With thirty minutes until he needed to depart, Touch pulled up Google on his laptop and searched "Dixie Mafia Kentucky." The relative diversity of entries among the top ten results surprised Touch: a claim that the loosely organized gang dated to the 1950s, evidence of an assassinated federal judge and his wife, links between Whitey Bulger and the Dixie Mafia, various true crime podcast advertisements, and a number of mentions of the F/X series *Justified*, which Touch enjoyed watching several years ago. Unfortunately, minus the judge assassination piece, most of it appeared to be bullshit. Like many other things in the world these days, Touch concluded, people needed a label by which to refer to something in order to take it seriously. Killing a judge was serious enough for Touch, though, and he suspected that was why Shel Richardson at the US Attorney's office also seemed to take the situation seriously.

Eventually, Touch discovered Wikipedia's Dixie Mafia page. Largely void of citations, the wiki page named Biloxi, Mississippi, as the group's de facto headquarters and a man of Croatian descent, Mike Gillich Jr., as its kingpin. Again with the labels ... Another couple paragraphs, and Touch learned that the Dixie Mafia associated with New Orleans organized crime as well—the old-school mafia. Further, one of the Dixie Mafia's more notorious members was thought to be behind the attempted assassination of

Sheriff Buford Pusser. Fleetingly, the thought of Dougie Delaney or Ricky Drummond attempting to assassinate Dwayne "The Rock" Johnson, who portrayed Pusser in the recent remake of *Walking Tall*, the story of Buford Pusser's life, tickled Touch.

Touch shut down and closed his laptop, wished Bonnie a good afternoon and a pleasant evening, and left the sheriff's office for the day. In a better, lighter mood after getting The Rock versus Dougie Delaney visual, Touch hopped into the Tahoe, fired the ignition, turned on the radio, and tuned it to WBVR. Alan Jackson and Jimmy Buffett were about halfway through their "It's Five O'Clock Somewhere" tune, always a good one to hear when one was on one's way to a bar. Several minutes later, Touch pulled into the Cooper Country Club parking lot the same as he had the day before, greeted the attendant, and asked how he might find Will Welch. The attendant informed him that Mr. Welch likely was either on the eighteenth green or had just finished up and therefore was on his way to the bar.

Touch thanked the young man and headed toward the bar, content that he would either meet Welch in the air-conditioned room or see him on his way there from the eighteenth green. Either way, he was plenty comfortable sharing an extra minute or two with Smiling Sarah, as Jerry Welch called her.

"Sarah, it's nice to see you again. I'll have another Knob Creek on the rocks, same as yesterday, please. You can put it on Mr. Barnett's tab as well." Touch said as he settled himself into a bar stool.

"Nice to see you again, Touch. You going to join the club or what? You seem to be spending as much time here over the past couple of days as our most active members," Sarah joked.

Game for witty banter after his computer search and listening to Jackson and Buffett on the radio, Touch replied, "No chance of that. One, golf's too slow a game for me, and two, Sheriffing doesn't come anywhere close to paying enough to cover the membership dues. Of course, I could just keep coming and mooching off the generosity of the fine folks who are already members of the club—sort of a 'why buy the cow if you can get the milk for free' approach to golfing and drinking!"

"Certainly a cheaper approach," Sarah said as she set the drink down in front of the sheriff. Several moments later, Will Welch joined Touch at the bar and ordered a Ketel One martini, just like his father had the day before.

"Sheriff Thomas, I just finished up my best round of golf of the year. I'm in a good mood, now. You're not gonna crap all over it, are you?" Welch greeted Touch.

Touch grinned at the thought of crapping on Will Welch's day, which basically boiled down to an afternoon golf game. Taking the high road, though, he replied, "Congrats on your golf game, Will. I appreciate you agreeing to meet with me on such short notice. I'm certainly not here to bring you down, but what I want to talk about isn't a pleasant subject. You were pretty young at the time, but I'm gonna hazard a guess that you remember the murder of David Barnett back in 1977. His case more or less haunted my father, and now it continues to trouble me as the sheriff office's most prominent unsolved case. You know Andrew Barnett and my family have always been close. Just in the past couple of days, a couple things shook loose, and I'm following them up. I had a chat with your father and Edmund Shakopf right here yesterday on the same subject, as a matter of fact. Interesting that your drink of choice is the same as your father's, by the way. Anyway, just a couple questions, and then anything you can share about your recollection of events and such from that time period would be really welcomed."

"Uh-huh, Touch, that's going back quite a way. What're your questions?"

"First, do you remember ever hunting with a .243? Second, do you recollect doing so out near Charlie Sprague's farm in the northwest part of the county?" Touch let those questions sink in. He could tell from Welch's facial expression that something had triggered a memory. The sheriff continued. "If you didn't recollect it, David was killed in June. So nothing really worth hunting at that time of year—squirrels, rabbits, varmints. Not to say that folks don't run out to blow off some steam shooting targets or groundhogs or crows, but doing so with a .243 would seem to be a little overkill, don't you think?"

Welch took a sip of his martini and looked into the mirror behind the bar, clearly thinking. Touch let him have his time and tried to read any change of expression from his reflection in the mirror.

Sarah placed a small bowl of bar mix in front of each of the men and inquired if they planned to also stay for dinner this evening.

"Thanks, Sarah, but I've got another conversation with Laceon Shakopf later this evening," Touch shared. He saw an eyebrow raise in Will Welch's reflection and a narrowing of the man's eyes. Sarah has perfect timing, just like an excellent barkeep should. He gave Welch a five count before following up his questions.

"Will, anything come to mind from back then? Jamie over at Fish and Wildlife also unearthed a deer tag Mr. Shakopf booked in late 1976, but it doesn't have any more info than name and date— no location. A friend of mine who lives out that way thought he remembered you guys hunting out that way back then. Maybe y'all saw something when you went back to take your stand out of a tree or to hunt coons, rabbits, or groundhogs in the spring or summer."

Will Welch turned to face Touch and said, "Laceon and I hunted all over the place when we were in high school. We were always together. Our families still spend quite a bit of time together. In fact, I'm surprised he wasn't golfing with me this afternoon; it's probably why I shot so well. Also, we definitely hunted with .243s. That was the most popular rifle of the time, I believe. We were such goofballs that there's no way our fathers were giving us anything better or more expensive to hunt with. Usually, we chose where to hunt, north or south, depending on a couple conversations with whoever our fathers were leasing hunting land from. It seemed like if the weather was warm, deer ran to the north, whereas colder weather had them concentrating in the south part of the county. Probably it was something to do with when farmers were harvesting crops, but I don't know anything beyond that. We'd go every afternoon after school and all day Saturday and Sunday until both of us tagged a deer. We still do it, as a matter of fact."

Touch nodded at Welch's recollections and pushed just a little bit more. "Any memory of going back out to that part of the county outside of hunting season? Did you guys shoot targets, rodents, or something else during the summers?"

"Sure, Touch, we shot targets at all those places too. Honestly, I'd probably have to see the place to remember if we shot targets or groundhogs or whatever there. Maybe you, Laceon, and I can schedule a time to meet up and see," Will Welch proposed. "Anything else from the case that might jog a memory? No one saw anything that I remember from the news coverage and talk, but did anything else ever present itself from an evidence or whatever standpoint?"

"Nope, you're correct, Will," Touch agreed. "Nothing else ever shook loose from an evidence point of view. No one that we've ever talked to saw anything. We found a .243 slug, as obvious from my questioning, but not a shell, a footprint, or anything else. My father and I have been grasping at straws on this case for over forty years at this point. David Barnett was autistic—harmless, basically: I'm guessing his getting shot was just a horrific accident. No one's ever come forward and claimed responsibility for it, though. With you and Laceon running all around the county back then, I just thought you might have seen something out of place around Sprague's farm. It's a long shot but worth a couple conversations, I think. Anyway, as I said, I'm speaking with Laceon a little later. We'll see if he remembers anything more notable or vividly than you recall. I really appreciate you giving me what you've got, though. Your father and Mr. Shakopf are checking their records to see if they leased that piece of ground west of Sprague's. I was just out there, and the woods and underbrush are dense as hell—tough to see anything other than the ground immediately in front of you. They didn't know about the rifles, though, so I'm glad you let me know .243s are what you and Laceon shot back then. If anything else comes to mind, you know how to get in touch with me."

With the heavy questioning out of the way, Touch switched gears and started chewing the fat with Will about his work, family, golf game, and other interests for the fifteen minutes the two men took to finish their drinks. Welch confirmed his responsibilities at the bank centered on community relations, volunteering, and related activities. His two kids—a boy, Jerry Jr., and Emma—were normal teenagers and into the usual kids' activities: sports, dance, band, and some forced Baptist church activities. All of this pretty much intersected with Shakopf's wife and kids as well, and the two saw each other multiple times a week in addition a standing golf game on the weekends and whenever in-week schedules allowed. The Welches also gathered for family dinners at the old man's house on Sunday afternoons.

Touch graciously allowed Will Welch to buy him his Knob Creek, saving Andrew Barnett eight dollars off his monthly bar tab from the Cooper Country Club. Sarah was prepared to comp it anyway, having acquired a soft spot for Barnett long ago. Touch thanked Welch again for his time, wished Sarah and then the parking lot attendant a good evening, walked to his Tahoe in the parking lot, and left to grab a quick bite to eat at home before meeting with Laceon Shakopf.

A serviceable cook but by no means a gourmet, Touch warmed the last of a smoked pork shoulder he'd barbecued Saturday and mixed it with some peppers, onions, and spinach to put on a couple tortillas and make burritos. The last of a bag of chili and cheese Fritos and a tumbler of sweet tea rounded out his evening meal.

Touch had married a couple years out of college. However, his young wife never took to the army's ways, and the two parted amicably a tour of duty later. Occasionally Touch dated, but no one had clicked with his lifestyle.

With a few minutes to spare before he needed to head over to Shakopf's house, Touch did a little impromptu housework, quickly vacuuming his living room, starting his dishwasher, and throwing in a load of laundry. He'd need to remember to run it through the dryer when he returned from Shakopf's. The three-bedroom, two-bathroom house Touch had bought eight years ago, thinking he would someday acquire the family to fill it up, felt larger than it was. Primarily it seemed that way because the man only got around to furnishing half of its rooms. Bonnie helped Touch pick out what little furniture existed in the house, at least guaranteeing a smidgeon of tastefulness.

Less than an hour later, Touch was in his Tahoe with "Crazy Train" blaring over WPKY, and he was on his way to Laceon Shakopf's house. Touch hoped he'd given the Shakopfs plenty of time to finish their evening meal and that the kids were into their evening routine so Laceon would not be preoccupied. Just as with Will Welch, Touch planned to play Laceon off of Will to see if memories of the two gallivanting around the countryside of Walter County shook loose any meaningful recollections. Despite nothing firm arising from his talks with the older Welch and Shakopf, as well as Will Welch, other than confirming their use of .243s, Touch had a feeling that something remained amiss.

Touch pulled into Laceon Shakopf's driveway about fifteen minutes later just as "Turn the Page" from Bob Seger concluded on WPKY. The man must've heard Touch cut the car's engine because Shakopf answered the raps on the door almost immediately: "Hey, Sheriff Thomas, I appreciate you coming over to me rather than asking me to leave the house. I like to have dinner with the wife and kids during the week whenever I can. Between all the summer activities, folks get pulled a dozen different ways nowadays."

"My pleasure, Laceon. Just part of the job," Touch shared.

"Will told me y'all had a good conversation at the club earlier this afternoon. I'd hoped to play golf with him, but I couldn't get away from the office today. I probably play too much golf, anyway!" Shakopf admitted. Touch had hoped to catch Shakopf flat-footed and unaware of his earlier conversation with Will Welch, but such surprises proved almost impossible to execute in the cell phone era.

Touch pivoted quickly, though, and went the "buddy-buddy" route, hoping to lure Laceon into a sense of comfort. "Yeah, Will said he he'd shot his best round of the season without you around! You guys' brotherly competitiveness must rattle him, huh? I assume that Will let you know I'm interested in anything you might remember from 1977 and the time surrounding the murder of David Barnett out at Charlie Sprague's farm. Anything notable come rushing back to you from then after Will spoke to you?"

Just as with Welch, Touch watched Shakopf's eyes and expressions for any minute twitches or reactions that appeared interesting. Despite the fact that cop shows and detective novels well publicized the markers for people lying, many individuals still lacked the discipline to control their reactions, especially if those reactions involved traumas to themselves or others.

As Shakopf pondered Touch's question, he looked away and closed his eyes. When Laceon started his answer, he looked toward a family photo on the wall to Touch's left and not directly at the sheriff. "Nothing specific comes to mind. You probably already knew that Will and I hunted all over the place. We weren't really good at much else—unlike you, no talent for sports. We were okay at working for our fathers. That's not something we'd go out of our way to do more of, though. I know Sprague's farm. We've certainly hunted out that direction off and on through the years. As for a specific year, that's anyone's guess, let alone shooting a specific time of year."

Touch interrupted Shakopf. "I appreciate that, Laceon, but David Barnett was shot in June 1977. Nothing's in season then. Whoever used a .243 then almost certainly had to be doing something at least a little out of the ordinary, I think—target shooting in the country, or hunting groundhogs or crows. It's a decent drive from town. There are probably easier, quicker places to do those activities closer to town, don't you think?"

"I hear you, Sheriff," continued Shakopf. "Will and I certainly shot plenty of targets and groundhogs. No one would use a .243 on a crow, though; that's shotgun work. Just to get away from folks, we'd head out to the country. Honestly, a few beers or a little weed motivated us to get farther out of town and out of sight."

"Have you been out by Sprague's in the past few years?" Touch asked. "The reason I ask is that the area from which Barnett was almost certainly shot would have required someone to either be visible in an open field or to shoot from a deer stand. David was autistic, but I gotta think he would have recognized the danger posed by someone pointing a gun at him in broad daylight while standing in the middle of a field. The density of the undergrowth in those woods, which I doubt changed at all over the past forty years, mandated that anyone looking for a view outside the woods would have to be above that undergrowth, in a stand. Do you remember any time you guys left a stand in the woods after hunting season?"

Touch hadn't posed the last question to Will. Laceon Shakopf narrowed his eyes as he searched for the best way to dodge the sheriff's question.

"Will and I probably had three or four stands in trees the season before that. We weren't the most diligent fellows back then. I can't remember what, if anything, we did with them. Some years we just left them where they were until my dad or his dad changed the hunting leases. Then we'd eventually go get them before the season started. Sorry I can't be of more use to you, but that was a long time ago. I'm sure you understand."

Touch thanked Shakopf for his time, bade him a pleasant evening, and took leave of the Shakopf house. As had been the case since he had knocked David Barnett's case file off his desk, Touch felt something out of place. He deliberated on details of his talks with the Welches and the Shakopfs as he drove home.

CHAPTER 17

Predictably, Touch slept fitfully after his conversations with Will Welch and Laceon Shakopf. Unlike before, when David Barnett's murder had appeared to be a puzzle without enough pieces, Touch started to view the case more and more as solvable. The deer tag, hunting lease, and accident trifecta fit together better than any previous explanations. Maybe getting Welch or Shakopf to stop feigning ignorance offered the catalyst to put all the pieces of the puzzle together. Touch failed to see how he could compel either of the men to step up and offer an explanation, though.

Touch worked through his morning weightlifting routine, showered, dressed, and headed to the Tiger's Den for breakfast. During that time, he continued to deliberate Barnett's murder and the Dixie Mafia's encroachment on Walter County. Breakfast concluded without interruption, allowing Touch to offload some anxiety by engaging in friendly, idle banter on community and athletic affairs with the café's regulars.

While ambling down the sidewalk towards his office and waving at a couple passers-by, Touch decided to release Hank, providing that Hank agreed to the terms laid out yesterday. The director of the women's shelter might push back regarding Hank's forced labor at the place, but Touch figured he could address that problem when it happened or find an alternative community organization in need;

there was no benefit in inventing hurdles when so many remained to be cleared.

Upon entering the sheriff's office, Touch greeted Bonnie. "Good morning. What's the good word, Bonnie?"

"Hey, Touch," Bonnie replied. "All's well around here. A couple DWIs picked up by the deputies overnight, and another theft by taking, but nothing too eventful. Hank's now got company, though."

Touch entered his office, turned on his laptop, and processed forty-three emails over the next twenty-eight minutes. Feeling accomplished, he decided he'd visit with Hank and see what he thought about the deal presented yesterday.

After pulling Hank out of the cell so as to avoid the new inhabitants overhearing the conversation, Touch escorted the smaller man to the same interview room in which he'd drafted his statement on Dixie Mafia involvement in Walter County. "Hank, did you come to a conclusion on the deal I offered you yesterday?"

"I'll take it," Hank replied without pausing a second.

"You sure you fully understand the terms, now?" Touch inquired. "You mess this up, and I'll come down on you like stink on shit. I'm nervous as hell that some Nosey Nellie in town's going to get wind of this and have me over a barrel with activist groups I've never heard of. I'm taking a big risk here."

"I'm on it, Touch. I feel terrible. I've had a ton of time in here to think on how to straighten things out and do better. I don't want to spend another moment in here or any other cell. I'm gonna get the help I need to be a better person," Hank pleaded.

"All right, Hank. Gimme a few minutes, and I'll get a deputy to take you back to your place. Anything you need out of that cell, or is it okay to stay here for a while?"

"Here's fine, Touch. Like I said, I don't need to spend another moment in that cell."

Before he released Hank with a deputy, Touch wanted to survey the immediate area around the courthouse for Dougie

Delaney, Ricky Drummond, or anyone else who looked like they might be associated with the Dixie Mafia. Several minutes later, after concluding that the coast was clear, Touch instructed one of his on-duty deputies to take Hank Benitez out the side of the courthouse opposite the sheriff's office and to his home. Further, Touch asked the deputy to wait an hour outside Hank's house, cruise the surrounding neighborhood, and then backtrack to the office, all the while being on the lookout for anything looking suspicious, especially Dixie Mafia thugs. Finally, Touch thought it prudent for a deputy to check in on Hank the following morning and instructed Bonnie to tell one of the deputies to do so as he exited his office.

Touch walked back into the interview room and gave similar instructions to Hank. "Hank, you and one of my deputies are going to exit the opposite side of the courthouse. He's going to drive you back to your place and cruise the neighborhood around your house for an hour or so. If you see anything out of the ordinary while he's there or after he leaves, call me and the Cooper police immediately, okay? Be careful."

Hank was dead twenty-four hours later, found face down in his living room with a small-caliber bullet in the back of his head.

CHAPTER 18

Laceon Shakopf and Will Welch were about as tight as two friends could be in the mid-1970s. They were sixteen in spring 1976, equally awkward and unknown to girls, and neither athletic nor particularly studious. The two boys relied on each other for their social existences. Golfing, hunting, and goofing off consumed much of their time. Each held a summer job, but with their respective fathers being their bosses' bosses, their jobs required nothing particularly arduous from them. Showing up defined the primary requirement and knocking off early for a visit to the lake or to scout hunting locations proved to be an entirely acceptable work absence. Their fall schedules were even more open-ended as summer work was in their rearview mirrors, co-opted by smoking dope, hunting, and other unproductive passages of time.

Through fall 1976, neither Laceon nor Will saw the trophy buck they'd hoped would offer the triumph of their deer hunting campaign for the year. Others took down large, multipoint bucks, but through the end of the year, sighting does and young spike bucks characterized the boys' hunting experiences. Most of the larger deer in 1976 were taken in the north part of Walter County, so playing the percentages and being somewhat contrarian, Will and Laceon focused their efforts to the south of the county. However, as the season neared its close in late winter 1976, the boys conformed to the trend of others bagging large deer and transitioned to hunting in northwest Walter County, at Sprague's farm.

Jerry Welch leased four tracts of land on which he and Edmund Shakopf and their sons could hunt for the 1976 season, which spanned August to March of the following year. Jerry and Edmund split the costs, but Jerry held responsibility for choosing where to lease. Will and Laceon would hunt squirrel and rabbit early in the fall, doves and quail later, and deer (their favorite game) for a limited number of weeks in November and then in January. Two of the tracts Jerry leased were on opposite east-west edges of the southern part of Walter County, and he leased corresponding tracts to the north as well.

One of those tracts in 1976–1977 was the wooded acreage to the west of Charlie Sprague's farm.

Giving up on their southern strategy for the last few weeks of the 1976-77 hunting season, Will and Laceon ventured up to the relatively unknown swath of woods Jerry Welch leased in summer 1976. They trudged through the property looking for the best sightlines for their deer stand. The stand, a two-person model that elevated hunters about ten feet off the ground, rose above the underbrush and offered Will and Laceon not only views of much of the forest floor surrounding them but also Charlie Sprague's front yard.

The Welch-Shakopf hunting party abided by a long-standing set of rules for hunting in pairs: the winner of a best-of-three rock-paper-scissors battle chose first to hunt or to spot. Will Welch won the rock-paper-scissors battle and chose to hunt first. Over their first hour, though, neither he nor Laceon spotted anything interesting. However, into their second hour of hunting, during Laceon's turn to shoot, the buck for which they'd been waiting over two months, an eight-point, thick-necked beauty, appeared less than one hundred yards away, traipsing through the trees. A two-count after Will spotted the deer, Laceon dropped it with an excellent shot from his

Remington .243 rifle through that thick neck and directly into the deer's heart—a clean kill.

Laceon and Will field-dressed the deer, dragged it through the ridiculously thick underbrush back to their pickup, and hoisted it into the truck's bed. They left the stand for future hunting as was the custom and in expectation of returning soon so Will could bag one of this beautiful buck's siblings. Alas, that luck wouldn't be in the cards for Will Welch, and 1977's deer-hunting season ended with the young man failing to tag a deer. While initially happy that he had sighted Laceon's kill, which Edmund Shakopf gladly transported to the butcher and taxidermist for processing of the meat and preservation of the head as a trophy, jealousy built in Will Welch through spring 1977.

Little changed for Will and Laceon through the spring and summer of 1977 as the boys moved from their sixteenth to their seventeenth birthdays and toward their junior year of high school. They resumed their usual rhythm of goofing off, driving around, smoking dope, and hunting squirrels and rabbits, with occasional forays to fish and swim with whatever girls showed up at Lake Barkley. At the suggestion of Jerry Welch to remove their deer stand in June 1977 and amid a little good-natured ribbing at the hands of Laceon Shakopf, Will Welch's jealousy for Laceon's big buck reached a climax. After climbing up the stand with his .243—a gun far too powerful for hunting anything smaller than deer—for some dumb, inexplicable reason, Will chose to observe his surroundings through the rifle's telescopic sight. He scoped through the 135 degrees of wooded area before rotating through the pasture that separated the woods from Charlie Sprague's house and yard. About a half-turn through his survey, Will caught sight of David Barnett mowing Sprague's yard. The unexpected movement of the man on a green and yellow tractor caught Welch by surprise. Distracted by his jealousy and amid this surprise, Will Welch frighteningly and bafflingly pulled the trigger of the .243. Why the safety was not activated, neither Will nor Laceon knew. To that point, despite not being the most thoughtful and diligent boys in Walter County, they'd been nothing but safe and responsible with their firearms. A split second after the shot, however, David Barnett fell forward on his John Deere lawn tractor, dead.

As with most traumas, neither Will nor Laceon immediately realized what had happened. The massive noise created by firing a high-powered hunting rifle like a .243 is impossible for even the most disciplined hunters to ignore. Outside of the deaf, such a disruptive noise startles everyone. It shocked Will Welch to the point of dropping the rifle out of the tree stand. Thankfully, the gun didn't fire again. Laceon shouted "What did you do!" to his buddy. The two took a few moments to collect themselves. Upon hearing no shouting and experiencing nothing else out of the ordinary and taking a while to settle down, Laceon and Will disassembled their deer stand and left the woods. Both remained oblivious to the death of David Barnett until the next day, when the news cycle of small-city Cooper and the relatively high public profile of David's father, Andrew Barnett, resulted in widespread awareness of David's death. Over the next several days, negligible detail surrounding the shooting of David - basically only its location - cycled through Cooper's gossip mill. Neither motive nor witness materialized.

Upon hearing of David Barnett's death, fear and denial consumed Will Welch and Laceon Shakopf. Visualizing their lives as they knew them coming to an end as they likely would pass much of those lives behind bars, Will and Laceon made a pact of silence that only the young and dumb ever think will be upheld. While shootings were entirely uncommon in Cooper, they did happen and usually involved domestic disputes or criminal activity. With neither of those explanations offering any clues to David's death and little other meaningful information forthcoming over the ensuing weeks, the Cooper and West Kentucky news cycle focused elsewhere. As time passed only Andrew Barnett and Dean Thomas – and later Touch – remembered David.

For almost forty years, and much to the surprise to both Will and Laceon, the pact of silence held. In fact, nothing to date had tested their silence as much as Sheriff Tanner "Touch" Thomas knocking a cold case file off his desk, chatting with a short-order cook, and doing a little old-school police work that, for whatever reason, had never entered prior officers' minds to do.

Solving David Barnett's murder, though, ranked as small potatoes given the magnitude of what else Touch was on the verge of solving.

CHAPTER 19

Touch's cellphone vibrated in his pocket as he forked the next to last bite of scrambled eggs, bacon, and cheese into his mouth. The call interrupted Touch ruminating about the new details brought to light in David Barnett's case. He was all but certain that the shot that had killed David came from the wooded area to the west of Charlie Sprague's house. Touch remained in the dark, though, as to the who and why of David's shooting. Did the young man see something he wasn't supposed to see? If it was an accident, who would have been that careless with a .243 rifle out of hunting season?

Momentarily struck by the decision to answer the phone with a mouthful of food or to return the fork of food back to his plate, Touch did the right thing and plated the fork and food. He answered his phone without looking at the caller ID and said, "Sheriff Thomas."

"Sheriff, Mike Menser. I'm over at Hank Benitez's house, checking on him like you instructed us to do. Hank's dead, Touch."

Touch was silent for a three-count but was quick of thought. "Take a quick look around the house for anything out of order. Go outside and do the same thing as best you can without touching anything: look at the front and back of house, a the windows and doors. Then go to your cruiser, call it in to Bonnie, and tell her to send two deputies over to secure the street and scene. I want you to drive the surrounding three blocks looking for anything out of place.

I'm going to call Chief Hauser and have him send the coroner and crime scene folks he's got over ASAP. Okay, Mike?"

"Got it, Touch."

Touch quickly finished his food, coffee, and water. Reva read the concern on his face and recognized the quickness in his movements. He paid his bill and wished Reva a good day. Two minutes after Menser's call, Touch was out of the Tiger's Den and on the phone with Chief Hauser.

"Chris, thanks for picking up my call. That Dixie Mafia thing got real, really fast. My deputy, Mike Menser, just found Hank Benitez dead in his house. I've got Mike canvassing the neighborhood and two deputies on their way over to secure the street and the scene. Can you have your crime scene tech and the coroner over their ASAP, please? I'll meet you there, if that works for you."

"Damn, you got it, Touch. Thought this was gonna be an easy day. Such a thing seems not to exist anymore."

Touch didn't even drop by the office to fill in Bonnie. He depended on her experience and understanding from years on the job to do what needed to be done after Menser called in Hank's death. For the seven-minute drive through Cooper to Hank's house, a route that Touch knew all too well from prior calls to the address, Touch reflected on his last conversation with Hank. Either he woefully misread how involved Benitez was with the Dixie Mafia, or Hank decided that giving himself up offered the only way to protect Mandy and his parents. Touch got a very bad feeling that things in Cooper were about to get a lot worse.

First things first: Hank Benitez was dead. Seconds after arriving on the scene, Touch learned someone had shot Hank in the back of the head with what looked to be a relatively small-caliber pistol. Powder residue around the entry wound indicated a close-range shot. Whoever executed Hanks almost certainly used a handgun with a suppressor: Menser's quick canvassing of the area revealed no one in the immediate vicinity had heard anything like a gunshot the prior night.

Touch hadn't worked too many prospective murder scenes in Cooper. The ones he had processed presented as fairly straight-forward. A domestic dispute unfortunately escalated rapidly to a stabbing or shooting with a known assailant. Similarly, a small-scale drug deal or robbery went askew, but again with a known or highly probable perpetrator. In a prior life with the army, though, Touch developed a protocol of sorts by which he mentally catalogued and evaluated crime and murder scenes. He started outside and worked his way closer to where Hank's body laid. Touch methodically inspected the area around Hank's house in tighter and tighter concentric circles, looking for anything out of place: broken limbs, rustled leaves, trampled flowers, and the like. He surveyed the house, looking for possible points of entry and exit. Touch mentally attempted to replicate the approach and process of the shooter. He thought doing so offered perspective prior to hearing analysis and opinions from crime scene techs, deputies, the coroner, and whoever else was on-site. The time it took to do so also allowed Touch to prepare himself for more closely viewing the deceased. In the case of Hank Benitez, a man Touch had tried to help much of his adult life, the adjustment period likely would prove insufficient. Touch never necessarily liked or respected Hank Benitez, but he had developed a personal connection with the man over the years and tried to aid Hank in transitioning to being a happier, more productive person.

Nothing looked out of place. To start with, Hank's house was nondescript: three-bedroom, two-bathroom red brick ranch purchased several years ago when he'd strung together enough uninterrupted work history to convince his parents to loan him the money to make the down payment on the house. Landscaping largely consisted of neglected boxwoods in need of trimming that lined the sidewalk leading to the front door. The front and back yards were 99 percent grass and low-lying weeds, also in need of a trim. From outside in toward the house, none of the window treatments—shades or curtains—looked disheveled. The front door remained a beehive of activity with law enforcement and techs shuffling in and out of it. After circling to the back of the house, Touch saw the backdoor remained shut and appeared to be undisturbed. A storm door fit in its jamb as it should, but Touch would make sure a tech dusted both inner and outer backdoors for fingerprints. After making his way around to the front of the house in his final concentric circle outside the house, Touch entered through the front door.

Spending time outside helped Touch get his mind around the fact that Hank Benitez was no more, but it hardly helped him reconcile that releasing Hank proved to be fatal for the man. Touch had assessed the risks to Hank far too conservatively, and now he was dead. Much more was in play than the sheriff had estimated. Fear and regret competed for Touch's subconscious mind as he entered the front door of the house.

The entryway opened to Hank Benitez's living room. Hank lay on the floor, face down, having fallen away from the front door and toward the interior of the house. Someone had thoughtfully pulled Hank's eyelids lower so at least Touch Thomas didn't have to endure the vacant stare of the deceased. Immediately, Touch thought the location and position in which Hank died implied he likely knew who shot him. Touch also hypothesized that Hank had been dumb enough to open the door to his killer. Two factors supported these inferences. First, scared people typically cowered away from their assailants but remained facing them as they stepped backward. Second, if Hank was running away from the shooter, he'd likely had gotten at least a few steps farther and, as a result, would have crashed, as momentum carried him forward, into either the doorway that gave way to a dining room or into the furniture in the corner of the room. Touch thought it highly unlikely that Hank, given his recent situation, would turn his back on anyone who presented a threat to him.

Touch visualized the assailant entering the house, raising a gun as Hank turned to walk toward the center of the house, and then firing into the back of Hank's head. Chris Hauser entered the house and started to speak while Touch kneeled to gain a different perspective on the crime scene.

"Touch, I'm sorry for your loss. I know you were working with Benitez to help him through things. I'm here when you want to review the situation."

Before rising and addressing Chief Hauser, Touch completed a full scan of the living room. As with everything else associated with the house, nothing looked out of place or unusual other than the dead man in the middle of the floor. Thankfully, the small-caliber shell created no exit wound, and as a result, the crime scene appeared far less grizzly than it might have if the killer had chosen a larger caliber firearm.

Touch turned and addressed Hauser. "Thanks, Chris. Looks like I could have done Hank a helluva favor by leaving him in that jail cell. Bad read of the situation. Hank either knew it and let it happen, or he thought he somehow could work his way out of it. I guess I should have taken more seriously those visits from the two mafia thugs. Can you give me fifteen minutes to walk through the rest of the house, please? I'll find you outside, if that's okay."

"Sure thing. We'll be on-site for a while, obviously."

After turning back toward the center of the living room, Touch made his way through the central hallway of the house, checking the bathrooms and bedrooms at the end of the hall and circling back toward the dining room and kitchen. As anticipated, Touch found nothing out of order in any of the rooms. Hank hadn't even taken the time to hang his towel up after his first shower upon returning home from the sheriff's office jail. Touch looked more closely in the kitchen and noticed no food in the refrigerator or dishes in the sink. Given the time since the deputy had driven Hank home, he either grabbed something to eat elsewhere or was killed before he ate. It was impossible to imagine a man not heading for food after a three-day stay in the county jail. Touch made a mental note to talk as soon as possible with Hank's parents and whoever worked the counter of their restaurant yesterday evening.

After dawdling at the kitchen window for a moment or two, Touch retraced his steps back through the kitchen, checking the corners and underneath the dining room table for anything out of place. Sadly, it looked as though Hank had spent almost no time in the house before being shot. As Touch passed from the dining room through the central hallway and back into the living room, Hank's lifeless body still sprawled on the carpeted floor, he taxed his mind as to why he felt such remorse for a man plagued by poor choices made for fifteen years not of necessity but of a misplaced sense of entitlement, placed in Touch's custody for abusing a woman—another poor choice. Simplifying his stream of thought, Touch concluded that his sadness resulted not from Hank's death or the situation that placed him in that precarious position but rather from the lost potential of the man. Although always at arm's length and without much more than the exchange of occasional pleasantries with the Benitezes at their restaurant or around Cooper, Touch watched the family struggle through the hard times only to ultimately achieve the rewards of financial independence and self-determination afforded them by hard work. Hank, tormented by the vice of indolence, never graduated from being a corner-cutting adolescent spoiled by the fruits of his parents' hard work and determination.

Lesson learned, maybe, for Touch: it was nigh-on impossible to make two positives out of a negative situation. The sheriff likely should have been pleased with his ability to remove Mandy from her abusive relationship and potentially dead-end job. Similarly, he should have left Hank to the mercy of the justice system. Possibly Hank would have met his demise in prison, but that wouldn't weigh as heavily on Touch as seeing the man dead in his own living room only hours after being release from a jail cell at Touch's complete discretion. Touch expected that single decision to weigh on him until he rectified this affair.

Shaking his head and sighing, Touch exited the house in search of Chief Hauser. Upon seeing the chief conversing with the coroner near his cruiser, Touch walked in Hauser's direction, scanning the adjacent houses and streets as he went. "Anything particularly of note surface yet?"

"Not a thing. It's as clean a murder scene as I've ever had. The two officers I assigned to knock on doors completed the neighborhood canvas. They unearthed nothing. No one saw anything out of the ordinary. No one heard anything unusual. No one seemed particularly distraught that Hank Benitez no longer lives on their street. I'm sure you saw much the same thing I saw inside. Nothing appeared out of place other than the dead body face down in the middle of the living room. It didn't even look like Benitez had the time to do much more than take a shower. We'll wait for the autopsy and interview results to see if he managed to grab a meal before that bullet entered the back of his head. At this point, that's the only potential clue I see arising from this scene: if he ate beforehand, maybe someone at the restaurant saw him with someone. The kitchen certainly didn't look like anything changed in it for the past week."

"I agree, Chief. Not that I've ever given it a great deal of thought, but eating and showering would be two of the first three things I'd look to do once I got out of a cell. I assume he showered before he left to get food, providing he actually made it out of the house to eat. I doubt Hank was the receipt-keeping kind, but maybe a quick search of his pockets could help us out sooner rather than later as well."

Touch turned to the coroner and inquired if she had happened to search Hank's pockets. She shook her head, so the sheriff did an about-face, headed back into the house, and rummaged through Hank Benitez's pockets. Unfortunately, Touch found only change, a wallet with cash and cards, and keys. After heading back outside, Touch invited Chief Hauser to ride with him over to the Benitezes' restaurant, where he expected they'd find Hank's parents working as usual.

Hauser and Touch had a quick chat with their respective lead officer and deputy on-site and then, converged on Touch's Tahoe. After firing the ignition, Touch turned off the radio: crime scene and next step discussions took precedence over WPKY's eclectic mix of music from the seventies, eighties, and nineties.

"Chris, this looks a little too crisp, clean, and professional for a Cooper-only job, don't you think?"

"Exactly. I'm concerned. Whoever did this knew what they were doing and how they wanted to do it long before they arrived at Hank's house. The precision of the job, the obvious understanding of human behavior, and I think more importantly, the apparent familiarity between Hank and whoever shot him scares me."

"I'm with you. Either Hank was in deeper with the Dixie Mafia than he let on, which I don't feel to be the case, or whatever the mafia's got planned for Cooper and Walter County is larger than we estimated. Of course, both scenarios could be in play. I'm unconvinced that any organization with any sense would employ Hank to be anything more than a mule or a local bagman. He never conveyed that degree of competence and, therefore confidence, to do much else. Regardless, I think we're in for more trouble."

"Agreed: more trouble's almost certainly on its way. We probably need to check in with the KSP and US Attorney's offices and start lobbying for a task force, if one doesn't already exist. If they've already got one, you or me, or both of us, need to get on it ASAP. After visiting with the Benitezes, how about you call the US Attorney's office, seeing as how you've already got a dialogue going? I'll call the KSP."

A couple moments of silence later, the two men pulled into the parking lot of *Mi Tierra*, the restaurant Hank's parents had owned and operated since the mid-1990s. In addition to being a popular name for Tex-Mex restaurants across the United States, for the Benitezes, the Spanish translation to "My Earth" or "My Land" served as a double meaning because the family owned the restaurant as well—an American dream realized. Now, Touch and Hauser were about to overlay that dream with every parent's nightmare.

Hauser entered *Mi Tierra* first, closely followed by Sheriff Thomas. Manny and Paula Benitez knew Chris Hauser and Tanner Thomas on sight because the two law enforcement officers had dined in their restaurant professionally in uniform and casually off-duty for years. As Paula emerged from behind the hostess station and Manny came from the kitchen, they knew the sight of both officers couldn't be good. They'd never seen the two men arrive at the same time. Paula showed the two men to a four-top in a vacant part of the restaurant near the front window. Manny joined them moments later. Touch asked everyone to please take a seat.

"Paula, Manny, I'm very sorry to tell you than we found Hank shot dead in his house several hours ago. Please accept my and Chief Hauser's condolences."

Touch and Hauser allowed Manny and Paula Benitez a few minutes to console each other. Both broke into tears. They hugged each other as lifelong partners did in tumultuous, terrible times. A longtime server, recognizing something serious had occurred, brought four sweet teas to the table and silently set one down in front of each person.

As the solemnity of Hank's death settled for his parents, and the two men in front of them intended to do their jobs, so Manny and Paula dried their tears with napkins from the table. Each turned to face Touch and Hauser and inquired how they might be able to help catch Hank's assailant.

Hauser started. "Paula, Manny, when's the last time either of you saw or spoke to Hank?"

"Hank came to see his mother immediately after Sheriff Thomas released him from prison," Manny replied.

"No, Manny, I don't think Hank came to see us immediately. He'd cleaned up, I'm certain, before he came here," Paula interjected.

Touch concurred. "I think you're correct, Mrs. Benitez. One of my deputies escorted Hank home and stayed in the neighborhood for about an hour after dropping him at his house. I'm guessing he came here after that hour or so passed."

Recognizing that the deputy might have seen Hank departing his house or neighborhood as he completed his drive-through of the area, Touch made a mental note to query that deputy if they happened to see Hank or Hank's car in the area. He followed up this line of thought with the Benitezes.

"Hank still drove a late-model, royal blue F-150 truck, correct? Would he have access to any other cars that you know of?"

"Not that we know of, Sheriff Thomas. On occasion he drove Mandy's gold Corolla, but he hated that car—too small. We saw Hank pull up in his truck last night, anyway," Manny Benitez answered.

Hauser chimed in on the questioning. "Did Hank meet anyone, talk with anyone, after greeting you?"

Paula Benitez responded quickly. "No, sir. Hank came in and gave me a kiss on the cheek and a big hug. I hugged him and then smacked him. I was so disappointed in him. You know, Manny and I tried as hard as we could to raise Hank right. We gave him too much. He was just too spoiled. We failed. Now, our son is dead—the ultimate failure. I know in my heart of hearts it's not my fault. It's certainly not Manny's fault. Hank simply never adjusted to accept what the world required of him. That does nothing to heal my heart, though. It does nothing to heal Mandy Herman's wounds. It's just brought more hurt to us and to Cooper. Bad. I'm so sorry and so sad."

Touch and Paula took a sip of sweet tea. Chief Hauser looked at the window to the parking lot. Manny stared at his shoes.

After another moment of silence following Paula's lamentations Touch asked, "Was there anyone out of the ordinary in the restaurant when Hank was here, anything appear out of place?"

Manny raised his head, "Yes, Sheriff. A man came in right after we opened yesterday morning. He took quite some time to order. Drank an entire glass of tea and ate a basket of chips before he ordered anything to eat. I'd never seen him before. He dressed a little more formal—what do they call it? Not a suit coat, but a ... it's also the name of a small SUV ... a blazer, yes, a blazer. He wore that over dark jeans with some sort of fancy western boots. His speech was different as well. You could hear more—please don't be offended— but more hillbilly in his voice than people in Cooper have. I didn't think anything of it until now. I don't remember much of anything else, unfortunately, because we got busy with the lunch crowd just after he ordered. He left a generous tip, cash, with his check. Let me call Juana over and ask, please."

After motioning to the same server that had brought sweet teas for everyone, Manny asked Juana Escovedo about the stranger she had served early yesterday. He rattled off a handful of questions in Spanish, which Juana dutifully answered, also in Spanish.

After relaying the questions and their answers to Touch and Chief Hauser, Manny said, "Juana says that the man was polite and well spoken. He ordered tacos al carbon with queso, drank three glasses of sweet tea, and ate two baskets of tortilla chips and an entire dish of hot salsa. He paid his bill in cash, left a large tip, visited the bathroom before he left, and did nothing else out of place."

The group could think of nothing more that might be of interest, so Touch and Police Chief Hauser again offered their condolences to the Benitezes. Upon leaving *Mi Tierra*, each of them surveyed the parking lot, the adjacent buildings, and the passing traffic in front of the restaurant. They climbed back into the Tahoe, and Touch started the vehicle. The radio remained off as the two men reflected on their conversation with Manny and Paula Benitez. Several minutes later,

Touch turned on the radio, and the lunchtime WPKY DJ signed off and gave way to the afternoon's drive-time DJ, who kicked off her shift with AC/DC's "Dirty Deeds Done Dirt Cheap." Again, Touch marveled at the coincidences that appeared every day in life. While the motivations for the song both Touch and Hauser thought deplorable, each man would admit that Angus and Malcolm Young, AC/DC's band leaders, did an awesome job creating a compelling beat with the song.

Touch dropped Hauser off at his cruiser near Hank's house, and the chief confirmed both man's fears. "Touch, this looks like a professional job. The man cased *Mi Tierra*, waited for Hank to visit his parents, followed him home, and killed him. As we agreed earlier, it looks like Hank also must've known the man but didn't think he was a danger. I can't imagine that he would turn and walk away in his own house from an unknown man wearing boots and a blazer, can you?"

Touch pursed his lips and silently nodded as Hauser closed the Tahoe passenger door and walked to his cruiser. Touch watched as Hauser executed a three-point turn and headed back to his downtown office. Then he returned to his own office. As Hauser exited the vehicle, "Dirty Deeds Done Dirt Cheap" concluded and gave way to REM's "Losing My Religion," which accompanied Touch for much of the drive back to the courthouse.

CHAPTER 20

Rafe Livingston employed two Dixie Mafia grunts in rotating surveillance of Hank Benitez's house as soon as the organization received word that the Walter County Sheriff had released Mandy Herman. One way or another—bail, lack of evidence, waived charges, or whatever—the Dixie Mafia was fairly certain that Hank would make his way back to the house sooner rather than later. Before four days passed, Livingston's hunch proved correct as a Walter County Deputy Sheriff dropped Hank off at his house.

With an extensive history of dealing with tweakers, pot heads, and junkies of various flavors, Livingston left the two grunts, Tiny Smith and Gordie Richards, with simple and explicit instructions. Work in twelve-hour shifts. Communicate via cellphone with each other one hour prior to swapping shifts. Rotate every two hours between the back and the front of the house. Park at least two houses to the right or left of the house. Never park on the same side of the house from one rotation to the next. Do not call Livingston unless you see Hank Benitez in his house. If you see the cops, casually leave, circle to the other side of Benitez's house, and return an hour later.

Upon seeing the deputy dropping Hank off at his house, Gordie Richards circled from the front of the house to the back via two right-hand turns. Along the way, Richards eyed the deputy escorting

Benitez into the house. Consistent with Livingston's instructions, Richards left the area after spotting Benitez and called Livingston.

"Boss, Benitez was dropped off at his house about ten minutes ago."

"Good job, Gordie, you're off-duty now. Call Tiny, and you two get out of Cooper ASAP. I don't care where you go or what you do. Just leave. Call the boss man, and he'll tell you your next job and when it starts."

"We're gone, Boss."

Rafe Livingston, who stayed at a Lake Barkley–area motel, readied to leave his room, the area, and the state. Highly trained by various branches and agencies of the US government, Livingston remained adept at traveling lightly, leaving no trace of from where he came or to where he planned to go.

After packing a small toiletries case in the bottom of an Osprey Farpoint backpack, Livingston covered it with a change of clothes, a portfolio of alternate means of identification, and two extra magazines, holding twenty-four rounds, for his Walther PPQ .22-caliber pistol. Schooled across international locations where preparation and planning often delineated life from death, Livingston rarely allowed his handgun to be farther than an arm's length away. Rafe packed three more items into the backpack: an iPad Air, an iPhone, and the charger for the devices.

Livingston ran through a final room check, ensuring he left nothing behind—a ritual of his for leaving all rooms. He grabbed his backpack and headed to the office of the motel to return his room key. Having done so, Livingston remotely opened the door locks and started the engine of his nondescript lightning blue Ford F-150 Lariat extended cab pickup. He never wanted to look like he was in a hurry, but experience taught Rafe Livingston that the ability to remotely start a vehicle was worth many times over the cost of the feature. Although West Kentucky wasn't Afghanistan or Africa, the flexibility afforded one by a fast exit could prove invaluable under certain circumstances. In a chase, every intersection placed between Rafe and his pursuers complicated exponentially the "turn, no turn" decision-making. At thirty-five miles per hour, an extra thirty seconds could put as many as six intersections between Livingston and his followers. That was a lot of turns someone in a chase had to predict.

Rafe Livingston jumped on the phone once in his truck to contact his Dixie Mafia handler. A for-hire gun, Rafe went out of his way to never lay eyes on the people who employed him. Cash changed hands, but never in face-to-face arrangements. Rafe instructed his client to call Hank and let him know that a member soon would stop by to check on him. Livingston stressed that the man use a tone and dialogue that placed Hank at ease. It would be far better and easier if Hank never suspected Rafe Livingston as having anything other than his ongoing utility to the Dixie Mafia in mind.

Livingston was dressed in western boots, Wrangler jeans, a button-down shirt, and a tasteful sports coat. He had close-cropped hair, a trimmed goatee, and looked like a gentleman farmer or a high school principal. Confident in his approach and friendly in his conversation, complete with a comforting Southern drawl, Livingston proved efficient in words as well as in action. He was lethal in tight spaces, having killed over two dozen enemy combatants in hand-to-hand fights, and he also possessed rare skill at distance commensurate with exiting the US Army as a sharpshooting member of the Marksmanship Unit before engaging in more covert missions for the US government.

Given the dossier Livingston had collected on Hank Benitez, the man had little concern that eliminating Hank would prove difficult. In his mind, the biggest question concerned why the Dixie Mafia would worry about such a low-level grunt as Benitez in the first place. Pleased with the payday and the relative ease anticipated for the task, Livingston chose not to ask too many questions of his client. The recent political environment combined with what appeared to be potentially warring factions of the drug trade in the Southeast United States appeared to offer Rafe Livingston very profitable prospects for the next few years.

The man neither enjoyed nor disdained the killing. Most of his kills ended up being sorry-assed motherfuckers whom very few, if any, decent people missed. Hank Benitez hitting a woman ranked up there on the SOB list, and Livingston doubted that anyone other than his mother and father would miss the guy when he was gone.

Figuring that a visit to mom and dad, who owned a Tex-Mex restaurant in Cooper, likely would be Hank's first stop after being dropped off at his house, Livingston aimed to visit the same restaurant right after it opened for lunch. After finishing his tacos al carbon, Rafe followed Hank home; their vehicles were quite close in year, make, and model. He allowed Hank a few moments to settle into his house and field the call from his Dixie Mafia contact. Then Rafe Livingston, as cool as a cucumber, knocked on the door, followed Hank into his house, pulled his silencer-equipped Walther PPQ .22 from a rear holster in the small of his back, and put a slug into Hank's head.

The execution went as smoothly as Livingston had anticipated it would go. Hank fell in-line with his walk pattern, not even creating a mess that Livingston would need to clean up. Forty-five seconds later, Livingston was in his Ford pickup, remote started before he had stepped out of Hank's house. Less than 10 minutes after the execution, Rafe merged onto the West Kentucky Parkway on his way to Interstate 24, Nashville, and points farther south. The second $12,500 payment for eliminating Hank Benitez would be available for pickup in a week at an already agreed-upon Thornton's gas station south of Lexington, off Tates Creek Road. If recent trends continued, Livingston might be able to combine trips, picking up his money as well as another job in Kentucky.

CHAPTER 21

Bonnie knew Touch would take Hank Benitez's death hard. She recognized Hank as a monumental fuck-up and not a great person, but also not a person due for a bullet in the back of the head. One of Touch's most endearing qualities was that he thought he could eventually fix almost anything and almost anyone. Hank Benitez now was well beyond being fixed. Bonnie thought Touch would now focus on how he could fix whoever had murdered Hank Benitez.

Furrowed brow, fast gait, door slamming behind him—Touch Thomas was pissed off. He thought he had put a plan in place capable of straightening out Hank Benitez. Now, not only had someone screwed his plan all to hell, but they'd killed someone in the process. Cooper, Kentucky, no longer was the idyllic community in which Touch Thomas grew up, but also it wasn't the type of place where people, even dumb-assed petty criminals like Hank Benitez, got shot in the back of the head. Touch needed to get this fixed, and fast, before Cooper's sense of community unraveled and the mayor, city council, and county commissioners started to get concerned. Nothing good ever came of city and county government meddling in law enforcement in Cooper and Walter County.

After a moment to accept that he was angry, emotionally raw, and generally feeling screwed, Sheriff Thomas picked up the phone and dialed Shel Richardson's office for the third time in a week.

These were three more times than Touch had ever before called the US Attorney. Touch didn't know if his dad, in all the time he had spent as sheriff of Walter County, had ever spoken with a US Attorney. Definitively times had changed.

Unfortunately, but not unexpectedly, Touch got an assistant and left his name and number for Shel Richardson to call him back ASAP concerning what appeared to be a Dixie Mafia–linked murder in Cooper. Next, Touch texted Chris Hauser and let him know about the call to Richardson and to gently remind him to check in with the Kentucky State Police.

To calm his racing mind, Touch took out a pen and notepad and commenced listing everything he knew and thought about Hank's murder. Release time, plan, deputy responsible for dropping him off, crime scene descriptions, review of his conversation with Manny and Paula Benitez—anything and everything that came to mind. Several minutes later, Touch had a short list of peculiarities on which he could dial in his efforts.

First, the killer had to drive to Hank's house. Mike Menser would have spotted anyone on foot; no one walked any farther than from their front door to their car in that neighborhood. Maybe time would jar something loose, or someone who hadn't been home during the initial canvassing of the neighborhood would come forth with something useful as word of Hank's death spread through the town.

Second, the man Juana Escovedo served at *Mi Tierra* linked up too well from an appearance and timing standpoint not to be involved, if he was not the shooter himself. Caught up in the emotions of the situation and in the reactions of Hank's parents, Touch and Hauser neglected to ask the Benitezes about security camera footage. Touch made a note to call on that point ASAP.

Finally, killing a low-level nitwit like Hank made little sense unless something much larger, and likely more complicated and meaningful, was in play. Did Hank know something beyond what he shared with Touch during their first conversation—the one that ultimately led to Mandy gaining the protection of the US Marshals? That move, at least, appeared prescient given Hank's fate.

Outside of crimes of passion and jealousy, the age-old adage of "follow the money" almost always applied to solving crimes. Occasionally, one could substitute "power" for "money," but even in those instances, the competition and coveting of power frequently distilled to issues of money. Drugs in Cooper certainly generated impressive cash flows, but to Touch's knowledge, nothing significant changed in that dynamic over the past few years. Unfortunately, in a town Cooper's size in the twenty-first century, illegal drugs existed, and Sheriff Touch Thomas wasn't naïve to the presence and use of them. Touch sensed that Hank's murder signaled a change in the money-power-drugs dynamic in Cooper. Thinking for a few more moments on the topic, he concluded that someone in Cooper funded the Dixie Mafia's move on Cooper and its drug trade. Hank knew something and someone intimately involved in this dynamic, and this knowledge got Hank killed. Postulating one step further, Touch assessed that Hank's arrest for assaulting Mandy and concerns among the Dixie Mafia and their partners that Hank would share this knowledge in exchange for avoiding prison made him expendable.

Touch kicked back from his desk, put his feet up, and cogitated on the limited number of people in Cooper wealthy and arrogant enough to thumb their noses at law, order, and decency—and to instigate expansion of the drug trade in Walter County. A couple criminal defense attorneys came to mind, but they made little sense because becoming deeper entrenched in criminal enterprises would actually cannibalize portions of their income. Widespread knowledge of *Breaking Bad*, its attorney Saul Goodman, and his spin-off, *Better Call Saul* also increased scrutiny of the profession's linkages, as silly as that sounded. Several small business owners could fund the enterprise, but Touch thought them doing so highly unlikely as he assessed their logistical skills as paling in comparison to their sales talents. As a result, the business owners also talked far too much. The vast majority of the balance of wealth originating in Cooper and Walter County chose not to reside in the area any longer; those folks relocated to Nashville, Louisville, or larger metropolitan areas even farther afield. Although he couldn't pinpoint the relationship, Touch thought he was on to something. He closed his eyes for a long moment, cleared his mind, and breathed deeply and slowly. The calmness that came from regaining control overtook him.

After stepping out of his office, Touch took a chair and pulled it up to Bonnie's desk. "Bonnie, who in Cooper and Walter County has enough cash and contempt for their fellow citizens to establish a new drug ring with a bunch of hillbilly criminals?"

"Well, you've been to the country club each of the past two days. Haven't you seen any possibilities? If I were looking for rich assholes, that's about the first place I'd check."

"Uh-huh, not a bad suggestion. Anything else?"

"How about staking out the best dive bar in town? Back in the day, my daddy would have said the bootleggers were the best source of info on the criminal element in town. Of course, that was back when Walter County was dry and the nearest bottle of booze for legal purchase was about forty minutes away. Now that the groceries and convenience stores sell Tito's and Knob Creek and whatever tutti-frutti wines or seltzers are in vogue, I think the bars may be your best bets. You used to play ball with Timmy over at the Roll'n Saloon, by the train tracks, didn't you?"

"I'll be damned. Aren't you just a fount of good information today? Let me call Chief Hauser and see if he'll join me at the Roll'n later this afternoon. Regardless of whether or not he knows anything, it'll be good to see Timmy. Wanna join me for lunch at the Tiger's Den? My treat."

Bonnie and Touch caught up on her doings over grilled cheeses and bowls of gazpacho—too damn hot outside for regular tomato soup. Reva took all of the recent events in stride. Touch swore nothing fazed that woman. Other tables, however, were all abuzz with speculation on Hank's death: drug deal gone bad, revenge killing by Mandy's dad for hitting his daughter, and some other even more far-fetched stories.

Touch walked Bonnie back to the office and settled in behind his desk. He dialed Chris Hauser and inquired if the chief had availability to join him for a beer or two at the Roll'n at five o'clock that afternoon. Chief Hauser was in, confirming in the process that it was a good idea. He would be able to review what he had learned from the Kentucky State Police about increased Dixie Mafia activities in the western part of Kentucky as well.

Reflecting on his earlier thoughts, Touch clicked off with Hauser and dialed *Mi Tierra*, asking for Manny Benitez when the hostess picked up the call. "Mr. Benitez, this is Sheriff Thomas. Thank you and Paula again for the time and hospitality earlier today. Again, I'm sorry about Hank. Regarding finding out who killed him, Chief Hauser and I failed to ask if your restaurant has security cameras. So few places in Cooper have them that it slipped my mind. Any chance you had them installed?"

Manny Benitez replied in the affirmative. With the loss of Hank, the presence of the cameras had slipped his mind as well. He agreed to preserve the recordings, and Touch said he'd be right over to review them. Touch hoped that at the very least, he'd be able to pull a photo of the man on whom Juana Escovedo waited to share with KSP and the US Attorney's office, if not the FBI.

Thirty minutes later, technology granted Touch's wish. A man in boots, blue jeans, and a sports coat all but smiled and waved at *Mi Tierra's* security cameras. He knew he stuck out and, it appeared to Touch, didn't give a good goddamn. The sheriff copied a digital black-and-white photo of the man Juana Escovedo had served and emailed it to his office account from his web-based email account. Within the hour, Touch imagined he'd have the photo in the hands of the Kentucky State Police and Shel Richardson's office.

Touch jumped into his Tahoe, turned the volume down on Brooks and Dunn's feel-good anthem "Boot-Scootin' Boogie," and called Chris Hauser on his smartphone. Hauser picked up the call on the first ring. "Chris, it's Touch. You're not going to believe this, but we forgot to ask the Benitezes if they had a video system for restaurant security. It hit me in a moment of calm as I sat at my desk. Turns out that not only do they have security video, but also we now have a still photo—black-and-white, mind you—but nonetheless a photo of the guy who spent so much time in *Mi Tierra*. Also, we've got a timestamp on that video that dials in the time of death for Hank Benitez."

"Nice work, Touch! What time does the video show this guy leaving the restaurant?"

"Looks like he left the restaurant at a little after 1:30 in the afternoon. So, time of shooting must be sometime between 2:00 p.m. and 9:00 p.m. given the state of the body. Not a huge improvement, but we might get lucky and find someone who sighted this guy leaving town as well. We can hit service stations and the like once we get a blow-up and copies of the photo. I'll pass it on to KSP and the US Attorney's office as soon as I get in front of my laptop as well."

"Thanks, Touch. Keep me posted, and I'll do the same for you."

"The only thing is the guy seems to know he's on the security camera but acts like he couldn't care less. I find it eerie. It's almost like he knows we won't be able to find him even if we've got video and a photo."

"Huh. I definitely don't like that," Hauser said.

"Well, I'll see you at five at the Roll'n. If nothing else, it'll be good to catch up with Timmy," Touch said as he ended the call.

CHAPTER 22

Edmund Shakopf watched news coverage of Hank Benitez's murder on the NBC affiliate out of Paducah's local news coverage. Apparently, it was a slow news day in the region. Edmund anticipated some coverage but hoped it would be restricted to the local radio station. He didn't think wider coverage of Hank's death on a slow news day would impact his plans; Sheriff Thomas likely would turn over every stone imaginable. The man was nothing it not persistent. Shakopf thought his network implacable to local obstructions. To date, none of the state- or federal-level law enforcement organizations had so much as sniffed the breadth and depth of his family's criminal enterprises.

Choosing to knock off Hank Benitez marked a long-planned advancement of Shakopf's retail drug trade in West Kentucky. Long the wholesale supplier for the region, Shakopf concluded that the local components of the drug network over the past year had grown too fat, happy, and complacent. Edmund concluded it high time to make a statement and bring these people back in line. Rectifying this situation, though, called for a work of art in applying pressure in combination with ruthless negotiations while not scaring off his lieutenants and having them run across battle lines to the authorities. By Edmund's analysis, Benitez ranked as well-known enough to garner attention among those in the trade but anonymous enough among the power players to not raise attention.

Touch Thomas and Chris Hauser may be able to pull in a few low-level bagmen and delivery mules, but Shakopf rested assured that the higher-up components of his operations would remain above the fray. For over thirty years, his family had utilized their network of service stations to run drugs from Alabama through Tennessee and into Kentucky, Missouri, Illinois, and Indiana. Strategically avoiding the densely populated towns and cities that larger, more powerful organizations controlled and fought over, Shakopf relied on poor communications, and thus poor coordination, to remain below the radar of the more sophisticated elements of the US drug enforcement apparatus. With little competition, impeccable community credentials, a geographically large business network capable of legitimately processing large amounts of cash void of scrutiny, and ready-made excuses for traffic flows at all hours of days and nights, Edmund Shakopf's decision to move into the drug trade thus far proved to be a thing of genius. Having his best friend, Jerry Welch, head up his community's longest-established bank hadn't hurt him and his businesses any either.

However, neither of the men's sons, Laceon nor Will, proved to be anywhere near as adept at business as their fathers. Both sons remained relatively discrete, but they drank too much, and as people say, "loose lips sink ships." Sheriff Touch Thomas stumbling upon the David Barnett situation had left Will and Laceon none too comfortable. Both men agreed, as they had countless times before these most recent inquiries, to remain quiet and allow the situation to fade into memories because the trail likely would lead nowhere yet again.

The operation had started small with Edmund Shakopf in the early 1970s—1973 or 1974—noticing the same late-model Chevy pickup pulling into his parking lot, never buying anything or engaging in any of the auto repair services Edmund offered, and then leaving several minutes later after meeting with another random car. As tired of offering free parking as he was interested in what the meet-ups were about, Shakopf cornered the Chevy pickup driver after about a month and the tenth free-parking instance, and asked what the guy was doing. The fellow was inordinately fidgety, so Edmund knew something peculiar was afoot when the guy stuffed something under his seat. A quick threat to call the cops, and the low-level weed dealer opened up like a favorite book. Shakopf told the fellow that for ten bucks a month, he could come and go as he pleased—as long as he continued to be as discreet as he'd always been. Ever the consummate businessman, Edmund also suggested the guy drop into the store for a pack of gum or something periodically to "legitimize" his operation.

It turned out that the weed dealer was a decent fellow, interested in Shakopf's experiences and knowledge. Six months later, Edmund Shakopf more or less obtained an associate's degree in drug dealing after chatting with the guy and inquiring as to how the supply side of the business worked, as well as how he acquired new customers. Most importantly, Shakopf learned how to keep the cops from ever suspecting anything but gas-pumping and car-repairing was going on at his shop. If one acted like nothing out of the ordinary happened, everyone else pretty much assumed nothing unusual occurred. As gas stations gave way to convenience stores through the 1980s and 1990s, the operation seemed even more at home running through gas station and convenience store parking lots. Plenty of regulars cycled through Shakopf's stations. As long as no one saw any peculiar "packages" changing hands, all was well. Folks buying a case of beer and splitting it into coolers so close to Lake Barkley seemed entirely natural for Cooper and Walter County residents. As Shakopf opened more stations around the lake area, it appeared just as normal there too. Eighteen months after meeting the initial pusher, Shakopf made first contact with the weed source for West Kentucky. Within another year and a half, Edmund Shakopf moved everything from pot to cocaine through the twenty-four service stations and convenience stores he operated around the area.

When the big cities like New York, LA, and Chicago experienced surging heroin use in the late 1970s Shakopf did everything in his power to restrict its encroachment on West Kentucky. Cocaine proved to be far more addictive than anyone imagined, ruining bank accounts and families. That was several years before things got absolutely crazy with the Colombian cartel inundating the US market with coke. Fortunately for Shakopf, the flood of drug enforcement money focused on the cities, and his operation more or less ran as it always had: under the radar.

The biggest issue became one of too much success. Jerry Welch, who agreed to take a cut of Shakopf's profits in the mid-1970s in exchange for helping the man "clean" his money, grew very concerned about the magnitude of cash Shakopf channeled through his bank. Asian competition set Cooper's small manufacturers on their ears while the farm economy was even worse—on its ass—through the 1980s. Welch feared that an astute regulator would start digging once they discovered the little bank continued its long run of success amid a terrible local economy. In another brilliant move, Shakopf advised Welch to "lose a little to gain a lot," and he loaned out a portion of his cash knowing that the businesses and farmers wouldn't be able to pay it back. Doing so offered Shakopf and Welch minor solace that their criminal enterprise wasn't entirely bad. Adding the age-old adage "If they weren't buying from us, they'd just be buying from someone else," the two men practically felt absolved of any wrongdoing for supplying illegal drugs to an ever-widening area of Kentucky and its adjoining states.

To date, Shakopf focused more on adding and consolidating territories than on defending turf. In almost forty years of operations, no other dealers of any size or means had really seen much opportunity in challenging Shakopf's organization, if they even knew about it. Suppliers never encountered reasons to question, let along challenge, Shakopf because he moved product and paid bills. Edmund Shakopf treated his people well and assured them comfort and, if they followed the rules, safety.

However, Hank Benitez started to get a little too big for his britches. Divulging operating secrets to a group from Eastern Kentucky, Benitez not only betrayed Shakopf's trust in him, which came at no small cost to Edmund as he stomached Hank's run-ins with the law related to roughing up Mandy, but also Hank placed the entire organization at risk of intensely higher scrutiny if it came to a drug war for Shakopf's territory. A meeting of the minds—Jerry and Welch and Edmund and Laceon—determined that Hank had to go for a variety of reasons even prior to his latest incarceration. That episode reinforced the necessity of removing Hank.

Edmund Shakopf discretely inquired of his major supplier as to the mechanics of planning such an action, as well as recommendations for personnel to execute that plan. After three phone calls, one each to Louisville, Lexington, and Atlanta, Shakopf possessed the plan and the people to fulfill it. After two more anonymous communications, one to supply a photo and background info on Hank Benitez and another to update that profile for Hank's recent arrest, the removal of Hank Benitez—and hopefully any threat from outside influences— was a done deal.

Welch and Shakopf wouldn't sleep soundly until Hank's murder disappeared from the news coverage, but the lack of any direct ties between them, Hank, the Dixie Mafia operatives, and Rafe Livingston provided some relief. No one anticipated that the other organization working with Hank would step up their involvement; messages had been sent, received, and acknowledged according to Shakopf's supplier. Everyone concluded comfortably that Hank's demise sealed off that threat.

CHAPTER 23

Touch Thomas knew nothing other than that Hank Benitez was dead and, even though he wasn't the greatest guy on Earth, he shouldn't be. Touch also sensed that something wasn't quite right with the Welch-Shakopf recounting of their hunting escapades. Nothing else existed for the sheriff to do other than his police work, though.

Fortunately, tonight Touch Thomas's police work involved hanging out with a couple of old buddies at one of his favorite Cooper dive bars, the Roll'n Saloon. Touch had known Chris Hauser, who had joined him at the Roll'n, since high school. However, Touch had known Timmy Robinson, the Roll'n's bartender, since they were five-year old boys starting school. Timmy had been Touch's center on every football team he had played on in Cooper until Touch left for college.

Timmy ran a tight ship, operating as "clean" a dive bar as he could, but those in Cooper in need of knowing about the town's criminal elements knew that the Roll'n was the place to go. As a result, it frequently had a cop or two and a journalist or two drinking at the bar, as well as a few folks looking to score a bag of weed, move hot farm equipment, monetize food stamps, or execute any number of other illegal money-making schemes.

Hauser and Touch knew full well that they likely could sweep up a handful of Cooper's more frequent ne'er-do-wells at the Roll'n, but without catching them in the act, the attorneys counseled the chief and the sheriff that the probability of the charges sticking was likely small. Also, by creating a relative "safe zone" for discussions of illegal activities, law enforcement established a repository for information on those activities. Theoretically, acquiring and acting on this information would place law enforcement closer to catching the thieves, fraudsters, and dealers amid their illegal acts. Long ago, the Roll'n's owner, Wendell Ford, made it more than well-known that even mentioning certain activities was off-limits at the Roll'n. Anything involving children, women, moving people against their will, or life and death was subject to "country" law with miniscule probabilities of friends, relatives, or law enforcement ever finding the perpetrators again. Ford instilled some "honor among thieves," which was enforced by Timmy.

Unbeknownst to Touch and pretty much anyone else, several years ago, a kncklehead made the mistake while at the bar of bragging about what he'd done to a teenage girl. It just so happened that the girl had grown up in Timmy's neighborhood. Timmy had been friends with the girl's father for almost as long as he'd been friends with Touch Thomas. After the guy drank a few beers and decided to leave, Timmy, who was the size of a small farm tractor with about the same amount of horsepower, took a break from the bar, followed the fellow out the door, bounced his head off a nearby tree two or three times, picked up the guy, and stuffed him in the trunk of his car. After his shift ended at two in the morning, Timmy drove to a spot he knew on an old bridge over one of the rivers feeding Lake Barkley, weighted the guy down, and disposed of the child molester. No chance of the guy getting off on a technicality. No need to waste Touch's or Hauser's, or a judge's and jury's, time with it—the guy had confessed to it right in front of Timmy. That was not the way everything should be handled, but in Timmy's book, some things demanded to be dealt with immediately and directly.

Touch arrived at the Roll'n just after five o'clock. A few early drinkers occupied barstools, but in general the place appeared fairly empty, as it probably did most Thursdays in the late afternoon and early evening. The Roll'n catered to a crowd generally known for starting and ending late. Touch planned it that way because he anticipated Timmy would be more comfortable chatting with him and Hauser with fewer patrons in the place. Plus, Touch remembered he needed to make an appearance at the county commissioner's budget meeting a little after seven.

The words of Dwight Yoakum's "Guitars and Cadillacs" twanged out of the Roll'n's famously old-school country jukebox, one of the few redeeming qualities of the bar other than Timmy's on-point service, as Touch walked through the door. Upon seeing him, Timmy came out from behind the bar and gave his old quarterback a monstrous bearhug. Towering about five inches over Touch and about half again as wide as the sheriff, Timmy dwarfed Touch.

"Touch, man, it's been way too long! It's great to see you. Grab a table. I'll get you one of those microbrews you like. This Tailgate Brewing Company in Nashville has a peanut butter milk stout that I'm betting you'll like. It's thick and dense, just like you!"

Touch sat down with his back to the wall, facing the bar with the Roll'n's main door to his left. Several minutes later, Chris Hauser walked in as well.

"Timmy, grab Chief Hauser one of those peanut butter cup beers too."

Hauser said, "Touch, I see you've still got Timmy doing your blocking for you. Well done! I appreciate you looking out for me on the beer front as well. Doesn't even matter what it is. After the last few days we've had, any beer's bound to be a good beer."

Several minutes later, Timmy returned to the table with two beers and a massive Styrofoam Sonic cup full of ice water, Timmy's drink of choice.

"Chris Hauser, it's damned fine to see you in the Roll'n. As you can imagine, we do not get many Black men coming through our door. If it didn't make you uncomfortable, I'd ask you to take a picture so I could hang it on the wall behind my bar. Oh, boy, I could get both of y'all in a photo and put some kind of sign over it, like, 'Roll'n: A Friend of Cooper Law Enforcement.'"

"Funny you should mention that, Timmy," Touch started. "Chris and I both wanted to come and hang out with you for a while, but we also were hoping you could help us out with a few questions on actions in Cooper's less-than-legal dealings. Specifically, do you have any ideas as to why someone would invite the Dixie Mafia into Cooper and Walter County? While you're cogitating on that one, throw this log on the fire as well: Who fronts the money for the drug trade in Cooper in the first place?"

Timmy gulped about six ounces of ice water in a single pull on his straw and placed the cup back on the table in front of him. "Damn, fellas, I was hoping y'all came in to talk about old times and such. I guess nobody ever wants to talk about what the bartender wants to talk about, though. All about the customers, huh?"

Dwight Yoakum tailed off the jukebox as "Guitars and Cadillacs" ended with "It's the only thing that keeps me hanging on," which Dwight drew out for an extra few seconds at the end of the song. As the jukebox moved on to its next song, Confederate Railroad's "She Took It Like a Man," Timmy formulated an answer to Touch's first question.

"You know, Touch, I should have known something was up earlier this week when those Mafia clowns got drunk and made asses of themselves at my bar. I'm sorry, I should have called you and Chris and let you guys know that there were some new dimwits to be on the lookout for. I was so concerned with not losing my cool and bashing their heads that I plum forgot they were out of place and likely up to no good. They had something to do with Hank Benitez's murder, didn't they? Hank was a damned fool and a pain in the ass, but he wasn't a terrible guy when he was sober. I tried to get him to keep his drinking under control, but he'd just leave and go somewhere else. I guess I'm not the conversationalist that I once was."

Touch stepped in. "Timmy, I don't think anything was going to help Hank. He was going down one way or the other. I blame myself too—I released him. By all accounts, he probably should have gone away for abusing Mandy again, but I struck an arrangement with him. When I think about it, if he'd gone to prison, he'd likely end up the same way. Someone marked him. Chris and I are trying to figure out why."

"Thanks, Touch. Those Dixie Mafia guys asked a few questions, mostly about low-level drug stuff in Cooper. Nothing I don't hear a few times a week, if not every day on the weekends. When Hank needed money, he turned into a dealer and bagman for the mover in Cooper. I think it's the same guy who's been working out of the convenience store on the west side of town for the past twenty years. I forget what his name is, though. Minus using the convenience store for dealing drugs, the guy's pretty professional. Almost has to be, or no way he'd be in the business for twenty years. He'd have disappeared long ago. If you think about it, drops at convenience stores are pretty brilliant, though, right? Tons of traffic in and out, and plenty of regulars buying beer, candy, smokes, lottery tickets, and such."

Chris Hauser shook his head. "Hold on a minute, Timmy. You mean to tell me that a guy's been dealing drugs out of Shakopf's convenience store for twenty years?"

"Sorry, Chris, didn't know this would be news to you. I figured you guys knew this. Monitored it or whatever for what you needed to know. Certainly, if folks aren't getting their stash from Shakopf's, they're just going to get it from somewhere else. Sure, Cooper's got a few problem souls who get a little too deep into stuff, but Cooper doesn't seem to be anywhere near as bad with drugs as a lot of other places. I thought you guys somehow had it under control. Shit, figures I give you two fools too much credit—QB1 and his big-play wide receiver."

Touch continued. "So, I guess you haven't seen those two Dixie Mafia fellas in here the last two days?"

"Nope, they were one and done. There were four of them, though, not just two. One was a mousy-looking little fucker."

"That'd be Dougie Delaney," Touch chimed in.

"A taller, more muscly fellow."

Touch identified him. "Ricky Drummond, the SOB who put his hands on Reva Dennis."

"Oh, hold on a minute, Touch," Timmy demanded. "Someone put their hands on Reva in your presence? Is he still breathing? Are you sure you're still eligible to be sheriff after what I'm imagining you did to this Ricky character? I mean, touching Reva's a capital offense in your book, isn't it?"

"Timmy, I don't mind saying that I was entirely composed as I put that bastard on the ground and threatened to remove his right arm from his body with an arm bar. I'm still shocked that his elbow didn't immediately pop out of socket. I was so composed that I helped Ricky to his car—by his hair. I promptly explained to him then that if I so much as thought I saw him, it likely would be the last time anyone would see him."

"I'll pretend I didn't hear that, Touch," Chris Hauser said with a smirk.

The other two guys, one really fat and one average, as Timmy described them, neither Touch nor Hauser had laid eyes on. Timmy hadn't seen them the last two days.

With the business side of the meeting over in the first fifteen minutes, the three men progressed to reliving old times. Cognizant of the city commissioners' meeting at 7:00 that evening, Touch and Hauser limited themselves to two beers. No limit existed, however, on the embellishing of back-in-the-day events.

Always one to deflect accolades to his linemen, receivers, and running backs, Touch noted that his favorite Timmy play came in their junior year against Mayfield. Tired of getting his ass kicked up and down the field, Mayfield's all-state noseguard went low on Timmy's knees late in the third quarter to create a pile-up on a fourth and short play that Touch ultimately turned into a twelve-yard gain on a naked bootleg run to the left side of the formation. The next play, which saw Touch and Hauser combine for a twenty-three-yard touchdown, Timmy "got fit" under the noseguard's shoulder pads—no small feat for a person five inches taller than their opponent—and drove the guy almost the entire twenty-three yards backward into the endzone.

Hauser's favorite high school sports memory came on the basketball court. In the regional finals their last year, a game that Walter County lost, Touch and Hauser almost managed to take the game over by running two-man plays. Hauser's favorite, though, was an alley-oop that Touch had thrown him early in the second half to spur their comeback. It allowed the shorter Hauser to dunk definitively on his significantly taller and mouthier defender.

For Timmy, his prized memory of Hauser was a reverse he scored on early in Timmy's senior year. In his mind, the play really set the tone for the year because it defined just how easily Walter County was going to be able to score that year. The play featured a devastating block that Touch—the quarterback, mind you—threw on Taylor County's middle linebacker. Touch de-cleated the guy. It was such a clean yet vicious hit that Hauser almost quit running to watch. The visual in Hauser's mind twenty years later still played in slow motion as the linebacker came into his peripheral vision just long enough for Hauser to see him before Touch, running like a freight train, blew him up.

Timmy revered how Touch protected those less able than him. If one was a bully around Tanner "Touch" Thomas, one had best turn tail and find something else to do—and somewhere else to do it. One of the first times Timmy and Touch had ventured out of Cooper on their own to catch a movie in Paducah—they must have been sophomores with maybe six months of driving history between them—a small group of older boys was teasing a geeky-looking kid and his date. It was obvious to Touch and Timmy that the teasing made the young man, and more importantly his date, uncomfortable. After telling Timmy to hold on a second before they entered the movie theater, Touch approached the group as though he knew the boy and girl, asking them if they were ready to see the movie. The leader of the group took offense to the interruption and grabbed Touch by the bicep. Touch, well on his way to being a man among boys at about five feet ten and 175 pounds of rippling muscles, flexed his bicep, shrugged out of the older boy's hold, and turned to leave with his new friends. This apparently aggravated the aggressor, who saw fit to push Touch from behind. Touch kept walking, but the fool followed and pushed Touch again, this time with a two-hand thrust. Touch offered him a warning, which the poor guy chose not to heed. Touch slipped the guy's first punch, caught the fellow's arm as it came over his shoulder, rotated into and under the older boy, and executed a textbook arm spin. The flashy yet simple wrestling throw resulted in the older boy landing flat on his back with a sickening thud about ten feet away from where he had previously stood. Touch, still standing, gently placed his knee on the kid's neck and kindly asked that he no longer be a bother. As Touch helped the older boy off the ground with an arm bar, he also extracted an apology to the boy and girl with a slight increase in pressure on the bully's wrist. For a fellow as hefty and, as a result, frequently as clumsy as Timmy, the fluidity with which Touch Thomas moved left Timmy—and most others—dumbfounded. He found it not unlike watching a bird take flight because it appeared to be something that should not be physically possible.

With reminiscences and their second beers finished, Touch, Chris Hauser, and Timmy Robinson bade each other a good evening, agreeing that it had been too long and that not so much time should pass before they did this again. Touch and Hauser had fifteen minutes to make it to the commissioners' meeting, which was no problem. After walking out toward their cars, the two heads of law enforcement in Cooper and Walter County agreed that they would commence undercover monitoring of two of Shakopf's service stations, one on each side of town.

CHAPTER 24

Touch Thomas and Chris Hauser walked into the county commissioners' budget meeting about ninety seconds apart and from different sides of the building. There was no reason to give the commissioners any idea that the two departments coordinated their comments at these meetings. Frankly, neither the sheriff's office nor the police department voiced much in the way of dissent or criticism of the commissioners and the way they went about their business anyway, but in the past, avoiding scrutiny seemed to be the most advantageous path to harmonious coexistence.

This meeting, however, would turn out to be different than the prior meetings the two law enforcement officers had attended. The death of Hank Benitez, rising drug activity, and a corresponding increase in hospital admissions related to that activity made its way into the public consciousness and thus that of the county commissioners. For the first time that either Touch or Hauser could remember, a reporter from the *Cooper Courier* attended the meeting as well.

Following a call to order, a review of past business, and a cursory request for any comments or concerns from the audience, which consisted of all of seven people, items that cumulatively consumed seventeen minutes of what typically was a one-hour meeting, the commissioners commenced to entertaining new business. The first item of new business: a proposal to fund a Cooper City Police Department and Walter County Sheriff's Office drug task force. The fact that neither law enforcement department instigated the proposal marked a first as far as Touch or Chris could recollect. Second, the willingness of the commissioners to spend money proved unprecedented as well. Finally, the rapidity with which the board reacted to very recent events caused a few raised eyebrows.

Reacting to the announcement, Touch approached the microphone, "I appreciate the board addressing this issue so quickly and aggressively. If I may, could the board provide some context as to the drivers behind this proposal? Also, in its analysis did the board identify any potential gaps in current law enforcement efforts that it anticipated these proposed new funds filling?"

"Thanks, Touch—ah, um, Sheriff Thomas," the board chairman started. "A couple local business leaders, Jerry Welch and Edmund Shakopf, voiced concerns about the area's escalating drug problems and advanced the idea of a task force. As for gaps in enforcement, initiating undercover resources, coordinating with other municipalities in the area, and interfacing with state drug and law enforcement agencies could be focus areas for funds."

"Ms. Chairman, I appreciate your candor. I, and I would guess Chief Hauser as well, welcome the opportunity to interface with you and the board to make sure these funds are, first, justified and, second, effectively allocated. Finally, we want to assure that we appropriately accounted for the funds as well."

Chris Hauser signaled his agreement with Touch with a nod of his head.

The Walter County Board of Commissioners addressed a few other far more mundane items of new business. The meeting ended with a commitment on the part of the board, Chief Hauser, and Sheriff Thomas to agree on a meeting time the next week to initiate the planning function for a Cooper-Walter County drug enforcement task force.

It was just before eight o'clock, so Touch and Chief Hauser agreed to grab a bite to eat and discuss the shock of Welch and Shakopf initiating and supporting a drug enforcement task force. The two men agreed on Big Bob's BBQ on the east side of Cooper.

Touch climbed into his Tahoe and fired the ignition. The radio entertained Touch with Dolly Parton's "Jolene." The "please don't take my man just because you can" line ranked as one of the most vivid song lyrics in Touch's recollection. On the ten-minute drive over to Big Bob's, Touch's mind raced between Parton's lyrics and the motivations behind Welch and Shakopf expressing concern for drug enforcement in Cooper. "Jolene" gave way to "The Night the Lights Went Out in Georgia," Reba McIntire's rendition of small-town revenge originally sung by actress Vicki Lawrence of *Mama's Family* fame. Touch couldn't imagine that any of the judges in the area had bloodstains on their hands, unlike the judge in the song. Somebody had Hank Benitez's blood on their hands, though.

Hauser beat Touch to Big Bob's by just a minute or two, long enough to grab a table and a couple of menus. No sooner had Touch sat down than a waitress arrived to take the two cops' drink orders. Big Bob always treated the law enforcement folks like royalty in his restaurant. It was the second reason why they kept coming, a distant second to Big Bob's out-of-this-world buttery brisket. Neither Touch nor Hauser were bashful about eating when it came to barbecue: both men ordered a pound of brisket from the point, potato salad, baked beans, cole slaw, cornbread, and sweet tea. Touch's workout in the morning likely would suffer, but Big Bob's was just too damn good not to indulge in it when one had the chance.

The business of ordering behind them, Touch and Hauser embarked on full throttle speculation as to why Welch and Shakopf would engage the county commissioners to establish a drug enforcement task force. "If Shakopf actually knowingly allowed drugs to be trafficked through his stations, why would he want law enforcement focusing on the issue in Cooper and Walter County?" Hauser asked.

"Furthermore," Touch said, "why in the world would a community banker like Jerry Welch motivate law enforcement to increase focus on drug dealing? I recently met with both Shakopf and Welch, and the two men failed to mention the idea. It strikes me as strange. I've got a long-running policy of investigating crimes on the basis of following the money. This reeks of dirty money."

Hauser continued Touch's line of thought. "How might Shakopf and drug dealing link with the murder of Hank Benitez and the arrival of the Dixie Mafia in Cooper and Walter County? Are Edmund Shakopf and the Dixie Mafia somehow linked or competing to run drugs in Cooper?"

"Chris, nothing from a population growth or demographic point of view would motivate anyone to view Cooper, or even Western Kentucky, as prime territory for drug dealing. We've been losing people, especially young people, to the surrounding cities for decades: Nashville, Louisville, Lexington, Bowling Green. Hell, I even left for twenty years."

"To some degree, lower operating costs and less risk of arrest could offset this negative," Hauser added. "If I do some quick math, I think it'd show relatively low potential profit too. Then again, for folks with few skills, there aren't a whole lot of jobs around here that'll pay the bills. I think we maybe need some different perspectives on this."

After finishing up his barbecue feast, Touch proposed a quick action plan. "I'll call Sam Stevens at the newspaper in the morning and set up another meeting with the *Cooper Courier's* investigative reporter. We can compare notes on the Shakopf drug links and see how Welch fits this puzzle."

"Sounds good to me, Touch," Hauser said. "I'll interview Laceon and Edmund Shakopf, in that order. Maybe you can do the same with Jerry and Will Welch?"

"Sure," Touch agreed. "I'll also make time this weekend to chat with Andrew Barnett and see what he thinks about Shakopf's and Welch's business and financial ties. That guy knows more about Cooper politics and family histories than anyone else in the county, I'd bet."

Touch and Hauser left their waitress a tip on the table, paid their bills, and exited Big Bob's after sharing handshakes with the owner. "Catch you tomorrow," Touch said to Hauer as he opened to door to his Tahoe and climbed into the vehicle.

When Touch got home, he was still too wired to hit the sack. Like he'd done earlier in the week documenting thoughts on the shooting of David Barnett, he grabbed pen and paper and commenced detailing everything he knew about the Shakopf, Welch, drugs, and Hank linkages. Looking to his "follow the money" method, Touch sketched out the flows of drugs to, through, and from Cooper and wondered how the cash flowed through his community. Even if the area proved to generate a fraction of the profit that larger, more metropolitan areas produced, it probably still represented a considerable sum of money compared to most of the area's other businesses. How did Shakopf, or whoever was responsible for drug dealing in Cooper, move their money without attracting undue attention?

It hit Touch then: If Shakopf moved drugs through his businesses, he likely partnered with Welch to move the resulting money through his bank. The two old men partnered on almost everything else, so why not on this as well? In addition to talking to Andrew Barnett, Touch needed to get Shel Richardson on board. With a homicide and what appeared to be a substantial drug operation, Touch doubted it would take much, if any, more than asking to get Richardson and his substantial base of resources behind him. If he was lucky, the *Cooper Courier's* reporter had at least some theories that Touch and Hauser's information and theories could confirm or deny.

Looking the other direction, Touch wondered what roles Will

Welch and Laceon Shakopf fulfilled in the organization. Their fathers were far too old to remain sufficiently active to run a multicounty drug ring in addition to continuing to oversee high-level activities for the bank and the service stations. Done correctly, a task force, complete with undercover officers, could possibly shed light on Will's and Laceon's day-to-day activities. Tying Laceon's physical presence at a convenience store when, say, a drug drop went down could provide Touch and Hauser the leverage needed to turn the younger Shakopf against the organization. Similarly, if US Attorney Richardson could enlist the resources of a forensic accountant to scrutinize the flows of drug-dealing cash through Walker County Bank, it could prove a boon to the investigation.

Finally, Touch thought that if the task force, should it come to fruition, could generate sufficient pressure to force one of the Shakopfs or one of the Welches to throw the other one "under the bus," they might name the murderer of Hank Benitez.

Touch held little hope, however, of actually being able to corral Hank's shooter. About the only way in which he envisioned that happening, given the level of professionalism the shooter employed in his operation – minus the flagrant disregard for being captured on video - was the man returning to Cooper to tie up loose ends should any materialize. Unless Richardson possessed far more information than he let on in Touch's prior conversations with the U.S. Attorney, Touch thought it improbable that they could penetrate the drug supplier to any degree sufficient to nab whoever that was in the security video. Hell, he didn't even know the shooter's name despite the fact that he had him on video. Again, maybe Richardson could help.

The incremental thirty-five minutes it took Touch to detangle the thoughts in his head proved to be almost as good as an Ambien for his sleep. The final knot to untie, which his mind chewed on as he closed his eyes and headed off to dreamland: what benefit would Shakopf and Welch gain from establishing a drug task force?

CHAPTER 25

Friday morning, Touch awoke far more refreshed than he feared he would just before he fell asleep Thursday night. The Big Bob's barbecue sat kind of heavy, but Touch commenced his weightlifting routine at the usual time and without modification. He cranked up the music, starting with Metallica's "Enter Sandman" just as he had for every Friday morning workout since the band released the album in 1991. He slid two forty-five-pound plates on each side of his squat rack's long bar and ripped off twelve repetitions. Feeling good with no balking from his knees, Touch added another big plate to each side of the bar and repped the resulting 315 pounds ten times with relative ease. To close out his squat work for the morning, Touch added another ninety total pounds to the long bar and ripped off eight reps of 405 pounds, the maximum he allowed himself to squat nowadays. In the not-too-distant past, Touch had noticed his form failing when he added more than 405.

Fifty-two minutes later, Touch was on the last set of his Friday lifting routine: eight repetitions of "cheat" curls with a forty-five-pound plate on each side of the long bar. The final beats of "Another One Bites the Dust" by Queen played through his home gym speakers as he reracked the bar, cleared and returned the weight plates to their spots on the weight tree, turned off the lights and his speakers, and headed to the kitchen for a protein shake before showering and heading to the Tiger's Den for breakfast.

Knowing Andrew Barnett to be another early riser, Touch called the old attorney after his shower to invite him for an eight o'clock breakfast at the Tiger's Den. Barnett picked up on the first ring and graciously accepted Touch's invitation. Parking next to each other near the sheriff's office at the Walter County Courthouse, Touch and Barnett walked into the Den at the same time. Reva beamed upon seeing the two men together. Andrew Barnett had been among her favorite people in Cooper since she was a little girl. With a particularly soft spot for all children after his son David died, Andrew Barnett never missed an opportunity to stop in and visit with Reva when he had the time. Touch ordered his usual egg concoction with coffee and water while Barnett enjoyed a stack of pancakes, bacon on the side, orange juice, and coffee.

"Andrew," Touch started, "what can you tell me about the history of Edmund Shakopf's service station business? Did you ever suspect that he dealt drugs or engaged in any type of illegal businesses and used the gas stations and convenience stores as a front? I know it's still early and those are heavy questions, but Chris Hauser and I have a ton of crap coming down on us as a result of this Hank Benitez murder. The county commissioners last night voiced support for a new drug task force. Get this: Jerry Welch and Edmund Shakopf instigated the idea."

"Wow, Touch, that's quite a mouthful there. Let me have another bite of pancakes and think on that or a while. Have a sip of coffee and breathe."

Touch watched Reva float from table to table, refilling coffee cups and clearing empty plates and glasses. He estimated that the woman must burn about a thousand calories an hour hustling and bustling from table to table during her breakfast and lunch rushes. No wonder she was able to maintain such a girlish figure despite working in what could easily be described as a greasy spoon.

"I've known Edmund Shakopf—and Jerry Welch for that matter; one might as well treat them as a tandem pair—for sixty-odd years. You'd never see one alone for long before the other showed up. I've never been a fan of either man, personally. Shakopf worked hard all his life and gained his wealth by bootstrapping that hard work. Welch married into his money and managed not to screw it up, from everything I can tell. I've not always been a lawyer. I have, however, always been an excellent judge of character. I never witnessed either man do anything blatantly wrong or illegal. I also never witnessed them do anything entirely selflessly and for someone else, not even their wives or kids. I always got the feeling that with those two, it somehow always came down to one palm greasing the other. When their sons were coming of age, it seemed to reinforce that feeling.

"So, no, it wouldn't surprise me in the least to learn that Shakopf and Welch had something going on the side. A lot of small-town living ends up being 'don't ask, don't tell' in that many times neighbors don't really want to know bad things about their fellow citizens. It sort of follows a 'don't rock the boat' philosophy of go along to get along: if we don't know anything bad about them, maybe they won't know anything bad about us. I've tried to live a wholesome life, even more so after David died. I was so grief-stricken that I didn't have the mental capacity for mischief. I had more than a few female accompaniments after my wife died, however. I'm sure neighbors and colleagues looked the other way. You know as well as I do that law enforcement frequently looks the other way if a problem appears small or they believe it soon will disappear. Not to pick at an open wound too soon, but the Hank Benitez situation offers an excellent example."

"Thanks, Andrew. I've accepted a portion of responsibility for Hank's death. However, if he'd not placed himself in that position in the first place, I wouldn't have had the opportunity to release him, either."

Andrew Barnett smiled. "I'm glad you made that connection,

Touch. Rarely is something entirely one person's or another person's fault. It takes two to tango, as they say. I'm sure you've already thought of this, but if Shakopf, and thus Welch, run drugs, where does the money go? Sure, those families fare well by Cooper standards, but they hardly look like Kentucky versions of Pablo Escobar or El Chapo. Where's the money go?"

"Amen, Andrew. Right after we finish breakfast, I'm calling Shel Richardson and executing a brain dump, or at least scheduling the time to do so with him. You'll know better than me, but I'm hopeful that the combination of Hank Benitez's murder, involvement of the Dixie Mafia in that murder, the appearance of a link to a drug ring, and a desire on the part of the Walter County Commissioners to establish and fund a drug task force will induce Richardson to commit resources to helping us. Chief among those resources, unless someone offers a superior idea, is forensic accounting talent to snoop through Walter County Bank's dealings with Shakopf's businesses in an effort to figure out where the money goes and how it gets there.

"Just between me and you, Andrew, Sam Stevens has a journalist who's been working some portion of this mess for at least a month. Also, we've got video of Hank Benitez's suspected shooter from the parking lot security camera of his parents' restaurant. The degree of disinterest the guy exhibits being recorded on video is unbelievable, but it looks like the shooter ate at *Mi Tierra* before following Hank home and putting a bullet in the back of his head. Thankfully, as far as my guys in the department and Hauser's people can tell, this psychopath left town immediately after executing Hank. We also have yet to witness any further Dixie Mafia presence. Until facts lead me elsewhere, I'm working under the premise that Shakopf had Hank executed in order to head off encroachment on his operations by some other drug-driven organization. It's a leap, I understand, given no more than we've got to go on at this point, but events, actions, and associations increasingly point to some derivative of these factors."

"Touch, you're going a mile a minute, but as I've witnessed over the entirety of your life, that's definitely when you're at your best. My only advice at this point is to try to not have anyone other than maybe Chris Hauser keep up with you … and maybe Reva, too. By the way, who wins a footrace between you and Chris?"

"Chris, all day long. I doubt it would even be close! I'd throw him around like a ragdoll and probably get him in the three-cone drill if we were doing an NFL combine thing. Straight-line speed, though, Chris Hauser was borderline world-class. It's unbelievable, but a guy who could move like that never really even liked to run! He simply liked being around everyone else, I think, and feeling like he contributed. My understanding is that's the way he runs the police department as well, very much as the servant rather than as the served."

"Touch, I've got to be on my way, but please keep me posted on how this is going. As I said, I've never gotten warm fuzzies from Shakopf or Welch—I only do business with them because they're local. I would love to have my theories on their social deviances confirmed."

Nodding, Touch replied, "I understand, Andrew, but I really hope we're both wrong. For a community like Cooper to have two leading citizens be as dirty as we're implying Shakopf and Welch are, would shake the town to its bedrock. Of course, if I'm wrong and someone else is behind all this, we may have a much larger problem than two leading citizens running a drug business under our noses for the past however many decades. Have a great day, and thanks as always for your time and guidance."

Touch grabbed the check before Barnett could do so. Reva came over to thank Andrew Barnett for stopping in and to voice her pleasure at seeing him offering sage advice to Touch, who could definitely use it in her opinion. Touch waited for her at the cash register to pay his bill.

"Touch," Reva said as she approached the counter, "how's progress on finding Hank's murderer?"

"Well, you know I'm not supposed to discuss open cases and all that mumbo jumbo, but we've got video of the guy we think did it. No idea who he is, and it appears from the video that he doesn't care if we know. We shuttled a photo off to the US Attorney's office. Hopefully, he's in an FBI database or something. As soon as I get to the office, I'm calling to lay things out for him and to see if he'll allocate resources to Walter County. Fingers crossed."

Reva grinned from behind the register. "I've not heard you talk this fast or seen you move this fast in months. If energy solves anything, you should be well down the right path. We've not seen any more of those thugs the past couple days, either. I appreciate you dealing with that for me. Johnny's getting a little old to be bouncing guys out of the Tiger's Den."

"I heard that, Reva," Johnny shouted from behind his cooktop. "Don't you worry none: I still got it. I can deal with it if it needs dealt with. I can't deal with it like no Touch Thomas, that's for sure, but I can still deal with it."

"Thanks, Johnny," Touch shared as he backed through the front door of the Den. The bell clanged as the door closed behind Touch.

CHAPTER 26

Touch fast-walked back to his office. First on his morning to-do list: call Richardson at the US Attorney's office in Louisville. Touch hoped that the fact that Louisville was in the Eastern Time Zone and an hour ahead of Cooper would mean Richardson already was at his desk with a cup of coffee and through his morning reading.

"Hey, Bonnie," Touch said with a smile as he entered his office. "How was your evening? Hauser and I ate about half a cow at Big Bob's last night, and I slept for crap, but my workout this morning was awesome. Today, I'm fired up!"

"That much I can see, Touch. Nice to see you with a spring in your step. I'm guessing you and Chief Hauser launched a plan to figure out and arrest who killed Hank Benitez and get Cooper back to its kinder, gentler character."

"Bingo, and first up this morning is another call to the US Attorney's office in Louisville. I'm hopeful Richardson's got a name for me on that *Mi Tierra* video as well as a treasure trove of resources he can dedicate to rooting around in bank financial records and the like."

With that foreshadowing of his morning agenda, Touch closed his office door behind him, carefully maneuvered around his desk, turned on his laptop, found Richardson's office phone number, and dialed. The call rang through to Richardson's assistant, who informed Touch that the US Attorney had just stepped out of his office for a cup of coffee and would be back momentarily. Touch chose to hold, and true to the assistant's word, Richardson picked up his call less than two minutes later.

"Sheriff Thomas, you've been busy over there in Cooper. How can I help you today?" Richardson offered.

"Yeah, more bad guys doing bad things around here than I'm comfortable with. It's them who keep me in a job, though. Did the FBI happen to get a name from that video I forwarded to you a couple days ago?"

"You're in luck that they did in fact pull a name from that video. Unfortunately, you're really unlucky that the man's name is Rafe Livingston. He's one bad son-of-a-bitch: US Army, maybe CIA, definitely soldier for hire, and now apparently hit man. He doesn't come cheaply, and as you're now aware, he's quite efficient at what he does. Whoever brought him in didn't care about cost and wanted to make a statement by retaining the best to do the job. Even worse, none of the federal databases has any more than basic information on Livingston. Either the guy lives underground, or someone wipes clean his file. From your description, it sounds like he knows he's a ghost too."

"Oh, boy, Cooper's hit the big time for hit men. Yay for me. What in the world would motivate a guy like that to take out an everyday joe like Hank Benitez? Now, I'm fairly certain that something bigger than immediately meets the eye is going on around here. Any chance you can direct me to someone in federal law enforcement who can investigate accounting practices and cash flows for a local bank and a company that runs a small chain of convenience stores? I think they may be in cahoots dealing drugs and laundering money—maybe doing so for decades."

"Sure I can, Sheriff. Why don't you give me what information you've got and a little color on where it came from? We can build out resources from there."

Touch took a moment to collect his thoughts and to decide where to begin. "Mr. Richardson, I'm first going to lead with the fact that my primary sources are an investigative reporter for a local paper and a bartender buddy of mine who was my center on all of my football teams since we were in middle school. Obviously, this came at us fast, and as such I've not enjoyed the time to investigate any of this, let alone do so thoroughly."

"Sheriff, I'm going to guess that your sources are at least as trustworthy as most confidential informants. Also, you didn't have to pay for your information, I'm guessing. So, please continue."

"I gathered that Hank Benitez made contact with a group looking to disrupt whatever drug trade exists in and around Cooper. My guess is that whatever group enlisted Hank plans to use the combination of Lake Barkley's multistate access and links to relatively undertraveled interstates to expand their trade into the entire area south of Chicago, west of the Alleghenies, north of Atlanta, and east of Kansas City. I think my geography's pretty good there, but I could be off a state or two. The reporter bird-dogged this piece of the story working undisclosed sources corroborated through a handful of prison interviews.

"My bartending former center told me that one of our local leading citizens, Edmund Shakopf, either deals drugs or allows drugs to be dealt from his network of convenience stores and service stations, which pretty much surround Lake Barkley and operate all over West Kentucky. If it's true, Shakopf supplies the entire western regions of Kentucky and Tennessee; potentially, he could deal into Missouri and Illinois as well. It sounds like this arrangement might date back decades. If one takes a moment to reflect on the nature of his business, it's an awesome front for dealing: high traffic, cash based, with a widely accepted regular clientele. Folks going in and out of his stores almost would never look out of place."

"Yeah, Sheriff, let's keep that between ourselves. I agree that convenience stores and gas stations offer a solid front for drug dealing. Any idea how Shakopf launders his cash?"

"Excellent leading question there, counselor. The families of Edmund Shakopf and Jerry Welch have been close for two generations now. Their sons, Laceon and Will, were and are bosom buddies—hunting, fishing, drinking, golfing. The fathers, Edmund and Jerry, have been pillars of the Cooper community for over fifty years. Jerry Welch ran Walter County Bank for the entirety of his adult life before passing off the reins to a nephew. Interestingly, while the industrial base of Cooper fell to shit, Welch's Walter County Bank never missed a beat. Have you ever witnessed anything this far-fetched before?"

"I've spent thirty-five years in various capacities of criminal law, defense and prosecution, in big and small cities. All too frequently, the bigger the sums of money, the more far-fetched the situation becomes. Remember Colombians smuggling cocaine in Cabbage Patch dolls in the eighties? How about Bernie Madoff swindling thousands of people out of hundreds of millions of dollars putting up seemingly unbelievable returns year after year with no one ever questioning or investigating him or his firm? When it comes to crime, it doesn't have to be believable for it to end up being true. So, if I were to request some forensic accounting talent, I would do so in order to investigate Walter County Bank in coordination with cash deposits made over decades from Edmund Shakopf and the gas stations and convenience stores that he controls. Is that about the crux of it?"

"Dead-on, Shel. And as long as I'm asking, do you think the FBI or DEA might be willing to participate in an area task force? I'm guessing I could use some undercover presence so none of my people get burned. Cooper and Walter County only have about twenty thousand total residents. It'd be pretty easy to spot local law enforcement, I think. One last little twist to the story: Shakopf and Welch actually suggested to the county commissioners that they launch a drug enforcement task force. Potentially big-time crooks asking for increased law enforcement is about as contrarian and as arrogant as one can get, is it not?"

With a little chuckle over the phone, Richardson concluded his conversation with Touch. "Sheriff, that's pretty audacious, I agree. It may be as much a defensive move as anything else, though. If Shakopf feels outside pressure, and he's flown below your radar for as long as you fear, increased law enforcement attention focused outwardly and away from his efforts could deter whoever's looking to encroach on his turf. I'm going to chat with the DEA and some others in the know on the drug situation in the Midwest and see if I can deduce what crew might be making for Shakopf's territory. We'll get back to you ASAP on the accounting, task force, and undercover personnel. We've already got the FBI on Rafe Livingston's trail, but that's been the case for some time now, to no avail. I'll be back to you early next week, if not before. Please keep me informed if anything else meaningful happens in the interim. I wish you luck, Sheriff."

Touch hanged up his phone, reviewed the two pages of notes he took, highlighted certain sections, and crafted a framework for presenting the details of his US Attorney conversation to Chris Hauser. Fifteen minutes later, Touch texted Hauser and asked him to meet again for lunch at the Tiger's Den.

CHAPTER 27

Saturday morning, the *Cooper Courier* ran its initial article on the town's drug situation, identifying their investigative reporter as Janie Drummond. Neither Touch nor Chris Hauser knew Drummond personally, but both recognized her name from past pieces she published.

Janie Drummond, Investigative Reporter for the
Cooper Courier:

Our town experienced a marked increase in drug overdoses in the past year, an unfortunate and readily apparent phenomenon for anyone visiting the Cooper Hospital Emergency Room. Although hospital officials chose not to definitively quantify the increase, interviews conducted by this reporter with numerous staff members documented this significant growth. Thankfully, the ready access to Narcan, the wonder drug capable of reviving those overdosing on opioids and their derivatives, vastly stemmed the number of fatalities. A relatively low body count as compared to the number of overdose cases, however, should not be interpreted as success on the part of law enforcement, health care, or treatment officials.

Based on proprietary interviews with individuals across the spectrum of the problem, including dealers, doctors, law enforcement, and addiction treatment professionals, the *Courier* anticipates that the problem probably will get worse before it improves. Two factors support this conclusion. First, local law enforcement appears to have little handle on the drivers of increased drug usage in Cooper and Walter County. Second, coordination efforts appear nonexistent between health care professionals treating addicts and those professionals focused on enabling addicts to recover and reclaim their lives. Notably, these challenges represent nothing new and persist in far larger areas with much more history combatting this situation with access to far greater pools of resources.

Recently, the Walter County Commissioners met to discuss with Sheriff Tanner Thomas and Police Chief Chris Hauser the potential for a task force to address drug-related challenges. Interestingly, leading citizens and longtime Cooper benefactors Edmund Shakopf and Jerry Welch instigated the county's inquiry concerning a drug task force. Though still very early in the discussion, the entirely law enforcement–focused tone of this initial meeting concerns this reporter as well as the *Courier*. Again, health care officials shied away from documenting the number of repeat overdoses, a shrewd position on their part given the ever-increasing focus on privacy of individual health care data. However, this reporter's conversations with frontline health care workers indicated substantial challenges posed by addicts incurring multiple overdoses. This reporter's future pieces will focus not only on the toll addiction takes on the addict but also on the addict's loved ones: spouses, children, parents, friends, teachers, and neighbors.

Extensive time spent speaking with incarcerated individuals at the state prison adjacent to Cooper uncovered several troubling facts. Speaking on conditions of anonymity, conversations with three former drug dealers serving anywhere from fifteen months to four years for their offenses, all of which occurred in West Kentucky, indicated a budding drug war likely commencing in or around Cooper and Walter County. Though only speculation at this point in time, initial investigations point to the recent murder of longtime Cooper resident Hank Benitez being linked to drug dealing. The apparently professional nature of Mr. Benitez's murder marks a particularly troubling development for the city given that its law enforcement efforts just recently commenced to form an organized response. Our understanding, however, is that Sheriff Thomas and Chief Hauser both voiced their support for the task force and may already have reached out to contacts at the Kentucky State Police, DEA, FBI, and US Attorney's offices.

The other troubling aspect of these conversations with former drug dealers and addicts stems from the absolute lack of alternatives to their prior lifestyles that these people perceive. Western Kentucky appears void of gainful employment options for former drug dealers. Yet these men and women carry the same responsibilities once released from prison as do other citizens. They care for and feed their children. They look after elderly parents, relatives, and neighbors. They need adequate housing, preferably removed from the elements that drove them toward the drug culture in the first place. Possibly most fundamental in rural areas like Cooper and Walter County that lack public transit, these citizens need transportation to shuttle themselves and others to and from jobs, treatment, doctors' appointments, and the like.

> Neither this reporter nor the *Courier* seeks to generate sympathy for former drug dealers or addicts. Rather, we propose that the expense and effort of reintegrating these people productively back into society likely will come at a lower level and with greater benefits than will be the expense of dealers and addicts reverting to their pasts and recycling back into the penal system. Potentially, Mr. Shakopf and Mr. Welch will see fit to benefit Cooper and Walter County by not only proposing

a law enforcement task force but also by leading fundraising efforts for a county treatment and reintegration center. This reporter and the *Courier* would gladly join their efforts.

After his first read-through of Drummond's article, Touch didn't quite know what to make of it. Her piece certainly had several markings of investigative journalism, but it also definitively crossed over into op-ed territory. Given the rawness Touch still felt for Hank Benitez, the sheriff harbored more than a little fear that Janie Drummond, by calling out Shakopf and Welch, might have put herself in jeopardy, even if her doing so focused solely on the direction of their community involvement. Touch reread the article. After picking up more on the community vibe and the article's focus on the drug problem from dealing as well as the addiction points of view, Touch settled down. Drummond in no way pointed a finger at Shakopf or Welch as a drug dealer.

Touch also couldn't get past the distinct possibility that his office had failed to effectively address drug dealing and use in Walter County. Given the apparently definitive increase in opioid-induced hospital visits, why had he and his deputies not been more aware of the impact on county residents? Maybe Touch's positive attitude led him to view with rose-colored glasses too many things in Cooper and Walter County. Regardless, Touch accepted Walter County's need for him to do more now.

CHAPTER 28

Shawna James signaled to make the right-hand turn into Shakopf's QuikPik convenience store parking lot. Her 2006 Pontiac Grand Am still ran fine, but its exterior incurred its share of bumps and bruises over the past fifteen years. Shawna had received the car as a graduation present from her father. It had proven to be the most valuable thing she had ever received from the man, unfortunately. Over the course of any given week, Shawna averaged visiting the QuikPik ten times: two for her own purposes of gas, smokes, and snacks, and the balance to fulfill demand for the weed and pills she pushed.

Shawna easily could have purchased a newer, better car, but what remained of the prudishness inherited from her poor mother, as well as a preternatural ability to avoid attention, told her the Grand Am was the perfect car for a drug dealer. No one would steal a beat-up, old Grand Am. No one would wonder where a thirty-five-year old woman, who appeared to be unemployed as frequently as she was employed, got the money to buy a fifteen-year-old car. No one would turn their head to look where the car came from or was going to; it was almost like she was invisible in it. She'd actually shelled out to have a new muffler installed on the car when the last one started making too much noise and drew attention.

The QuikPik attendants never paid Shawna any attention either.

She was pleasant and always said hi to them, but the cashiers seemed to turn over as frequently as the seasons. She bumped into many friendly folks from her neighborhood as she met with customers, which offered Shawna a sense of comfort. Everything flowed naturally as a result, and over the past twelve years that she had been dealing out of the QuikPik, no one thought her presence out of place. Given how the TV shows portrayed drug dealers, she'd initially gotten an eerie feeling that things seemed to go so smoothly. After the first few months passed without incident, though, Shawna's sense of comfort grew, and as a result, the frequency of her visits and her "chance" meetings achieved a sense of normalcy. She passed marijuana, cocaine, and pills to her customers as easily as she grabbed a soda from the cooler or asked the cashier for a hard pack of Marlboro Reds.

Users in Cooper remained comparatively consistent. Recognizing that a live and unincarcerated client proved to be more profitable than a dead or jailed user, Shawna did her best to manage her customers. She also retained a clientele composed largely of regulars.

On this day, Shawna serviced four clients in the three minutes she spent inside the QuikPik in the morning and another three clients during the four minutes she spent in the store in the evening. Shawna assigned potential new clients a protocol of instructions to execute their first purchase: money left in one location, verified, and followed by a "leave" in another location. It was a process she had developed on her own a couple years into the trade, and it had worked almost flawlessly since then.

Shawna had seen some terrible exchanges in her day. Buyers dropping wadded-up bills in entrance ways followed by dealers grabbing the wad of bills and dropping a baggie in exchange on their way out the set of doors they entered. Like a parent leaving a set of spare car keys for a teenager, buyers left bills on top of a car's rear tire with dealers leaving drops on an adjacent car's tire.

In Shawna's mind, the store arrangement came across as more natural with the opportunity to service more clients in a shorter amount of time. The criminal element also seemed vastly reduced: anyone could have left a drop on top of a box of tampons or a bag of Doritos. Shawna was a regular in the store; the clerk could attest to that. Shawna also knew that the QuikPik's security cameras only showed the door and the cash register. Not even the bathrooms appeared on the cameras. As Shawna added sugar and creamer to a cup of coffee in the morning or refilled a soda in the afternoon, her clients came over to visit with her. As she collected their cash, she worked locations for their drugs into their casual conversations: "Aw, I just came in for some peanuts," or, "I needed some of those Armor All car cleaning rags." She ran about a third of her business by dropping these dime bags. The other two-thirds of Shawna's business centered on Cooper's more well-heeled clients. She fronted as a house cleaner and dog walker for these clients.

The method of operation Shawna employed mimicked much of Edmund Shakopf's operation as similar situations occurred at all of Shakopf's twenty-four area stores. Twenty-four stores multiplied by twenty drops a day, seven days a week, and ten dollars a drop equaled about $1.7 million in drugs dealt just through Shakopf's QuickPiks. As evidenced by Shawna's operation, that $1.7 million represented only the small retail component of Shakopf's almost $6 million retail drug trade.

Also, he moved wholesale volumes through the bulk fuel transport operations that supplied his service stations. Five truckloads a week with $400,000 of drugs at a 20 percent cut for transportation amounted to another $20.8 million in earnings per year to Shakopf. Truck drivers for Shakopf likely ranked among the best paid in the United States. In addition to executing their usual refueling duties, they also made weekly deliveries to the stores in nondescript cardboard boxes that Shawna and others like her at the other stores picked up like so much trash. Retail allowed Shakopf to monitor the pulse of the market. However, wholesale definitely was where the money resided. Maintaining a retail presence also afforded command of the local market; it enabled Shakopf to deter anyone outside his network from encroaching on his territories. Market control absolutely offered the greatest returns. Any threat to control had to be met with maximum deterrence. Hence the murder of Hank Benitez: he'd described Shakopf's network to a Chicago-based group, and that could not be tolerated.

CHAPTER 29

True to his word, US Attorney Shel Richardson acted quickly, imploring the FBI to deploy two agents in separate cars to West Kentucky to investigate drug dealing through Shakopf-owned entities in connection with the murder of Hank Benitez. The agents departed their Louisville home office Friday afternoon and arrived in Cooper three hours later in the early evening. The agents consolidated into one car, dined at *Mi Tierra*, and took a thirty-minute tour of Cooper and Shakopf's area stations before retiring for the evening to the local America's Inn motel. The next morning, one agent deployed to a Cooper location while the other drove thirty minutes to another Shakopf location on Lake Barkley. The agents planned to monitor the "morning rush" if such a thing existed Saturday morning, and then tour adjacent areas. Their supervisor allocated four days to the undercover operation with the thought that dealers likely serviced different groups of users every day. If the agents failed to identify dealers and their patterns within a four-day period, the process likely would require a different approach.

Richardson picked up his phone and dialed Sheriff Tanner "Touch" Thomas. Bonnie answered Touch's line. "Good afternoon, Walter County Sheriff's Department; this is Bonnie. How may I help you?"

"Hi, Bonnie, this is Shel Richardson in the US Attorney's office. How are you today?"

"I'm just fine, Mr. Richardson. How 'bout yourself?"

"I'm great. Is Sheriff Thomas in the office today?"

"Unfortunately, Mr. Richardson, Touch—um, Sheriff Thomas—just left the office to check out a minor accident in the north part of the county. If you'll hold on just a sec, though; I'll see if I can patch you through to Touch's—dadgummit, Sheriff Thomas's—cell phone." She dialed him into the call. "Touch, I've got Shel Richardson on the phone. Mr. Richardson, you've got Sheriff Thomas. You have a nice day, sir."

Touch said, "Shel, thanks for calling. How's it going?"

"Sheriff Thomas, I've got great news for you. I don't think Walter County's going to need a drug enforcement task force after all. The two FBI agents the Louisville office allocated to the investigation identified a dealer at one of Shakopf's Cooper stations, with another agent discovering the dealer at a convenience store closer to Lake Barkley. It also looks like from the forensic accounting investigation that Shakopf is moving significantly larger volumes across a much larger geographic area through his wholesale fuel trucking operations."

"Wow, you must think we really suck at law enforcement over here in Walter County, Mr. US Attorney," Touch said.

"Not at all. Actually, when I conferred with my counterpart at the FBI, we lamented the lack of resources at the disposal of local law enforcement. Anyway, the Cooper agent identified the dealer after the morning drops of the second day; it took the other agent until the evening of the second day. The wholesale trucks only made weekly drops, so the process proved to be of too short a duration to spot that arrangement. The FBI wouldn't mark it until a second, multiweek operation meant to document the enormity of the business made the box drops by the wholesale fuel transporters."

Touch asked, "Where did the money trail lead?"

"Concurrently, it did not take the FBI hackers long to identify a significantly large anomaly in the magnitude of cash flowing through Shakopf-linked accounts and into Walter County Bank. The sheer size and frequency of the large transactions should have alerted bank regulators long ago, but because the transactions proved to be comparatively consistent, no red flags ever materialized. The disconnect between cash out for bulk fuel and store inventory, plus an acceptable margin, proved to be far too low in relation to the magnitude of cash flowing into Shakopf accounts. However, the fact that all the money appeared to be of domestic origin with balanced accounts and comparatively large outgoing expenditures on legitimate fuel, foodstuffs, consumer goods, and the like, failed to raise questions. Largely, it looked like a successful service station and convenience store operating normally unless one peeled back a few layers of the onion. For years, Shakopf's financial transactions rose in concert with expansion of his business operations: more stores, wholesale fuels, remodeling and renovations, marine fueling operations, truck stops, and truck and car repair. The cash flowed and flowed. Bank regulators lacked the resources to track funds across accounts like the FBI could. In a matter of days, the FBI's hackers and forensic accountants crafted a detailed report of the manner in which Shakopf laundered the cash from his drug-dealing operation. Having so many cash-based businesses easily allowed Shakopf to place his drug money alongside his legitimate money. He probably then layered in legitimate and sham transactions among and between his various companies, overcharging for wholesale fuel, expensing auto and truck parts that never arrived, and funding renovations that never happened. These bogus transactions enabled Shakopf to integrate his drug money with his legitimate money, which in turn funded further layering as Shakopf purchased substantial swaths of real estate in other states."

Richardson continued, "I'm impressed with the results from just a week of surveillance and investigating. Given how quickly and how much a relatively small FBI team—four individuals—managed to find in such a short period of time, I fear how much illegal activity goes undetected in small cities and towns across the country. I know from vast experience dealing with sheriffs and chiefs of police across Kentucky that law enforcement lacks sufficient funds to truly be effective at fighting crime, Touch. Tons of funds flow into acquisitions of ridiculous looking riot gear, bigger guns, and other superfluous crap that defense company lobbyists managed year after year to convince politicians to jam into budgets. An abundance of research shows that funds spent on education and training yield far higher dividends for communities than riot gear acquisitions. Nonetheless, every time we turn on the news, we see coverage of big guns and riot gear and next to nothing about education and training programs; they just don't sell as well with lobbyists and voters. When's the last time you used your riot gear, Sheriff?"

"I proudly used that riot gear last Halloween, I'll have you know. It won me first prize at the Cooper Baptist Church's costume competition."

"Nice to hear taxpayer funds continue to flow to meaningful community engagement activities, Sheriff Thomas. Anyway, our forensic accounting pros also tracked down substantial funds Shakopf laundered through Walter County Bank and several other banks in other states to acquire real estate and other assets. To the point you mentioned in our discussion last week, this looks like it's been going on for some time."

"This is one of those situations that makes you feel giddy and disappointed all at the same time. I'm thankful for yours and the FBI's help, but I'm upset that two long-serving leaders of the Cooper community participated in the drug trade for decades, unbeknownst to me and most likely my father."

"Your father?" Richardson repeated.

"Shel, my father was Walter County sheriff for about thirty years. One poor soul served for a few years in between us, but otherwise a

Thomas has been Walter County Sheriff for much of the past forty years."

"Aw, just as we discussed a little while ago, your department and so many others across the state—and likely the United States remain, so underfunded and understaffed that it's all you can do to apprehend those people blatantly breaking the law. I can tell you from personal experience working with the FBI and DEA that capturing and prosecuting the biggest criminals consumes more than all of their resources. As you can see with the depth of the effort Shakopf went to launder the money and the length of time those efforts went undetected, it's extremely difficult to catch the really good criminals. Most of the time, it's all we can do to capture those who are really bad at committing crimes. Unfortunate, but true.

"So, Sheriff Thomas, here's what I propose we do in order to cast the widest net and hopefully catch the most crooks. With an apparent link between Shakopf, Hank Benitez's murder at the hands of a well-skilled hitman, and the involvement of Walter County Bank, we can demand quite a few resources from Louisville FBI. I've spoken with the head of office preliminarily, and he's agreed to dedicate six agents to this effort for a planned four-month undercover operation. They'll commence with surveillance, identify weaknesses in the organization, seek to penetrate the organization if that avenue looks fruitful, and build a case through those efforts. Concurrently, at least one of those agents will seek to identify the organization looking to compete for Shakopf's drug business in your area and elsewhere, or possibly create a shadow organization with the allusion of a threat to Shakopf. Maybe, if we're very good at what we do, Shakopf will bring Rafe Livingston back in to redefine his stronghold, and we can shut down the entire operation in a matter of months. Wishful thinking, maybe, but I'm guessing that decades of acting undetected resulted in at least a little contempt for law enforcement. I presume that's the impetus behind the task force request."

"Shel, I don't know if you have or haven't done this before, but it sounds to me like you've worked this plan, or one quite similar, previously. I and my staff—and I'm hazarding a guess that Cooper Police Chief Chris Hauser and his people—are all on board with this. I can't speak for law enforcement in the other municipalities around Lake Barkley, but you've got our support in Cooper and Walter County."

"Good deal, Sheriff. I'll relay that to the FBI and be back to you with a plan to meet and nail down details on a formal launch of this investigation. You have yourself a good rest of your day."

"You too, Shel."

Upon hanging up, Touch got a fresh line on his phone and dialed Chief Hauser. Fifteen minutes later, Hauser had the high-level details on Richardson's plan, and as Touch predicted, he had the chief's buy-in on the plan to bring down Shakopf and Welch.

CHAPTER 30

As they usually did, Edmund Shakopf and Jerry Welch finished their round of golf at the Cooper Country Club just about the time everyone else in town got off work, at five o'clock. The two men, each approaching eighty, played a round of golf at least four days a week, typically teeing off just after lunch.

Edmund and Jerry had limited their golf to weekends and special occasions prior to advancing to semiretirement. At the age of retirement, however, and with middle-aged sons, the two men agreed to restrict their weekday work schedules to the mornings and the occasional afternoon. Each turned over the nuts and bolts of operating their businesses—Edmund a medium-sized chain of gas stations and convenience stores with the fuel-moving logistics to support them, and Jerry a relatively small community bank—to trusted lieutenants. In Edmund's case, he turned the filling stations and QuikPiks over to Laceon, his son. As for Jerry, he lacked the confidence in Will, his son, to effectively run the Walter County Bank, and he instead turned over management of the bank to a nephew, Davis Welch.

Laceon proved adept at managing Shakopf's stores, fuel inventories, and logistics. Edmund held off on adding the drug trade to Laceon's management responsibilities for the first couple of years. The theory Edmund evolved in doing so related to the necessity of running the legitimate operations well in order to generate sufficient above-board cash flow before introducing the illicit businesses into the equation and potentially bringing undue scrutiny to the operations should the stores fail to pay the bills. Laceon and Edmund incurred a few bumps and bruises along the way, but all in all, the transition progressed relatively smoothly. The boom-boom economy of 2006–2008 saw the family generate obscene amounts of cash, especially for a sparsely populated area like West Kentucky. Doing so allowed the family to substantially consolidate power in the region through the Great Recession and then significantly extend it through the ensuing recovery period of 2010–15. At that point, the drug operation reached natural geographic boundaries that Edmund judged to be too risky to exceed—the larger cities of St Louis, Nashville, Chicago, and Louisville. He decided long ago it was best to settle for what one had and could easily defend than to challenge for more and invite unknown risks and repercussions.

Unfortunately for Will Welch, community banking proved to be more complicated than he could grasp. Interest rate spreads, net interest margins, credit risk, economic cycles, and an inability to judge a solid operator from a stellar storyteller proved too much for him. Fortunately, Will recognized his deficiencies early on in his professional career, agreed with his father that he likely would never be top management material, and instead relished at throwing himself into Walter County Bank's community relations and marketing efforts. At these tasks, Will proved more than adept. As a result, he harbored no hard feelings with respect to his cousin running the bank once Jerry Welch turned over the reins to the next generation. The primary challenge in doing so, however, did not involve teaching a nephew the ins and outs of community banking and all the various pitfalls extending credit to slothful farmers or to drunken manufacturers. Instead, the principal challenge for Jerry Welch evolved around when and how to coax his nephew into continuing to aid Edmund, and now Laceon Shakopf, in laundering their drug money—Walter County Bank's most profitable operation. Davis Welch presented the perfect opportunity with a ready-made mechanism that enabled Jerry to convince him easily. Davis had a head for business, but his personal life left much to be desired. An affair, complete with an illegitimate child, led to a subsequent divorce by which Davis' wife absolutely cleaned him out. In exchange for agreeing to keep mum about the reason for the divorce, Davis's wife took all his assets and left the man incapable of connecting the dots financially. Jerry Welch, in response, presented Davis an offer he could not refuse: assume presidency of Walter County Bank and maintain Shakopf's money-laundering mechanisms, and his financial problems would quickly and painlessly disappear. The arrangement would leave the man wealthier, if not healthier and wiser.

The passage of time over the fifteen or so years since Jerry and Edmund had commenced transitioning leadership of their operations to the next generation only strengthened the execution and thus the quality of the businesses. A solidifying local economy played its part as well. Initially, as with Davis Welch, the two elderly men encountered some bumps, but patience and planning allowed each of these hurdles eventually to be surmounted. It helped to no end that Will and Laceon enjoyed a lifelong friendship and that Davis and the other two men, if not necessarily friends, always got along well.

About twelve months into the updated arrangement, the three younger men settled into their new routines. The legitimate businesses functioned as they always had with no turnover in key personnel. Cash flowed through the system as it always had, with only minor oversight and marginal adjustments made at the instruction of Edmund Shakopf. The drug operation clicked along more or less as it previously did. The same laundering mechanisms worked as they always had. Under threat of severe penalty, Davis Welch minded his Ps and Qs with his newfound wealth and avoided the additional scrutiny that could bring the whole operation to its knees if any of the three brought unwanted attention to themselves.

With little variation in operations internally, the view from the outside changed little as well. The operations presented no reasons to expect anything out of the ordinary, so Cooper and Walter County law enforcement paid no heed to Shakopf and his operations or to Welch and his bank. Drugs persisted in the area, but the usage and impact appeared to be little, if any, different than the balance of the area until recently. Little did Chief Hauser of Sheriff Thomas know that this largely resulted from the fact that Edmund Shakopf supplied the entire area. Because Shakopf's operation maintained a startlingly consistent level of execution over a decades-long period of time with an almost unparalleled degree of discipline, he and his lieutenants kept their runners and dealers in line. Shakopf paid relatively well and ran his drug operation much as he did his legitimate businesses: he put a great deal of effort into recruiting, hiring, training, and valuing trustworthy employees. Very infrequently, as with Hank Benitez, a rogue employee required swift action—and as it also appeared to be with Hank, Shakopf's method of dealing with these problems kept the balance of the organization in line for a substantial period of time.

Dealing with Hank-like problems in this way allowed Shakopf to keep his local operations organized and working efficiently with little threat of insiders disrupting harmony. On occasion—every three to five years—an outside organization would make a run at Cooper's drug trade. Then the true genius of Shakopf's low-volatility operating model showed through. As Shakopf paid his bills on time; moved product quickly, accurately, and covertly through his territory on its way to other locations; and on occasion took care of other requests from his suppliers, Edmund Shakopf enjoyed a significantly heightened level of respect with his supplier. Frequently, dealing with encroachment on his territory required only a phone call to Atlanta or Chicago, and the problem swiftly disappeared. In the very few instances over the past forty years when the big-city bosses failed to deal with his problems with simple phone calls, they sent their Rafe Livingston–type operatives to solve Shakopf's issues directly. Aiding rapport with law enforcement, Shakopf maintained a long-running absence of anything approximating a drug war in Cooper or in any other part of his almost five thousand square miles of operating territory.

The two men dropped off their golf clubs at the roundabout near the clubhouse. From there, the teenaged attendants cleaned the clubs and shuttled the bags back to the storage room the Cooper Country Club offered its most exclusive members. Leaving the cart for the attendants to park as well, Edmund and Jerry headed to the bar like usual. The game concluded as it almost always did with Welch winning by a couple strokes. A hundred dollar bill also traded pockets from Shakopf to Welch.

"Jerry, any word out of the county commissioners meeting on that drug task force idea we proposed?" Shakopf asked Welch.

"Haven't heard anything yet, but strangely both Chief Hauser and Sheriff Thomas seemed to be all for the task force. No concern about meddling in local law enforcement or anything was voiced. I don't know that we played that as well as we thought we would. Time will tell, I suppose. Did you happen to see the piece on drugs in Cooper published in Saturday's *Courier*? Reporter wants you and me to help fund rehab centers and the like."

"Yeah, I anticipated some pushback from Thomas, at least. I've never known him to ask for, let alone welcome, outside help. Maybe the Benitez thing shook him up more than expected. Something feels a little different, that's for sure. Maybe it was him snooping around last week on that old David Barnett case. Something's certainly got his dander up, though. Possibly it's time for a distraction over by the lake. I didn't even hear about the *Courier* piece; that's how few people read the paper nowadays."

"I don't know, Edmund. It might be time to lie low, let time pass, and try not to draw any more attention to things. We've managed these operations phenomenally well for a very long time, but you know as well as I do that getting on the wrong side of Touch Thomas has damaged more than a few folks. That son of a bitch has an otherworldly ability to go looking for shit to step in, jump in it with both feet, and come out smelling like rosewater. The athletic shit is one thing, but the stories I've heard about the guy's military career scare the snot out of me. I'm still shocked we managed to keep things under wraps for as long as we have with him around. That alone is the greatest testament to your management abilities."

"Honestly, I thought of packing it in and going legitimate the minute Thomas won that damned election, so I agree with you entirely. Then I thought, shit, I'm a thousand years old. If things start to go south, I'll just take the rap for it, clear the kids out of the operation, and ride off into the sunset. I fear that the opportunity for me to 'go down with the ship,' so to speak, may have passed with Laceon and Davis so intricately tied to the operations. Do you think the FBI or DEA would believe that an ancient codger like me could run a multi-million-dollar drug operation for decades without at least one layer of younger management? The abilities of these assholes to trace everything through the internet is really what scares the hell out of me. Privacy's a damned illusion. How you continue to move that much money through the bank without raising a regulator's eyebrow boggles the mind. I guess if the books balance and you're not losing money, no one asks questions, huh?"

"More or less, that's the situation. Not making or losing much of any more money than neighboring banks really defines the pièce de résistance, though. In your best years, funneling that much cash through our little bank should have raised more than a few questions on the part of bank examiners. Nope, they just glossed over balances, looked at origins and destinations of inflows and outflows, and apparently concluded that Cooper businesspeople must be that much better than the rest of their counterparts statewide. It's been truly fascinating."

CHAPTER 31

Richardson suggested that Touch and the FBI agents meet in Elizabethtown, about 120 miles east of Cooper. Chris Hauser rode over to Elizabethtown with Touch to meet with the agents at the US Department of Agriculture's regional office building. With a modestly shorter drive down from the Louisville FBI office, the agents, who drove in two cars, picked up two travel boxes of coffee and a dozen and a half donuts. The team budgeted about two hours for its initial meeting.

"Sheriff Thomas, Chief Hauser, I'm Special Agent Carter Diaz. It's a pleasure to meet you. The other special agents and I look forward to working with you. We've detailed Special Agents Arthur, Zook, and Zgutowicz. They allocated us two more agents back in Louisville to work the banking and money laundering components of the case as well, which I gather you already know about from your conversations with US Attorney Richardson.

"Thanks, Special Agent Diaz. I look forward to working with you and the other special agents as well," Touch said as he stood and turned to wave at the other people in the conference room. "I thought it might be best to start with how this operation came about and where we in Cooper maybe see it going. Is that all right with y'all? I'm happy to go in another direction if you guys think it more productive."

"Sure, Sheriff, please take us through the situation from first clue through the latest developments, if you would," responded Special Agent Diaz.

Touch walked Diaz and the other agents through the shooting of Hank Benitez and how he and Hauser had gathered information on Cooper's drug activity. He documented the Dixie Mafia's arrival in Cooper and his interactions with the gang.

Agent Zgutowicz said to Touch, "I understand from a briefing we got from Richardson's office that you and Chief Hauser maybe were first let on to a local drug-running operation by an investigative journalist for your local paper. Can you fill in details on this? Is there additional information on this front that might prove useful?"

"You're correct. A meeting with the owner and publisher of the *Cooper Courier*, a subsequent follow-up with the journalist, and a short article she published confirmed that a local operation moves drugs through Cooper and, probably, much of the rest of Western Kentucky. The journalist picked up the lead from an inmate at the state prison in an adjacent county. Chief Hauser and I subsequently confirmed that detail and gathered a good deal more intelligence through a contact we share at a local dive bar.

"Agents, we've got no details on the source of the drugs coming unto Cooper. We think one man, and now likely his son, run this operation: Edmund Shakopf, the father, and Laceon Shakopf, the son. Edmund's old now, approaching eighty, and Laceon's in his mid-forties. The father's sharp and quite shrewd, skills honed from almost six decades of running and building first a gas station and auto repair shop and then a chain of stations and convenience stores, QuikPiks. From the work your office did a while back, it appears that the Shakopfs supply much, if not all, of the western part of the state with every drug short of heroin. Your office's work also uncovered what appears to be a more extensive operation moving significantly greater volumes of illegal drugs through all of the contiguous states via the company's fuel logistics operations, which they also use to supply their local dealers. The method appears to be relatively ingenious: drop a box off with a week's supply at a convenience store to be picked up by the local dealer, who in turn supplies the local clientele through that same convenience store. They've apparently done this under our noses for decades because it appears that everyone's just a regular at the store, passing through for coffee, smokes, lottery tickets, snacks, booze, and gas. Nothing out of the ordinary and, I'm embarrassed to admit, no apparent reason to expect anything illegal going on. Whoops."

Arthur piped up. "Chief Hauser or Sheriff Thomas, do you think the Shakopf person has a monopoly on drugs in West Kentucky? It sounded like their operation stopped short of dealing heroin. Does another organization supply the harder stuff, or does Shakopf supply everything that's available and shut out the heroin trade?"

"Thanks, Agent Arthur," Chris Hauser said. "We think Shakopf operates as a monopoly with protection from either his supplier or his bigger volume customer, or both. We're aware of no heroin making its way into Cooper or elsewhere in the western part of the state. We think this protection from competition, wherever it's coming from, also supplied Livingston for the Benitez job."

Touch explained how he thought the money flowed from Shakopf's drug operations to Jerry's Welch's bank. He described the two families long-standing associations and friendships for the agents.

Diaz, the senior agent in charge, said, "Let me see if I can set up a semblance of an action plan and initially delegate duties. It'll probably be best to lay this out before we discuss options and alternatives, just to allow for an integrated overview of the operation and its strategy. Double Zs, Zook and Zgutowicz, I suggest you two divide Shakopf's retail territory by east-west and north-south locations and work to identify as many retail pushers as you can via photos."

Touch asked, "Y'all share those photos with local police?"

Diaz replied, "Definitely. I'll coordinate that data from local police with what Arthur pulls from the trucking operation. If we can get some photos from Arthur on delivery and pickup people, we can correlate those photos with our database, FBI field agents in those areas, and the DEA as well. We'll coordinate with local enforcement at this point in the process to arrest as many of these people as quickly as possible, barring a DEA operation we don't know about at this point. I'll rule that out ASAP but know that we'll have to adjust if something's going on outside of our operation."

"That's a good idea," Hauser said.

"After arrests are made," Diaz continued, "I recommend we let Shakopf, Welch, and the others in the organization stew for a day or two. They can think about which of their dealers will be most likely to turn on others in the organization, like with Hank Benitez. It's a dangerous angle to play, but as we all know, it's one that worked extremely well in the past. We should have a mountain of cash flow and financial data on the operation by then that will shed light on suppliers and customers, or at least their locations. We also ought to apply maximum pressure on Shakopf, Welch and their sons and nephew under this strategy. I'm certain we'll get some cracks in the organization with this pressure."

"We could run into some jail capacity issues," Touch said. "I guess we can request additional capacity at adjacent counties, though."

"That should work, Sheriff," Diaz said. "There are a few more threats we want to remain cognizant of as we build this case out. First, leaks happen and covers get blown. I suspect that whoever tried to hoard in on Shakopf's territory still expects to have the opportunity to do so again in the future despite Benitez's death. We may have to call in more agents to combat that threat if it materializes. Also, if we miss dealers or middlemen, things could turn violent. Same if competitors see opportunities to take territory. Finally, it's entirely possible that Sheriff Thomas's and Chief Hauser's counterparts in other counties are on the take. We're not at this point coordinating with all of these areas, so everyone be on the lookout for threats from friendlies. Feedback?"

Chris Hauser spoke first. "That sounds like a solid plan initially, Special Agent Diaz. It seems you expect no initial input from with my department or Sheriff Thomas's, is that correct? If so, why? Also, how often and where do you think we should get together as this plan rolls out to review things?"

"Correct, Chief. I wouldn't say a single word about this operation to any of your personnel in Cooper or Walter County. Everyone wants to think the best of their cops and deputies, but one never knows who had debts to pay or relatives in need. Loose lips sink ships. I'd keep this on the down-low until we're ready to coordinate with other area departments on the sting operation. As for meetings, I think a weekly—Sunday, maybe—group review at a location outside of the focus area should work. Anything else?"

Agent Zgutowicz said, "Carter, how much support from Louisville, DC, the US Attorney, and the DEA can we anticipate? Has anyone coordinated with any of the other law enforcement agencies—DEA, ATF, state police—to make sure that we're not stepping on anyone's toes? Sounds like no from your earlier DEA comment, but any other thoughts on these entities' involvement? I assume given that we want to create a sting operation near the end of this, no way exists to learn of local law enforcement's investigations? What happens if, in the course of our work, we discover more than a few cops on the take?"

"Thanks, Randy," Diaz replied. "We've all dealt with dirty cops before. I can't see any way to exclude them from the net at this point. They could be our greatest source of pressure on the higher-ups in the organization, as a matter of fact. As a result, we may want to sting them earlier than we plan with the wider net. The risk is that the dirty cop is just a part of a larger corrupt organization, and we miss a chief or sheriff who's also taking payoffs. Again, we may need to bring in another agent or two to bulldog those additional investigations. I advocate for maintaining discipline on the dealers like we just discussed, to avoid potentially breaking cover and spooking anyone. Remember, always check your six and make sure local enforcement isn't surveilling us as we're surveilling Shakopf's operations. Discrete, discrete, discrete. Anything else?"

Sheriff Thomas and the four other people in the room shook their heads. The FBI agents, Chief Hauser, and Touch had an action plan.

CHAPTER 32

Touch, Chris Hauser, and the FBI agents hammered out a few minor details in the USDA's Elizabethtown office. Three hours after arriving in E-town, Touch and Hauser climbed back into the chief's cruiser, hit the highway, and headed west, back toward Cooper. Touch tuned the radio to WBVR, which included Elizabethtown in its coverage area. Zac Brown Band's "Chicken Fried" blared over the cruiser's speakers for a few minutes, giving way to "Come Over" by Kenny Chesney.

"That song sounds like a stalker's mantra. What the hell was Kenny thinking, recording it?" Hauser asked.

"Probably something about his time with Zellweger. Still wonder what happened there. That was just weird."

"How screwed do you think we are, Touch?"

"What are you talking about, Chris? We've got the US Attorney on board, at least six FBI agents working with us, an opportunity to coordinate objectively with other law enforcement offices in the region, and most importantly a likely chance to bag the two largest criminals in Cooper and Walter County history. To boot, we just have to sit, wait, and stay out of the way until the fun starts! Screwed? Far from it, my man."

"Well, aren't you a breath of fresh air. Just like old times, huh?

Jump on the Touch Thomas touchdown train? Never steered me wrong, then, so I guess it won't now either."

With Hauser driving, Touch sat back and collected his thoughts. Diaz ran through a solid initial plan, and the responsibility for executing it firmly rested with the FBI. With Hank Benitez's murder and the drug trade appearing to be a little tighter than it'd been before, crime in Walter County had been pretty staid for about a month. David Barnett then popped into Touch's mind. Again, he had the eerie thought that some connection existed between Barnett and Welch and Shakopf hunting near Charlie Sprague's farm. He closed his eyes and ruminated on the facts of David Barnett's death: springtime, a .243 rifle, deer tag for Will Welch, and evidence that Shakopf and Welch leased adjacent land to Sprague's farm to hunt. Touch let his mind spin for a few minutes as the radio cycled through songs by Alan Jackson, Confederate Railroad, and the Georgia Satellites.

After about thirty minutes, Hauser decided he'd had enough country for one morning and flipped the station over to the National Public Radio affiliate, operating from the campus of Western Kentucky University also in Bowling Green. It was a Saturday and midafternoon, so *Lost River Sessions Radio* filled the car with fiddle, mandolin, and banjo. Later, Hauser and Touch giggled like schoolgirls on the drive from Elizabethtown while listening to Bill Kurtis and Peter Segal and their antics on *Wait Wait … Don't Tell Me* on the same NPR station. That was something he could look forward to with these weekly Sunday meetings: *Wait Wait* and some banjo music. All he needed was to find a decent diner, and the trips would be damned near like a weekly vacation.

"Touch, you think you've got any bad deputies in your department?"

"Is that what you've been so quiet about over there? Running through your department in your mind and deciding who could be bent? Man, great minds do think alike. I've been doing the same thing. I've done it backward and forward, and I can't see any of my people being dirty. I went through the same exercise after Hank was killed too. All of these people are either mine or my dad's. None of the others hired by that other guy stuck around. No one shows any out-of-bracket expenditures. You know we've not had any complaints about favors or excessive force. How about you?"

"I think I need to do a review of my office. I don't think I know my people as well as you know yours. There are a couple I can't vouch for because I don't know them well enough. It's not that I think they're turned, but they're relatively new. Do you think one of your career people might be able and willing to help me, if needed—kind of keep it an arm's length sort of thing, so to speak?"

"Sure thing, Chris. I'd have no problem asking Mike Menser to check a person or two for you. He'll absolutely understand, I think, and not consider it a breach of personal trust or anything like that given the situation."

"Thanks, Touch. Anything else you can think of that we ought to start planning around this thing? It seems like it could become an awfully big undertaking for municipal law enforcement with an unprecedented level of coordination required to get it anywhere close to right. Sitting around and doing nothing has never been a strength of yours or mine."

"I think it sort of plays to our strengths, Chris. In essence, we're supposed to protect the public. When folks start to jeopardize public safety, as it looks like Shakopf and his partners are doing, it's our job to remove that jeopardy and reestablish public safety. Even if we don't get everyone in this drug ring, I think as long as we cut off the head of the snake, the rest of the thing will die. Sure, we'll need to look for opportunities to help those who may be addicted and try by every means possible to make sure we don't eliminate one devil just to allow another one to take its place, but those're just more examples of us doing our jobs well. Keeping everyone safe while we determine how far and how deep this operation runs seems like the most complicated action to me given what already happened to Hank Benitez."

"I guess when you view it as doing our jobs and not allow yourself to get caught up in the fact that it could be an entire quarter's arrests in one day, it doesn't seem so daunting. It would be nice, though, if we had a little more help than just six FBI officers, two of which are involved remotely."

"Yep. We'll see if they can pull some more ATF or DEA presence in once Louisville gets wind of potentially how large and far-reaching this thing might be. Of course, the more headcount from additional agencies involved, the more nightmarish coordination becomes. It'll probably end up being a benefit that we're only set to take directions and not make decisions in that case."

With the NPR segment over and classical music taking to the airwaves, Touch reacquired WBVR just in time to hear the opening of Garth Brooks's "Friends in Low Places." By the first time the chorus came around, Touch and Chris Hauser were singing at the tops of their lungs, content that Cooper and Walter County could handle whatever Shakopf and his drug empire could throw at them now that they knew about it.

They'd be correct too, but the type of effort being right required would be quite a bit different than what either Hauser or Touch expected.

CHAPTER 33

It turned out that the dirty cop was not in either the City of Cooper's police department or the Walter County Sheriff's Office. Instead, it was all the way over in Louisville at the FBI's regional office.

Carter Diaz developed a gambling problem in 2010. After coming out of the US Army, which he had joined in the late nineties out of high school, and going to college on the GI Bill, the then twenty-two-year-old Diaz missed the adrenaline rush of combat. Intramural sports didn't do it for him. Diaz was relatively athletic and had always been undersized for truly competitive sports at five feet six inches and 150 pounds. The thrill of carrying a gun and the joy of firing it more than made up for the lack of competitive sports for Diaz in the army. However, the firing range failed to create the same delight for him once Diaz left the military.

Diaz discovered the joy of poker in college at the University of Louisville. Winning more than he lost against ill-equipped, testosterone-junky college students four years his junior, Diaz soon took to the riverboat casinos in the area for larger games. His wins still mostly outnumbered his losses, but the fix diminished without regular escalations in the size of the pot. Soon, Diaz's need for a gambling fix well outpaced his card-playing abilities, and his losses began to outnumber his winnings. For several years, he managed to work enough legitimate jobs to fill the gap, but then he discovered the excitement of sports betting, and he never looked back to the poker table.

Diaz started out gambling on college football. A penchant for picking upsets in the SEC and Pac-12 led to an impressive winning streak and a regular bookie. Utilizing the maturity he gained from military service and the related ability to achieve and to maintain extreme focus, Diaz did very well in his studies. He majored in criminal justice and considered attending law school. One of Diaz's professors suggested that the still-young man apply to the FBI. Diaz did so during a period of low unemployment with solid academic and military service records, the ability to speak Spanish, and adequate agility despite his small stature. He made it through the FBI's training academy relatively unscathed. However, he remained hooked on gambling throughout his training and early employment. Once his bookie discovered what Carter Diaz did for a living, he started to work the man, recognizing the value of a law enforcement insider to those on the other side of the law. Within six months, Diaz was into his bookie for one hundred thousand dollars and saw little to no legitimate way out of his debt.

In exchange for periodic favors in certain investigations spearheaded or assisted by the Louisville regional office of the FBI, the bookie not only allowed Diaz to continue betting—albeit at smaller, nickel and dime levels—but also knocked off ten thousand dollars from the outstanding debt for each useful turn Diaz managed to do for the underworld.

Prior to prepping for the meeting with Touch Thomas and Chris Hauser in Elizabethtown, Carter Diaz had never heard of Edmund Shakopf, let alone known that the man ran an eight-figure drug empire out of a podunk town in West Kentucky. Diaz spent his entire youth in Kentucky, but he had no idea where Cooper was, and until then he had never cared. However, with years of experience feeding drug-related information to gangs from the entire Midwest and Southeast United States via his bookie, Diaz well understood the value leading up an effort like the Shakopf bust held for him. While driving back to Louisville from E-town, Diaz thought he might have hit on the way to have the entire balance of his outstanding debt eliminated.

By this point in time, Diaz knew well what to do and how to do it in order to best manage his situation. With his bookie as a go-between separating himself from the end-user of whatever information Diaz provided, the FBI agent empowered himself to pick and choose what got passed on and when and at what point in the operation he passed it to the bookie. Rarely did Diaz interject himself in the process beyond passing information unless it jeopardized the safety of one of his partners. Anonymity had its benefits. Most of the time the outcome related to a bust thwarted by inside information regarding its particulars—when and where the FBI or local law enforcement planned to spring its traps. In the few instances where an operation met resistance, Diaz knew what was coming and thus far had managed around those challenges.

However, the wheels of criminality started to spin the minute Diaz learned how large Shakopf's organization might be. He called his bookie. "How about some action on that early season Virginia Tech game?"

The bookie responded, "We'll see. What else do you have for me?"

"Does the Shakopf name mean anything to you or your people? Some kind of West Kentucky drug dealer, I believe," Diaz said.

"I'll run it up the flagpole and see what I get. No VaTech action until I confirm, though," the bookie said.

The bookie hung up on Diaz and immediately placed a call to the head of the Dixie Mafia in Atlanta. "Shakopf name in West Kentucky mean anything to you?" the bookie asked.

"Yeah, why?" the Dixie Mafia boss answered.

The bookie continued, "I got an insider that may think something big's going on. I'll be back to you in ten."

"Diaz," the FBI agent answered the bookie's return call.

The bookie said, "VA Tech action's good for a dime. What do you have on Shakopf?"

"Big bust on his entire organization likely to go down within the next month or so," Diaz replied.

"Thanks. Go Tech," the bookie said as he ended the call.

It took Diaz's bookie a moment to redial Atlanta. The Dixie Mafia boss answered on the first ring. "Yeah?"

"My guy says the Feds are gonna hit Shakopf's operation within the month."

"Thanks," said the boss, ending the call.

No sooner did the head of the Dixie Mafia end his call with the bookie than he placed another call to Rafe Livingston. "I need you back in Kentucky ASAP, please. Same rate, similar job."

Rafe Livingston never expected to be called on again to visit Cooper, Kentucky.

CHAPTER 34

Two days after the Elizabethtown meeting, Diaz and two of the other FBI agents were on-site in West Kentucky, spread out over three locations around Lake Barkley: Cooper, Paducah, and Ballard. Agent Arthur, consistent with the plan Diaz originally laid out, trailed one of Shakopf's tanker trucks. Not knowing whether all of these tanker trucks ran drugs defined a key concern for Diaz and Arthur. If only select trucks incorporated drug runs into their legitimate fuel-delivery operations, it could take Arthur more than a few days to get lucky and latch onto a truck making a drug run versus a normal fuel run.

To give the illusion of being in town on business, the agents checked into local motels near Shakopf's stores. They started their mornings with a stop by one of the gas stations or QuikPiks in an effort to get the lay of the land. After filling up with gas and grabbing a cup of coffee or a snack, each picked a nondescript surveillance point for the store's front door with as much of the parking lot as visible as possible. Figuring that Shakopf's dealers likely made morning and evening deliveries, the agents started their days fairly early, at 7:00 a.m.

By 9:30 a.m., the two FBI agents identified several dealers in Paducah and Ballard. Diaz tracked the Cooper dealer, which the operation had previously identified. After knocking off for the rest of the morning and the early afternoon, the agents passed the time by checking out Shakopf's other locations in the towns. With the exception of Paducah, which contained several times the population of the smaller surrounding towns, almost certainly the same dealers serviced all of the stores in one town. Likely at least half a dozen dealers met the demand in Paducah. Diaz wanted to guard as much as possible against missing any part-timers in his sweep. Providing the agents could identify the dealers in a day or two, the next step of the plan was to photograph them and run the pictures through the FBI's database to pull any names and addresses. Once all locations were covered, they would coordinate the sting with local law enforcement. If things went well, maybe this piece of the operation would take a week, or ten days if things got bogged down.

Diaz thought that if the surveillance team could nail dealers in six towns, in combination with details on the trucking operation, it would be sufficient to generate pressure for a dealer to turn on Shakopf and give up the old man. Keeping the operation under wraps to manage the exact opportune time and type of information to leak to his bookie maximized the value of the information Diaz fed to the man without having his cover blown. Diaz was no fan of drug dealers and would like only one thing more than taking Shakopf's entire operation down: having his entire gambling debt erased. Though he had never executed an operation this large and complicated, Diaz guessed that the best time to spring his trap would be immediately after one of the arrested dealers or truck drivers turned on Shakopf. Diaz thought having the name of the flipped dealer and leaking the plan to take down Shakopf right before it occurred would amplify its value to the bookie and his contact, whoever it was.

Four variables complicated Diaz's execution: Jerry Welch, Will Welch, Laceon Shakopf, and Davis Welch. The FBI's forensic accountants in Louisville trying to track down Shakopf's money laundering could vastly complicate Diaz's plan, possibly rendering it worthless. If the four men at the top of the operation got scared and feared for their freedom, they could easily turn on each other. In that case, Diaz feared the value of his information would approach zero.

Shakopf and Welch also were ancient. If they chose to take the rap in exchange for slaps on the wrists for Laceon, Will, and Davis, then Diaz would likely be on the outside looking in with respect to the value of his ratting on the operation. Shakopf and Welch, despite the magnitude and length of time of their drug-running and money-laundering operations, would likely be sentenced to minimum security time at one of the "Club Med" prisons the United States maintained in choice locales several places around the country.

The open-ended, unoccupied time during surveillance when no one went into or out of Shakopf's store left Diaz with far too much time to chew on all these various scenarios and the degree to which he'd be screwed if they went against him. Diaz offset these mindfucks with much more pleasant thoughts of his gambling debt being paid off and being free and clear to mess his life up in some as-of-yet new and exciting and undefined way. He could even go clean; he was getting too old for all of the added angst on top of being a rising FBI agent.

Just then, Diaz got a text that Agent Zook had made the dealer at the Ballard location she had under surveillance. By Diaz's count, that put the operation about one-quarter of the way to completion. They would stake out another location or two in each town to confirm that the same dealers serviced each of a town's stores, get their IDs, and then execute the same plan in three more West Kentucky towns: Sterling, Paulsboro, and Iola. With any luck, Diaz would be in position to have the surveillance piece of the operation wrapped up in a week to ten days, largely depending on Arthur's ability to identify a drug-running trucker.

By the fourth day, Diaz, Zook, and Zgutowicz had made the dealers in Cooper, Ballard, Sterling, Iola, Paulsboro, and Paducah. Each of the agents who identified the dealers in the respective towns now planned to circle back through the town and photo the dealers to submit to Louisville for ID and address info. By Day 4, Arthur identified three drug-running truckers logging over 1,200 miles across four states and following eight different trucks. He'd gone ahead and taken the liberty of photographing the drivers to avoid the difficulties of guessing the three truckers' future schedules. As a nod to Arthur's outsized level of effort tracking the truckers, Diaz assigned Arthur to surveil one of Shakopf's marine fueling terminals on Lake Barkley to see if anything out of the ordinary occurred on the lake.

CHAPTER 35

"Hey, Laceon, Touch Thomas came to visit me again yesterday. Did he stop by your house again as well?" Will Welch asked his longtime best friend.

"Yeah, he was over to the house again. I don't know why the hell he's got a bee in his bonnet for David Barnett all of a sudden. That whole mess was ages ago. Do you even remember what happened? It's all sort of fuzzy to me."

"You know damned well what happened. We made a pact to never discuss it, remember?" Will said to Laceon with more than a tinge of anger in his voice.

Laceon took a moment to let tensions subside. "Will, you can think what you want; it doesn't matter a hill of beans to me. We've been friends far too long to worry about shit like this that Sheriff Touch Thomas wants to stir up. We'll talk tomorrow at the golf course. This too shall blow over."

Will, ever more emotional than Laceon—likely because he'd never lived up to his father's expectations—didn't buy into the younger Shakopf's thought that this latest episode of Touch Thomas's Goody Two-shoes dance would blow over. Will had known Hank Benitez for most of his life, and Hank's murder had shaken him. Once comfortable in his marriage, involved with and proud of his kids, Will now feared that maybe his wife wasn't as fond of him as she'd once been. His job at the bank offered a decent community profile, but everyone in town recognized that Will would never meet the expectation that someday he too would become president of Walter County Bank. More than a few comments shuffled around the country club—and made their way back to the ears of Will's wife—that Jerry Welch remained the only reason Will worked at the bank. If his cousin, Davis Welch, had his way, Will would have been gone some time ago, replaced by a smarter, more attractive PR person with out-of-state connections capable of bringing interest into Cooper from national and international manufacturers. About the only connections Will's ever developed outside Walter County involved vacations to Florida or Colorado. The thought that a business not already in Cooper would choose to build a new plant there was about the furthest thing from Will's mind.

Relatively simple-minded and all but void of creativity, Will Welch sure as hell had no idea what his father and Edmund Shakopf hoped to accomplish in proposing to the county commissioners a drug task force. In Will's mind, the proposal sounded akin to inviting the fox into the henhouse. Will's confusion quickly gave way to fear.

Will Welch and Laceon Shakopf bantered about the usual community news and events through the first three holes of their regular once-a-week golf match. The heat of the prior evening's conversation had yet to resurface. By hole four, though, as the two men ran out of current events and business topics to discuss, Laceon commenced a personal fact-finding mission on how much Will knew about his father's drug business, the money-laundering efforts that Walter County Bank enabled over the past forty years or so, and his thoughts on a Walter County drug task force.

Without going into too much detail on the specifics of where the drugs came from and how much the Shakopf family moved on retail and wholesale levels, Laceon educated Will on the family drug empire over the next three holes. By the time the two were on the ninth green, Laceon convinced Will that he had largely taken over the operation from his father. Jerry Welch, in contrast, discussed very little on the particulars of the Walter County Bank money-laundering efforts: ignorance was bliss, in his opinion. Plus, if Will didn't know much about it, he'd be less likely to get involved and screw it up. Jerry Welch, as he'd done for a few years now, left the details to Davis Welch, who remained paid exorbitantly well for managing things as compared to other small-city bank presidents. Will benefited by virtue of a decent sized trust that effectively doubled his monthly salary. Having never given the origins of the trust much thought, Will assumed that most multigenerational banking families commonly enjoyed such financial benefits.

On the back nine of the golf course, the demeanors of the two men began to change. Will Welch gained comfort with the increased information gleaned from his conversation with Laceon. The question as to why neither of the men engaged in the topic earlier never crossed Will's mind. That fact marked the primary driver of Laceon's fear as the realization came to him that Will understood next to nothing regarding what their families had been up to since the late 1970s: selling drugs and laundering money. A lack of desire to rock the boat, among the most endearing qualities of Will Welch, kept the topics far removed from the discussion list for pretty much forever. Hunting, fishing, SEC sports, and girls—and then wives, kids, and their parents—largely dominated conversations for decades, peppered with minor observations of their legitimate businesses. "Don't ask, don't tell" pretty much described the drug business, which was exactly how Edmund Shakopf had set it up with his first dealer all those years ago in his service station parking lot. Now, though, Laceon worried that Will's fears and sudden interest in the operation represented clear and present dangers.

As Laceon let this observation roll around in his mind through holes ten, eleven, and twelve, he bought himself some time by attempting to explain that their fathers' interests in a Walter County drug task force amounted to nothing other than a bait-and-switch operation. The two old men hoped that by baiting the county commissioners with an interest in limiting drug flows into Cooper and Walter County, they'd successfully switch the target of that interest from their operations to those of new organizations attempting to move into West Kentucky. Hank Benitez's cooperation with one of these outfits resulted in his execution, though Laceon left this last fact unsaid. Based on his read of how scared Will was earlier that afternoon, Laceon concluded it was best that Will know nothing about outsiders potentially encroaching on the Shakopf drug empire. With that explanation apparently satisfying Will's curiosity, the two men headed to the bar as they usually did after finishing a round of golf. Laceon had the feeling that drinks would flow easily that evening and suggested he and Will call their wives and declare the evening a guys' night out, with instructions not to wait on dinner or even wait up for them.

CHAPTER 36

When his smartphone rang, Rafe Livingston had just reentered the log cabin he inhabited on a several-hundred-acre compound to which he retired between jobs. Surprised by the ringing—Livingston had constructed the cabin so far from civilization that the phone infrequently acquired a signal—he decided to go against his usual reaction to silence the phone and allow the call to go to voicemail, and instead he answered it.

"Mr. Livingston, this is your friend in Atlanta. We've got another job for you. It's an area you're already familiar with: Cooper, Kentucky. You may have laid eyes on the target before too: Sheriff Touch Thomas of Walter County, Kentucky. I don't know how partial you are to repeat business in a town, but the job pays one hundred thousand dollars. I think that's a considerable raise compared to the last gig in that area. Call me back at this number by six this evening, please."

"I'm appreciative of the call, as always. I'll give it some thought and be back to you well before six tonight. Have a good one," Rafe concluded the call.

The call from the head of the Dixie Mafia, Don Lipscomb in Atlanta, perplexed Rafe. The only law enforcement officers he'd assassinated in the past were dirty cops on the take who threatened to turn the tables on their drug-running partners if their percentage didn't substantially increase. Or that was the situation laid out to him, at least. Rafe incurred no moral dilemmas taking out people corrupted by power or money. More or less, those people defined the primary reason he got into the business in the first place. Taking out rogue drug dealers or others limiting market expansion represented logical extensions of his operation.

Rafe decided he'd require some additional information regarding Sheriff Thomas, a figure he knew next to nothing about and thus far had heard nothing about regarding corruption. The little bit of time he'd spent in Cooper led Rafe to think it a generally pleasant place. He knew some of the backstory on Hank Benitez. Although he thought Touch releasing Hank was a stupid move, Rafe also possessed the inside information—his plan to kill Hank—that defined the move as stupid. Cogitating on the decision as he left Cooper after he finished the job, Livingston concluded that Hank's release was a fairly stand-up move. Given the risk Hank assumed in helping Sheriff Thomas, it seemed a balanced trade given the potential risk to the sheriff's reputation incurred by releasing Hank if he managed to find trouble again.

Having just finished his workout, a cross-country run through the trees surrounding his cabin, Rafe decided to take a cooldown walk to mull over in his mind Sheriff Thomas before calling back Don Lipscomb for more information. As Livingston descended down the wooded and heavily shaded path behind his cabin to the river, he reflected on how and why he had originally entered the military. Although it was over twenty-five years ago and during a period of relative harmony in the world, the US-Iraq skirmish of the early 1990s occurred during an impressionable period for Rafe Livingston, who was in his second year of high school. He was not quite old enough to drive but had a solid sense of right and wrong then. Opportunities to travel the world, learn guns and computers, and be part of a team appealed to Rafe. He was not necessarily great at following directions but was very good at getting things done.

College never appealed to Livingston because it seemed to be a whole bunch more sitting in the same place. By the time he'd arrived in high school, Rafe Livingston already had all the sitting in one place he thought he'd need for a lifetime.

The Livingstons were never necessarily pillars of the community, but nonetheless they abided by law and order. Rafe's father had served in Vietnam, and his grandfather had stormed the beaches of Normandy. Military service, at least right after high school, seemed to be a foregone conclusion for Rafe, before he arrived at high school. He never minded the thought and in fact found it something to which he looked forward.

As it turned out, once Rafe enlisted in the US Army, the following of directions turned out to not be a big deal at all; in fact, doing so seemed to make everything easier. He never worried about what to do because someone else already told him, or soon would tell him, what to do. Sit tight, take it easy, and wait for instructions? No problem. Predictably for a boy from the sticks of Georgia, shooting and trekking came naturally to Rafe. He was athletic but had no affinity for the dumbass coaches who always seemed to be barking nonsense at his classmates when he was younger, so the physical training component of the army came easily to Rafe. He tracked right into Ranger School and was damned glad that he'd done so.

Unfortunately, Rafe's relationship with the US Army turned to shit after 9/11. Idiots flooded the army, seemingly pushing bigger idiots into ever higher positions of command. After two tours in the desert, Rafe looked for a way out. The CIA too happily obliged with plenty of contract work for Rafe. He continued to excel, utilizing his sniper skills and supreme physical conditioning. With each subsequent kill in the Middle East, though, Rafe's detachment from humanity edged further and further away. He acquired a reputation of heartlessness, and assignments of increasingly questionable targets—women and teens—finally caught up with Rafe's sense of propriety. Notifying his handlers that he was done, Rafe Livingston took months-long tours of India and Southeast Asia to clear his mind and reset his life.

After returning to Georgia with a relatively fat bank account but no prospects for gainful employment, Rafe commenced reaching out to former army and, eventually, CIA contacts. In so doing, word of mouth brought his skillset to the attention of an elite network of for-hire assassins that operated entirely domestically and, as far as anyone knew, solely within the confines of major drug-running organizations. Almost like an OPEC of for-hire hitmen dedicated to the major cartels of the world, over the subsequent eight years, Rafe's bank account grew exponentially. Most of the work centered on controlling territories by eliminating rogue dealers, greedy politicians, or overreaching cops. To his knowledge, Rafe had yet to eliminate a truly "clean" individual.

Rafe's computer skills, via Ranger School and the CIA, were no match for his professional skills but were more than serviceable. In addition, prior experiences placed him in touch with a cadre of elite hackers and information gatherers around the world. Early on in his newly chosen career, Rafe learned that knowing his target often defined the ease with which he could achieve success. Knowing that a rogue dealer served three tours in Afghanistan and fell into the trade only because he no longer could service an opiate addiction with conventional income streams mattered to how one planned to eliminate him.

Remembering the catalyst for retiring from the CIA, Rafe decided that taking out a fortysomething, small-county sheriff ranked differently than taking out women and children. Obviously, Sheriff Touch Thomas ran afoul of someone who had paid some of Rafe Livingston's bills in the past. Now it was time to remove Sheriff Thomas. Rafe decided he'd take the job and double down on his background research as he made his way back uphill, away from the gurgling creek, and toward his cabin. He'd return Don Lipscomb's call as soon as he grabbed some water. With another one hundred thousand dollars pocketed, Rafe contemplated full retirement.

After dialing Lipscomb through the encrypted app he used to conduct business, Rafe raised the Dixie Mafia leader on the third ring. "This is Don."

"Don, it's Rafe. I'll do it, but this may be my final job. Just letting you know. As you've probably gathered, I'm not a fan of taking down clean cops. I struggled with this one quite a bit. I think I'm getting too old, and maybe too soft, for much more of this. Last time I was in Cooper, I was too brazen. I doubt it'll matter, but it was unprofessional."

"I appreciate the quick decision, Rafe. You've never been one to fuck around, though. I tell you what: you just say no when you're done, and we'll be fine with that. I understand, believe it or not. I usually would never send anyone back to the same location so quickly after previously working in it for us, but you're the only guy I trust with this one. Even a crackpot organization like mine really only wants folks doing things if they want to do them. Everyone's got to do a little shit work here and there to earn their stripes, but ultimately if you force people to keep doing what they don't want to do, mistakes will be made. No one's got that degree of discipline anymore. Probably shouldn't have had it in the first place."

"I appreciate the understanding, Don."

"Anyway, we're all good. We need Sheriff Thomas done by the end of next week. Usual terms. We'll make payment in the usual manner?"

"Usual means of payment will work. Thanks, and have a good one."

CHAPTER 37

It was Sunday. Touch, Hauser, and the FBI agents were in Elizabethtown, munching on donuts and drinking coffee.

Typical of a large-scale drug bust, the FBI collected photos of the major players in Shakopf's organization. Diaz arrived at the USDA building early and organized the photos by level within the organization and their geographic locations. Admiring Diaz's work, Touch stepped back and leaned against a fold-up table in the front row of the large meeting room. The team remained certain that several players would flitter through their fingers, but they were equally convinced that those arrested would easily turn over names of others in exchange for preferential treatment or modestly lighter sentences. Experience indicated this proved a simple and fruitful trade for all to make.

Touch reflected on the group's work. "Agent Diaz, it looks like your plan of action for enlisting local law enforcement officers is going to work. Hauser and I had concerns about coordinating activities across nine locations in three states. Casting a net that widely usually leads to snags. Agent Arthur identifying Shakopf's truckers seemed to be key—bigger shipments and more dollars, I guess. You'll call ahead and be on location in Cooper when we commence the arrests?"

Diaz replied, "Yep, I'll be on-site. The final component of the sting we're waiting on, Sheriff, are our computer people notifying me that they completed their traces on Welch's laundering operation. They want to identify where Shakopf's money was and how it got there."

Diaz wouldn't mind so much if Shakopf managed to flee in exchange for the forgiveness of his gambling debts, but he'd be damned if the old codger got to run away to fantasy island with tens of millions of dollars of drug money too. *Fuck that!*

"Folks," Touch said, "Chris and I know our counterparts in West Kentucky pretty well. I anticipate no problems with them making their arrests. We're excited to see this case coming to a close. Y'all have done a helluva fine job thus far."

Diaz said, "I briefed my bosses in Louisville and the US Attorney on the operation Friday afternoon. We've got soft approval to proceed with the planned arrests, which at last count involved nineteen people once the computer techs give the go-ahead that they've tracked everything of Welch's and Shakopf's that they needed to find in order to round out that component of the case."

"Any idea what the hang-up there is, Carter?" Touch asked.

"No details provided on that. It sounded like they'd have it finished up today, though, and we'll be ready to roll tomorrow early afternoon. Providing that this timeline sticks, I think we should be on the phones to the chiefs and sheriffs of our target areas tomorrow afternoon."

Touch said, "We should plan to follow-up with drive-to meetings for each location tomorrow night for Tuesday arrests. That's really tight, but it looks like we're ready to go except for the tech people."

"Agreed, Sheriff," Diaz said. "The other FBI agents and I will reproduce photos, names, and addresses by area for each town and decide which of us will visit which town today. For Arthur's truckers, we'll phone folks in those areas and have locals make those arrests on their own or in communication with the staties, if needed."

Special Agent Arthur said, "I think that maybe it'll be a better idea to just go directly to the state police in Tennessee, Kentucky, and Illinois and have them arrest the truckers. The staties might want to include larger area search warrants or something else beyond the scope of our operation."

"Possibly doing so could ensnare some third-party actors or information that could prove fruitful in other investigations," added Chief Hauser.

Diaz, noting the bobbing heads in the room, agreed with Arthur's point. "No reason that I can think of to not give the state police a heads-up so they can get rolling. Good idea, Arthur. Sheriff Thomas and Chief Hauser, we'll leave it to you two to take down the two older men, their sons, and the other banker guy, Davis Welch. Anyone have any problems with these plans? Then I think we're good to go, people" Diaz drew the meeting to a close and polished off the last donut.

Hauser hooted at Touch as the two walked to the car they shared from Cooper to Elizabethtown. "Your turn to drive now, Thomas. I took one for the team early this morning driving over here."

"I guess that's only fair, Chris. You might want to glance over every once in a while, though, because I had a nap on my to-do list for the drive back this afternoon. What say we slide by that joint on the Dixie Highway—what's it, again? Mark's Feed Bag, or something?—and grab some fried chicken sandwiches for the road? Reva mentioned something about it the other day when I was in the café. She read something about the place and thought about adding a similar sandwich to her menu, not knowing that I was heading this way today."

"Sounds like a damn fine idea to me. Nothing like washing down a few donuts with some fried chicken! Thank goodness it's a cheat day. Too much traveling with you, and I'd lose my girlish figure in a heartbeat. How is it that you maintain your waistline eating like you do, anyway? Barbecue at Big Bob's, steaks at the club with Mr.

Barnett, fried chicken sandwiches on the road, and whatever Reva's specials are day after day."

"Six a.m. workouts, my man. Get that metabolism up early in the morning, and don't let it drop over the day as I engage in the good, honest work that the people of Cooper elected me to do."

"Oh, I see now: you blow through several thousand calories a day generating, and then shoveling, bullshit. Yeah, I could see how one would need to eat to keep that BS machine going hour after hour."

Touch adjusted the seat for the extra couple inches he had on Hauser, fired the ignition, and dialed the radio in to WBVR. An oldie but a goodie came over the airwaves, with Jerry Reed crooning about his ex-wife getting the "Goldmine" while he "got the shaft."

Hauser grinned at the words of the song and said, "This that guy who drives the truck of Coors Light in that Burt Reynolds movie with Jackie Gleason and Sally Fields? What was the title of that movie?"

"You mean *Smokey and the Bandit*?"

"Yeah, that's it. Loved that movie. I still want a damned Firebird!"

"You can have the Firebird. I'd like to have the truck."

"Touch, you actually think we're going to rope in Shakopf and Welch with this mess and get anything to stick?"

"Hard to say, Chris. Half of me just wants to see the old men ride off into the sunset, so to speak. The other half is mad as hell that we let this go on as long as it apparently has. I keep thinking that Laceon and Will also have something to do with David Barnett's shooting. Too many loose ends point to those two bumbling something up years ago and making a mess of things. The fact that they invited this, to a large degree, with their request to the county commissioners for a drug task force offers poetic justice as well."

"That's still a weird exchange in my mind as well. Do you think Shakopf's behind Hank Benitez's murder as well?"

"Sure do. No other scenario makes sense. No reason I've come up with why another organization would care what Hank did or didn't do. He wasn't deep enough involved anywhere, as far as this investigation shows, to be of use elsewhere. Bringing those nitwits from the Dixie Mafia into town also brought unwanted attention to the situation. Some part of me thinks the old man wants to get caught to put an end to this."

"If that was the case, though, wouldn't he have been smart enough to come forward and admit his guilt? He could have copped a deal to save his son and the rest of the folks from arrest and prosecution, couldn't he? I mean, at most he's got to have five years left, don't you think? Why not turn over your source and save your son's and his best friend's asses?"

"Beats me. Maybe the old guys are just losing it and managing all of this just got to be too much for them."

Chief Hauser and Sheriff Thomas swung by Mark's Feed Store and got chicken sandwiches, fries, and cokes before they headed west back toward Cooper. Jerry Reed gave way to Martina McBride's "Independence Day" on the radio, which couldn't help but put community-conscious lawmen like Thomas and Hauser in a sour mood with its message of unassailed violence against women. McBride's lyrics momentarily brought back thoughts of Mandy Herman and Hank Benitez and how Hank's idiocy and lack of discipline had led the two men to where they were at the moment: it seemed like a year ago that he'd walked into his office after breakfast at Reva's to learn Hank was in the county jail again for beating on Mandy. The thought also reminded Touch of how weird things had gotten in Cooper since then.

"Chris, what say you and I stretch our legs with a short run when we get back? Then we can polish off this Sunday with a cold beer and a quick chat with Timmy over at the Roll'n. I get the feeling that it might be a good idea to get the lay of the land around town for the elements that fly below our radar."

"Sounds like a solid idea to me. I'll swing home to say hi to the wife and kids, change clothes, and meet you back at the football field around five. That okay with you?"

"Sounds like a plan to me."

With that, Chief Hauser pulled his hat over his eyes and enjoyed the nap that Touch had hoped he would have.

CHAPTER 38

Touch and Chris Hauser arrived back in Cooper just before three in the afternoon. Touch drove Hauser's cruiser directly to his house as Hauser had picked him up in the city police cruiser earlier that same morning for the drive to E-town. The two men agreed to meet at the high school in an hour for a short run.

After having stretched out their legs, broken a sweat, and more or less recovered from driving about three hundred miles earlier in the day and eating donuts and fried chicken sandwiches, Hauser and Touch covered their three-mile run in a little less than twenty-seven minutes. The two men agreed to meet for the third time that day, at the Roll'n at seven. Both also decided that they'd eat a healthier meal for their final repast of the day.

Touch was showered and felt the fatigue of a five o'clock alarm, a long drive, and mental exhaustion associated with executing what likely would rank as the biggest drug bust ever in West Kentucky. He decided that he needed a predinner nap. An hour later, aided by his alarm for the second time on a Sunday, Touch groggily awoke from a deep sleep. Shaking off the mental fog of his nap, he headed to his kitchen to see what from his fridge looked healthy. Sparse pickings appeared, and Touch decided to go with a tried-and-true combination for himself: carrot sticks and a bowl of Golden Grahams and milk. He had all of his food groups covered in one meal for the first time all day.

Just before seven, refueled with his supper of champions, Sheriff Touch Thomas pulled into the Roll'n's graveled parking lot, expertly avoiding the potholes. Touch parked toward the back so as not to scare off any of Timmy's clientele for the evening. He knew, though, that Sundays typically were slow nights at the Roll'n.

Shortly after Touch arrived, Hauser pulled in behind him. The two men walked into the bar together. Seeing them brought a wide smile to Timmy's face, and two cold beers came to the counter shortly thereafter.

"Fellas, what a pleasant surprise! As usual, sit anywhere you like: I'll be right there."

"Hey Timmy," Touch and Chris Hauser greeted in unison as they headed to a table near the jukebox, about midway the length of the bar and near the farthest wall of the building. The two officers wanted to avoid any of the usual riffraff drinking at the Roll'n eavesdropping any of their conversation with Timmy.

"Wow, what a treat: the two of you in my bar for the second time in less than a month. I doubt that bodes well for the crime statistics in Cooper, but it certainly makes my evenings go by faster. What's on your minds, fellas?"

"Thanks for the beers, Timmy," Touch started. "You noticed anything peculiar over the past two weeks around Cooper or the county?"

"You mean other than you two coming into the Roll'n twice?" joked Timmy.

"Yeah, Timmy, other than that. Geez," Hauser replied.

"Well, fellas, nothing really sticks out to me. I will say that a couple grungy-lookin' guys I'd never seen before—similar to the two you asked about last time you were in here, but different guys—stopped in last night for a couple drinks. No trouble, mind you, just different-lookin' fellas."

Touch caught Hauser's raised eyebrow and said, "Just the two of them, Timmy? No one met them? You didn't happen to catch sight of the car they drove, did you?"

"Saturday night, guys—way too busy to be ducking out and checking license plates. I leave that bar unattended for thirty seconds, and these bums will tear down the joint. Should I be on the lookout for something, though?"

"We'd appreciate it if you could give Touch a heads-up if you see those two guys again, or anything else that looks out of place tonight or tomorrow."

"Definitely, guys, no problem. Y'all aren't expecting another incident like Hank or anything, are you?"

"No, we're not expecting anything like that. It sounds like something big may go down over in Paducah or those parts. Chris and I are just trying to stay aware of any potential spillover in order to avoid anything like what happened to Hank. Hush-hush and on the QT, of course."

"Yep, I gotcha. No problem. I like y'all stopping by and everything, but I'd just as soon not see you two for another month or so. Things got kinda topsy-turvy after Hank's murder, y'know."

"Exactly. That's what we're trying to avoid: no more topsy-turvy."

Timmy, Touch, and Hauser shared a few old-time stories, chatted about who the up-and-coming troublemakers might be in the under-twenty-five crowd, and called it a night after Touch and Hauser drained their beers. In less than an hour, Hauser and Touch learned of another potential Dixie Mafia sighting and got Timmy's eyes on the prize before the Shakopf drug busts went down tomorrow.

With a full day's work completed despite the fact that Sundays should've been off days, Touch Thomas and Chris Hauser shook hands in the Roll'n's parking lot and agreed to touch base first thing in the morning. Each man's head hit the pillow before ten with alarms set to go off at five the next morning.

CHAPTER 39

Agent Arthur's suggestion that the FBI bring the state police into the fold on arrests and search warrants expanded the potential value of Diaz's insider information to his bookie. The agent decided it was time to execute his plan and collect his final payday. His bookie picked up on the second ring. "Special Agent Diaz, what can I do for you this evening?"

"My man, I got some things that I think you can use to clear my debt with you. We've got a major sting set to happen first thing Tuesday in West Kentucky. Our investigation shows that one individual will find information about this extremely valuable. For payment in full of my outstanding debt, I'm willing to convey the focus and depth of this operation. Only the kingpin gets away, though, and his assets almost certainly will be entirely frozen. Ain't nothing I can do about either of those things. This is too big to protect anyone or anything else. Go through your channels and let me know if we've got a deal or not. I need to know by midnight, though, because this goes off first thing tomorrow morning."

"Good deal, Agent, I should be back with you within the hour. I know who you're talking about and where to go with it."

"Gimme just another minute. I've got more, believe it or not. I think this is worth some extra for you and for me. Maybe a hundred thousand—fifty to me and fifty to you?"

The bookie snickered a little as he said, "Uh-huh, wanna go out with a bang now, do you, Diaz? Another fifty in addition to a full write-off of the prior balance requires something really special. Whatcha got?"

Diaz continued. "In addition to the Kentucky thing, the FBI also plans to bring in the state police in Tennessee, Illinois, and Kentucky. This drug dealer also ships via fuel delivery trucks into and out of these states. I've got no information on anything additional, but I'm guessing that when the state police conduct their searches, they'll find more than a few other dealers involved with this operation."

Diaz never really gave it much thought, but somehow his bookie always knew where to go with the information provided to him. Operating under "ignorance is bliss," Diaz always considered it best that he know as little as possible about the bookie's operations outside of direct dealings with the man. Snooping around likely would get Diaz in trouble either with the bureau or the bookie— or possibly both. Nevertheless, the concept of a "godfather" figure presiding over affairs from Chicago, Atlanta, or wherever fleetingly passed through Diaz's mind.

With that, Diaz went into waiting mode. He whiled away the time by reviewing what arrests were set to happen in which town, as well as who would execute the arrests, local or FBI. Even if Shakopf took the deal, Diaz thought the operation likely would rank as the most successful of the year for the Louisville office. Just tracking the cash through Walter County Bank and to Shakopf's various other accounts marked a relatively huge win for the office. The duration, depth, and breadth of drugs that moved through Shakopf's network offered the potential to significantly disrupt the dealing of every drug short of heroin, and maybe it as well, over much of the Midwest.

As most residents of West Kentucky drifted off to dreamland, FBI Special Agent Diaz's phone rang. Diaz grabbed the iPhone off the night table next to his motel bed. "Diaz."

"Special Agent, this is your bookie, calling back as promised. We have a deal on the Kentucky thing, but as you're aware, this needs to go down quickly. Here's the number you need to call ASAP. We are now all square on that piece. As for the additional information, fifty thousand to you is a done deal as well. Just let me know when you're back in town to receive it. You'll be better than all square with me—you'll be fifty grand richer," said the bookie. "As such, I'd appreciate it if you'd lose my number and never call me again. Have a nice life, Special Agent Diaz."

"Deal. I appreciate you remaining straight up with me. This will be our last call, guaranteed. Be good."

Diaz rubbed the palms of his hands over his face, taking a moment to reflect on how long and heavy that albatross had hung around his neck. For pretty much the entirety of his professional life and nearly all of his nonmilitary adult life, he'd been in to someone for gambling debts. It had taken the equivalent of selling his soul to a devil to finally clear his debts. One last call to make, and with any luck, he'd be done with nothing to worry about ever again. Of course, because he was dirty, the risk remained that someone would rat him out. Diaz had been living with that threat for at least ten years, though. After grabbing a drink of water to wash the moment away, Diaz pulled the burner phone out of his suitcase and dialed the number the bookie had provided.

"Yes," came the answer. From the waver in the voice, Diaz concluded it was an old man: Edmund Shakopf.

"Is this Edmund Shakopf?" asked Diaz.

"It is. Who's this?"

"Doesn't matter who it is. We've got a mutual acquaintance in Louisville, I believe, who instructed me to call you about an operation the FBI plans to execute tomorrow. Am I talking to the right guy about that?"

"You are. I appreciate you calling me and giving me the opportunity to make a choice. I think this may turn out as well as could be expected for both sides, believe it or not. Please tell me what you know."

"Mr. Shakopf, Tuesday morning at first light, the FBI, local law enforcement, and state police will arrest the vast majority of your drug distribution network. They'll take down your dealers in Cooper, Ballard, Sterling, Iola, Paulsboro, and Paducah, as well as your wholesale movers in Tennessee and Illinois. They've got financial records on how you and Jerry Welch used his bank, Walter County Bank, to launder money. In the morning, there will be knocks on your door, your son's door, Jerry Welch's door, his son's door, and his nephew Davis Welch's door. They're coming for it all."

"Thank you. Anything else."

"That's all," Diaz said as he concluded the call.

Diaz took the burner phone outside, deleted its history, wiped it down, removed the battery, broke the phone in half, and threw it in the dumpster behind the motel. He thought he'd feel a sense of great relief. Instead, he felt kind of hollow, the same as he'd felt the other times he'd sold information to pay off debts.

"Last time," Diaz muttered to himself.

CHAPTER 40

After agreeing to kill Touch Thomas for Don Lipscomb and the Dixie Mafia, Rafe Livingston hammered out a handful of additional details with Don Lipscomb, including the procurement of two Dixie Mafia soldiers. Livingston liked a front man as well as someone watching his backside. Lipscomb offered no resistance to sending a couple of his guys to meet up with Livingston outside Cooper. The two men agreed that Paducah, about forty minutes west of Cooper, represented the best rendezvous point.

Livingston left for West Kentucky the day after speaking with Lipscomb. By his calculations, it would take him roughly eight hours of driving time to get to Paducah. He'd gain an hour, though, because the drive moved from the Eastern Time Zone of North Georgia to the Central Time Zone in West Kentucky. The benefits of living in the middle of nowhere in his line of work were multitude. Short drive times, however, did not rank among them.

Leaving at nine, Livingston planned to be in Paducah by four in the afternoon, local time. By his estimate, a four o'clock arrival provided plenty of time to check in to a motel and get the lay of the land. He planned to visit Cooper as well and complete some initial reconnaissance with the two men Lipscomb sent to work with him. For the Benitez job, Rafe had spent some time in Cooper, but he had focused on the locations he knew Hank frequented. Rafe knew nothing of downtown Cooper, its sheriff's office, or Touch Thomas's travel patterns.

Livingston knew the *Mi Tierra* security camera had captured him dining at the restaurant. He also knew two additional things. One, no records existed of his activities after an honorable discharge from the US Army. Two, nothing other than appearing on *Mi Tierra's* security cameras linked him to the death of Hank Benitez. Rafe Livingston was brazen and bold, but he was also calculating,

In West Kentucky, Rafe Livingston and the two Dixie Mafia grunts Timmy saw at the Roll'n Saturday night relaxed in separate rooms, paid for with cash, at the Paducah Day's Inn on Hinkelville Road. It took Livingston twice as long to get from Paducah to Cooper as compared to the last motel he had used for the Hank Benitez job, but he wanted more distance between him and his target for this job. Touch Thomas was no slouch like Hank Benitez. Sheriff Thomas's experience almost mimicked Livingston's in terms of military service and security details. In fact, Rafe Livingston thought that with just a couple decisions going the other way for him over the past twenty years, he easily could have been in a similar seat as Sheriff Thomas. Now, though, Rafe Livingston plotted how best to take out a small-county sheriff.

The two lackeys cased the Walter County Sheriff's Office, its proximity to the Cooper Police Station, and major roads into and out of town in each of the cardinal directions. Livingston reviewed Touch's service records, committed a recent photo of the Walter County Sheriff to memory, and studied aerial and other photographs of his house pulled off Google Earth. Given the girth of Thomas's neck and the degree to which his biceps bulged from under the service polo he wore in the photo Livingston had, Rafe wanted nothing to do with a close-up encounter with the sheriff. By his estimate, Thomas must by at least thirty pounds heavier, four inches taller, and at worst equally fit. Given his history as a sports fan, Rafe Livingston couldn't avoid reading up on Touch Thomas's heroic activities on the football field and wrestling mat. He also noted the sheriff's Medal of Honor and Purple Heart from his time with the US Army. The more Rafe Livingston read about the man, the worse he felt about taking the job. There was no backing out now, though. Livingston decided he'd do it from afar and impersonally, using his .300 Remington 7. It was not as sophisticated as many tools he had used in prior careers, but it was widely popular among hunters and thus difficult to track.

CHAPTER 41

Edmund Shakopf, a night owl in long standing, exited his house Monday night and climbed into the shiny black Cadillac CTS parked in its spot in the garage. After backing out and clearing his driveway, Shakopf piloted the car to his son's house, which was about a seven-minute, one-stoplight drive away.

Shakopf rapped on his son's door. Luckily, Laceon was awake and watching the end of a West Coast baseball game.

"Dad, what in the world are you doing here at this hour?" Laceon inquired.

"Son, let's got for a short walk. We've got a couple pieces of business that need to be addressed now."

"One minute while I grab some shoes. Do you want a glass of iced tea or anything?"

"Nope, not the kind of business one does over a glass of iced tea. Thank you, though."

Laceon Shakopf ducked back in his house and returned ninety seconds later with a pair of flip-flops. He walked toward his father and the end of his driveway. "Dad, what's going on?"

"Laceon, it's all going to come to an end tomorrow. The feds, the sheriff, and the police are going to arrest everyone. They're going to come for us, Jerry, Will, and Davis."

"Oh."

"Listen to me, now. I think I can get you out of this. I'm old and am going down, as I should have long ago. It was a helluva run, but we knew it'd eventually end. You don't have to go down with the ship, though."

"Dad, I don't want to do it."

"Don't be a damned fool, Laceon. That idiot Will would do it to you, if given the chance. I think I've got enough squirreled away in hard assets that the FBI can't find to take care of everyone's kids. Jerry's got the same thing as well. We talked about this years ago. I don't know that he's still onboard with it, but what's done is done."

"Dad ..." Laceon trailed off as he thought about his wife and kids, and Will Welch's kids. No one gave a damn about Davis Welch; he'd always been a self-important, pompous asshole.

"Laceon, we're going to get in my car, drive over to Touch Thomas's house, wake him up, and lay out how Will Welch shot David Barnett. I know it was an accident, but that family's had a bug up its butt about David's death for forty years now. I think Touch will take it easy on you for finally sharing this with him. Either way, it can't hurt at this point, I don't think. I've got plenty more I can share with the Feds in exchange for leniency for you and Will."

Laceon took a moment, staring at the ground outside his house and standing there in the dark. "I guess I knew it would always come to this. I just refused to ever accept it. Everything came so easy to me with you around, Dad. I figured the David Barnett thing had faded into the past long ago. Now, not only does it come up but the drug running too—and both at the same time. It's a little much to take."

"That's the way it goes, son. When it rains, it pours. I'm old and without much time left anyway. I'm going to do my best to take the brunt of this and deflect attention from everyone else, if I can. Jerry's always said he'd do the same thing. We'll see if he sticks to it when this Barnett issue surfaces. At worst, that should be a negligent homicide, but I think most likely it'll be viewed as a horrible accident. We probably should have come forward long ago and given Andrew

Barnett some peace of mind. Fear does strange things to thinking, though. We'll do this, though."

The two Shakopf men got into Edmund's Cadillac. Several minutes later, they arrived at Touch Thomas's house and knocked on his front door.

CHAPTER 42

"Oh, good lord," Touch whispered to himself when he looked through the peephole in his front door to see who knocked. Touch threw the dead bolt, opened his front door and the screen door, and addressed the two men in front of him. "Mr. Shakopf, Laceon, what can I do for you fellas this evening? It's a little late for a social call, don't you think?"

"Sheriff Thomas, may we come in, please?" asked Edmund Shakopf.

"Well, sure. I apologize for not being more hospitable. The knock caught me by surprise. It's been a long day despite it just being Monday night."

"We understand, Sheriff. No reason not to be entirely forthcoming: I know what's going down tomorrow morning. My goose is cooked, and I plan to act like it. You'll not get any trouble from me. I brought Laceon over here with the hope of trying to lessen troubles for him. I think he's got an explanation to an issue that's long troubled you, your father, and one of your family's closest friends. Laceon, why don't you walk the sheriff through why we're here? Touch, I'd appreciate it if you'd listen to Laceon with an eye toward helping him out of as much of this mess as possible. I understand I'm not in an asking position, but obviously Laceon and me coming over to speak with you is not without risk and is of our own volition. Laceon?"

"Sheriff Thomas, Will Welch accidentally shot David Barnett. Your recent questioning was barking up the right tree, literally, but it was an accident. I don't know how you figured out we had a deer stand over by Sprague's farm. We left that stand in the tree too long that season. I guess one could say that Will and I frequently lacked motivation in our teens. Anyway, by the time we made it back out there that spring to remove the stand, all of the trees leafed out, and the underbrush was thick. I don't even know why we had a gun out there that time of year—squirrel hunting, maybe? Anyway, Will slipped or stumbled without his gun on safe, and he fell, and the gun discharged."

"Oh, my God," Touch breathed.

"Yeah, Will scared the piss out of himself, honest. He's lucky he didn't shoot himself or me. David Barnett wasn't so lucky. It was just a terrible accident. We weren't even screwing around with the guns or anything. Just dumb to try to carry something through that much undergrowth and stuff."

"Yeah, I hear you, Laceon. Obviously, I went out there myself in the past few weeks, and the leaves and underbrush are so thick, you can't see in or out of that piece of land. Just damn unlucky. Why not come forward immediately when it happened, though? I have to admit, it really doesn't look good coming forward now looking for some sort of deal. Sure, better late than never, but geez, Laceon."

"I'll be honest with you, Touch. I'd all but forgotten about the whole thing before you started asking questions again recently. Just one of those things you'd like to forget, as selfish as that sounds. My dad said this was the thing to do, though. Clear everything out and see what happens, I guess is the strategy."

Edmund Shakopf told Touch, "Sheriff, I contemplated this course of action for days—since you came to the country club and spoke to me and Jerry. I got a feeling that I knew what you were up to.

I've watched you from afar all your life. I know that once you get into something, you finish it eventually. I hope to deflect from everyone else as much attention from this drug business as possible and take full responsibility for my past actions. I should never have gotten into it, should have exited long ago, and never had the gumption required to do so. Sure, the money was enjoyable. I feared that if I let it go, then that heroin would make its way here. Little did I know that those opioid pills would do more damage around here than heroin could ever hope to do. Just way too cheap and easy to get, and to hide. Anyway, I hope that you'll view Laceon coming forward positively, help him out, and put me at the front of the line for responsibility and punishment."

Touch stared at his bare feet for a moment and then replied. "Edmund, I appreciate all of that. Laceon, I thank you for telling me what happened to David, even though it's several decades late. It's somewhat comforting to know what happened and to know that David Barnett wasn't targeted. I think Andrew Barnett may find some solace in that as well. Any idea why Will Welch didn't come and tell me, though?"

"Touch," Edmund Shakopf started, "neither Jerry nor Will know what's going to happen tomorrow. I wanted to speak to you first and share my plan not to challenge anything, in the hope that you could find a way to lessen the burden on everyone else. I know my dealers and runners will have to do some time, but Laceon, Will, and Jerry … No one gives a shit about Davis Welch; he's an ass. I hope I'll have some information that will help Laceon, Will, and Jerry gain some leniency."

"Edmund, I appreciate all of that. We'll go through the process, though, and see how everything shakes out. I can promise you that everyone will be treated equitably in my jail and in Chief Hauser's jail. Depending on what information you've got to share, we'll do the best we can to have it figure into the process of determining how the punishment best fits the crime in partnership with the court system as usual. That's all I can do or have ever done.

"Normally, each of you would now be handcuffed, escorted to the backseat of my Tahoe, and hauled off to jail. As you know, though, these are not normal times. I've got no idea who's got eyes on the jails. Obviously, someone with a lot of power knows something big is about to go down. As stupid and wrong as it feels, I can't risk all of that by hauling you two into jail and having a reporter or some other nitwit blab about it and blow up weeks of work completed by the FBI, Walter County Sherriff's Office, Cooper City Police, and the US Attorney's office. If that happens, I'll do everything in my powers to shitcan any deal you could ever hope to strike for anyone. Understand?"

"About all we can ask for, Sheriff. Don't you think so, Laceon?"

"Yep, Dad. About the best we can hope for. That's a deal."

"All right, then. I think y'all should just settle in right here—chair, couch, spare bedroom, whatever—and ride into the office with me first thing in the morning. Everyone comfortable with that? I doubt anyone was gonna get much sleep tonight anyway,"

"Sheriff, I haven't had a full night's sleep in twenty years. I doubt it was going to come tonight. We'll stay right here. Any chance we can make you a cup of coffee?"

"No, gentlemen, I'm still going to see if I stand any chance of getting some shut-eye right there on that couch. I'd appreciate it if you go about your coffee making as noiselessly as possible, though. Coffee maker's right there on the counter. Coffee's right above it along with sugar. I think I've even got some cream in the fridge. Help yourselves—quietly, please."

CHAPTER 43

The activities of Sunday and Monday left Touch utterly exhausted by nightfall. Initially, the weirdness of the Shakopfs' visit unleashed a rush of adrenaline. The thousand thoughts running through his head usually would keep Touch awake half the night. However, the combination of exhaustion and the usual crash after an adrenaline rush resulted in Touch falling asleep the minute his head hit the pillow. He managed six straight hours of solid sleep before his alarm blared at five. Edmund Shakopf already had a pot of coffee brewed with a fresh cup sitting next to the coffee maker, ready for Touch.

"Morning Edmund, Laceon," Touch said.

"G'morning, Touch," Edmund said as Laceon waved his greetings.

Touch continued. "I take it y'all didn't sleep last night."

"Nope, too many thoughts to rest, Sherriff," Laceon said.

"Understandable. We'll be going in an hour or so. Feel free to shower, if you'd like. It might be your last one for a day or two. I expect things are going to get chaotic and crowded today. I'm going to get my workout in and shower up, and we'll be on our way to the jail."

Always benefiting from morning exercise to elevate his energy level and to focus his mind on the day ahead, Touch knocked out three miles in about twenty-four minutes, outpacing his prior day's performance. By the time he returned home from his usual three-mile loop, sweat soaked through the sheriff's Cooper Cavalry Football T-shirt.

Touch spoke to the Shakopfs after entering his house. "I'll run through the shower, and we'll be on our way in twenty minutes or so. I suggest you make a lavatory visit. One never can tell how clean those things are in a jail, even one I run."

Twenty minutes later, Touch, Edmund, and Laceon exited the house and walked to Touch's service Tahoe. Laceon helped his father into the vehicle's back seat and then took the front passenger seat. Touch hit the ignition, and the radio crackled to life, playing Hank Williams's "I'm So Lonesome I Could Die." By the time Touch pulled behind the jail so he could shuttle the Shakopfs inside without anyone seeing them, WBVR had worked through the morning news and weather and played "If Tomorrow Never Comes" by Garth Brooks as well as Tim McGraw's "Live Like You Were Dying."

"Here we are, fellas," Touch said as he backed up to the jail's rear door. "I doubt anyone's paying attention yet this morning, but just in case, I would appreciate it if you would walk in as nonchalantly and casually as possible. Just walk right through the sheriff's office like you own the place and go all the way to the back. I'm going to chat with Bonnie for a quick second, then I'll be back to accommodate you. Okay?"

"That'll be fine, Touch. Won't it, Laceon?" Edmund Shakopf said.

Situating the Shakopfs went as smoothly as it could have. Touch was correct: no one in Cooper was out and about this early in the morning. Fifteen minutes later, Touch headed to the Tiger's Den for breakfast. Eggs and bacon felt like excellent fuel for arresting a bunch of drug dealers.

As Touch walked through the Den's front door, Reva smiled and greeted the sheriff. "Hey, Touch! Now I know it's going to be a good day."

"Good morning, Reva! Hey, Johnny, how's it going this morning?" Touch asked as he took a table looking out the diner's front window.

"Just fine, Sheriff, just fine," Johnny replied as he turned around with a smile.

Touch ordered his usual, adding sugar and cream to the fresh cup of coffee Reva poured him. As he sat awaiting his food and enjoying his coffee, he reviewed his plan for the day. He'd phoned Bonnie Sunday evening during the drive back from Elizabethtown and asked her to alert all his deputies that their services would be needed at 8:00 a.m. Tuesday morning. Touch figured he'd need about fifteen minutes to brief everyone. Of the arrests to make in Cooper and Walter County, only two were out in the county and not within the city limits. Chief Hauser's city police would act on the other eight warrants, including for the Shakopfs and the Welches. Touch assigned a deputy as backup for each of the Shakopf and Welch warrants, just in case. The sheriff planned to be "on call" to address any unexpected happenings.

Chris Hauser, unaware of the conversation between Edmund and Laceon Shakopf and Touch Monday night, had already instructed two of his sergeants Monday night to be on location at Edmund Shakopf's and Jerry Welch's houses by 6:00 a.m. Tuesday morning. Similarly, Diaz planned to be on-site with Touch and Hauser as officers brought in the Shakopfs and the Welches.

No one involved in the operation knew it, but US Attorney Shel Richardson, who got wind of the impending execution of the Shakopf operation, decided to venture to Cooper for the arrests. In fact, after checking in to the American Inn in Cooper, Richardson walked across US Highway 62 and grabbed his supper at *Mi Tierra*, unaware of the significance to the operation of dining in the restaurant.

Edmund Shakopf proved true to his word: the process of making the arrests went smoothly. One of the dealers out in the county attempted to make a run for it out the backdoor of his mobile home. Hungover or high and about forty pounds overweight, the running dealer managed to make it about thirty-five yards into the woods before a footfall landed poorly on a large root, and he took a violent tumble on a severely sprained ankle. Other than that, the other arrests went as though the targets expected to be apprehended. Arrests in the other locations, which were fewer in number, also went down without problems. State police in Tennessee and Illinois managed to nab the truck drivers red-handed early in the morning as they were getting the final pieces of their shipments situated in their trucks.

Departmental policies dictated that related prisoners be separated by at least a cell. To abide as consistently as possible with this policy, Touch and Chris Hauser separated the Shakopfs and Welches by age, pairing Will Welch with Edmund Shakopf at the county jail and Jerry Welch and Laceon Shakopf at the city jail. Touch also housed Davis Welch at the county jail. Upon the Louisville FBI office receiving news that the agents had overseen all the arrests, the head of the office notified US Attorney Richardson. Richardson packed up his travel kit, adjusted his tie in the mirror of his America's Inn room, and made his way to the Walter County Sheriff's Office.

Fifteen minutes later, Richardson arrived at the sheriff's office, which was abuzz with activity. Bonnie looked up from a growing pile of papers on her desk to see a man in a suit and tie—an outfit that definitely stuck out in Cooper and, even amid the morning's outsized level of activity, still looked out of place.

"Hi, I'm Bonnie. Can I help you?" Bonnie addressed Richardson.

"Good morning, Bonnie. My name's Shel Richardson. I'm the US Attorney for the District of Kentucky. Could you let Sheriff Thomas know that I'm here when you have a chance, please? I know there's a lot going on this morning and that the sheriff may be busy. No worries, though; I'm prepared to wait. Thank you."

"While I'm doing that, Mr. Richardson, can I get you a cup of coffee?"

"That'd be great. I'm happy to get it myself, though, if you'll direct me to your break room."

"Well, aren't you helpful?" Bonnie joked with the man. "Break room is right this way. Follow me, please, as I go let the sheriff know you're here."

Four minutes later, Touch Thomas entered the break room.

"Shel Richardson, Touch Thomas. You picked the busiest day, maybe ever, to drop in for a visit to the Walter County Sheriff's Office," Touch said as he extended his hand to the attorney.

"I'm sure you know mine is a well-calculated visit, Touch," Richardson said as he flexed his fingers after shaking hands with the vice-gripped former wrestling star.

"Certainly. Just pointing out that everyone else should know it as well! How can I help you this morning?"

"Sheriff, I'd like to speak with Edmund Shakopf as soon as I can, please."

"How about you give me ten minutes? Can you let me know what you're looking for, Shel? Maybe I can make things a little more efficiently for you, and possibly for us as well. I need to let you know that Edmund Shakopf and his son, Laceon, came to see me late last night. They informed me that they plan to admit to everything and that, as a result, Edmund Shakopf anticipated this entire operation would go very smoothly."

"Wow, that's quite the late-night visit, isn't it? Did that catch you by surprise, or does stuff like that happen all the time around here to a local legend such as yourself?"

"First time, ever, Shel," Touch replied with a smirk. "Sure, name recognition and past history buy me some time and respect with a lot of folks around here, but no, criminals don't just turn themselves in to me most of the time."

"Okay, so most of the time, things are normal around here, then. Good deal. Sheriff, what I'm looking for is Shakopf, Welch, and whoever to give up their suppliers in exchange for lesser sentences, or whatever we might be able to negotiate on that front. I'm sure you're not surprised by this. Given the aged profile of both Edmund Shakopf and Jerry Welch, this particular operation offers significant opportunities to bring down kingpins of larger organizations than other cases with far younger principals."

"I understand entirely, and, better yet, I think Edmund Shakopf understands that. One other extenuating circumstance you should be aware of: Laceon Shakopf admitted to me in front of his father last night that about forty years ago, Will Welch accidentally shot and killed a young man by the name of David Barnett. You may know David's father, Andrew Barnett; he's a renowned attorney in these parts as well as my dad's best friend. David was a special young man—now he would be known as autistic, I think—who mowed grass and tinkered with small engines. His death was just a case of wrong place, wrong time, but it plagued Mr. Barnett, my dad, and me for decades. I've investigated it from every angle since I became sheriff and armchair-sleuthed it for some time before I became sheriff. The weight of knowing continues to lift off my psyche, but I've not shared Laceon Welch's confession with Mr. Barnett or anyone else because I wanted to wait for the details on this Shakopf drug situation to fully come to light. We've got lots of moving parts here, to say the least."

"Yeah, you've had a full plate. That's another part of the reason why I'm down here. I'd have advised you to do the same thing with respect to Mr. Barnett. That being said, do you mind if I meet with Mr. Shakopf?"

"Again, give me ten minutes, and I'll have you in front of Edmund Shakopf in one of our interview rooms."

"Ten minutes it is. Thanks, Touch."

Ten minutes later, Touch returned to the break room, fetched Shel Richardson, and shepherded him to an interview room where Edmund Shakopf awaited him.

Touch took position behind the interview room's mirrored wall, facing Edmund Shakopf. Not only did Touch want to see Richardson in action, but he also wanted to hear what Shakopf would say and how he would say it.

"Mr. Shakopf, I'm Shel Richardson, the US Attorney for the District of Kentucky. I assume that Sheriff Thomas, one of his deputies, or another law enforcement official informed you of your rights?"

"Yes, Mr. Richardson," Edmund Shakopf said "Sheriff Thomas informed me of my rights earlier this morning. I appreciate you asking to meet with me so early. I have information that I'm willing to share with you that I believe you will find both enlightening and useful. In exchange, I want one thing and one thing only."

"Well, Mr. Shakopf, I assume you've watched enough TV and movies, read enough books, and such to understand 'give and take' defines this entire process. You give me a little, and I may give you a little. You give me a lot, and I may give you a lot. Understand, however, that I hold all of the high cards here. You know that someone of my stature being here this early in the process means I expect a great deal of valuable information from you. Typically, the US Attorney's office would not spend its time on a regional drug bust. However, the FBI surveilled your operation for some time. Hank Benitez's murder and some information stemming from it raised an eyebrow or two as well. The intricacies of your business, in combination with the length of time you've run it and the degree of money Mr. Welch appears to have laundered for you, indicate you potentially possess a treasure trove of details, including names, dates, and places, that could implicate many individuals involved in multiple criminal elements across the Midwestern and southeastern United States. I'm sure that those people whom you could name well understand this, making time of the essence. So, Mr. Shakopf, start wherever you'd like: your Atlanta supplier, your St. Louis and Chicago customers, and any points in between. I'm all ears."

Three hours of recorded conversation, four cups of coffee, and ten pages of handwritten notes later, Edmund Shakopf divulged enough detail for Shel Richardson to build immediate cases against the leaders of the drug trades in Atlanta, Nashville, Memphis, St. Louis, Chicago, and many points in between. The man's forty years of involvement included dealing not just with the current operators in these markets but also all of the predecessor dealers in those areas. Allusions to and indications of other illegal activities ranging from extortion, bribes, and blackmail to murder left Richardson's head spinning with respect to how far-reaching he could extend Shakopf's knowledge to criminal prosecutions.

Midway through Edmund Shakopf's confessional, the man paused, calling a timeout of sorts, and stated to Richardson his one request: immunity for his son and for Will Welch. This request came as no surprise to Richardson given his experience and Shakopf's age. As a sign of his good faith and in recognition of the value of the information already provided, Richardson picked up his iPhone, dialed his office, and instructed an assistant US Attorney to draw up papers granting Laceon Shakopf immunity from prosecution in exchange for his and his father's cooperation with the US Attorney. Upon completion of the document, Richardson borrowed access to a computer from Bonnie, remotely logged into his email, and printed the documents for signatures by the Shakopfs and by Will Welch.

By midafternoon, both sides received what they wanted. Touch Thomas needed a statement from Laceon Shakopf, getting the details of David Barnett's death delineated in a signed and sworn statement. To take a statement from Laceon, however, Touch needed to go to the city jail. As he walked out of his office for the first time in five hours, one of the Dixie Mafia grunts working with Rafe Livingston noted it and phoned Livingston with the details. Rafe instructed the man to tail Touch, which he dutifully did to the Cooper Police Station. Fifteen minutes later, Rafe Livingston took up surveillance across the street and a half block west of the building. With good sightlines created by empty parking spaces due to the

"Cooper Police Parking Only" signs in front of the station and the absence of vehicles in those spots, Livingston could easily keep tabs on the comings and goings at the station. He noticed Sheriff Thomas leaving the building an hour later, complete with a written and sworn statement detailing the death of David Barnett.

With the statement in hand and exhausted from six hours of executing arrest warrants and taking statements from people he'd known and respected his entire life, Touch Thomas decided it was as good a time as any to tell Andrew Barnett that the death of his son finally appeared to be solved. Twenty minutes later, Touch pulled into Barnett's driveway, killed his Tahoe's engine, and walked up to the front door of his father's best friend's house to tell the old man how and why his son had died. Touch rapped on the door with his knuckles three times. A minute later, he heard Andrew Barnett say, "Coming," as footsteps plodded along the floor toward the house's front door.

"Touch, what a pleasure! Little early for a social call on a Monday, isn't it?" the old man asked.

"Andrew, earlier today, Laceon Shakopf wrote a statement detailing what happened to David all those years ago. I've got the statement right here, if you'd like to read it. To paraphrase: Laceon and Will Welch ventured out to that wooded area near Charlie Sprague's farm to remove a deer stand from the prior season and to do a little squirrel hunting. Will tripped or slipped in that stand. He fell, and his gun discharged. David was just in the wrong place at the wrong time. The slug hit him, and neither Laceon nor Will even knew he was there, let alone that he'd been hit by the shot. I've been out there myself, and the underbrush and foliage are so heavy, you can't even see out of that thicket. I believe Laceon. What I can't come to grips with, and likely never will understand, is how neither Will nor Laceon ever said anything to anyone. Complete speculation on my part, but I suspect that both of their fathers knew something wrong happened then as well. They've certainly known for some time since then. We both know that it's frequently impossible for a parent to risk doing the right thing if it means their child could get sent off to jail. It's a story as old as time."

"Oh, Touch, that's a lot to take in for an old man in a short period of time. You got a minute to come in and sit down?"

"Good Lord, Andrew, I'm so sorry. That was terrible of me. Of course I can come in and sit for a while. I should have asked first if I could come in and recommended that we sit down. It's been some kind of day, let me tell you. Doesn't excuse my impoliteness and lack of consideration, though, Andrew. Please accept my apologies."

"You've got nothing for which to apologize. You've just solved the major mystery of my life! It might not look like it now, but you've lifted a major weight off my chest. You know how long I've struggled to accept what happened to David. Your dad and even you shared my burden. He was such an angelic child. The thought that someone purposely would do something hurtful to him, let alone kill him, almost consumed me. To know it was a freak accident perpetuated by a couple dimwitted, spoiled boys by no means makes not admitting it right, but knowing exactly what happened soothes me. I hope it provides similar solace for you too."

Andrew Barnett put his hand over Touch's as a symbol of his thanks as the two men sat at Barnett's dinner table. Knowing that Andrew Barnett would gain some comfort from the news concerning Edmund Shakopf and Jerry Welch, Touch relayed a CliffsNotes version of the morning's events to the old man over the next twenty minutes.

"I'll be damned, those two old fools!" Andrew Barnett exclaimed once Touch concluded his story on the depth and reach of Shakopf's drug empire and the magnitude of money Jerry Welch had laundered for him over the course of the operation. "I knew something screwy went on between those two, but I always found myself on the other side of the law from where they operated. From the outside looking in, they appeared as two successful businessmen, maybe on occasion screwing over the little guy but by no means being drug kingpins and shuttling millions of dollars in drug money through international accounts."

Hoping to return to his office before Shel Richardson departed and to witness Shakopf signing the papers that would grant immunity to Laceon Shakopf, Touch took his leave of Andrew Barnett. The two men promised each other to meet up later in the week for dinner and further discussions later in the week at the Cooper Country Club.

CHAPTER 44

Early Monday, Rafe Livingston watched Touch work his way through his morning run from afar. Consistent with the background research indicating that Sheriff Thomas remained an elite physical specimen, the man showed Livingston nothing that would lead him to think otherwise.

Livingston toyed with executing Touch Thomas first thing Monday morning. Certainly if he had, it would have thrown that day's entire drug bust operation into a furor. Livingston remained entirely unaware of the Shakopf affair and all of the planned arrests. By waiting and avoiding Monday morning, with all of the area law enforcement operations on high alert, an FBI presence in town, and even the US Attorney only a couple miles away in Cooper at the American Inn, Livingston appeared to have gotten lucky in deciding to take his time.

Now, though, Rafe Livingston took aim from the cover of a deeply wooded area about 250 yards from Andrew Barnett's front door. Having followed Touch to Barnett's house, Livingston spent fifteen minutes scoping out potential setup locations that would facilitate taking out Touch from a safe distance. Livingston noticed the area immediately east of Barnett's house after he turned around in a neighbor's driveway and retraced the path he and Thomas drove from Cooper to Barnett's house. Livingston pulled off on the shoulder about five hundred yards from Barnett's driveway, grabbed his rifle case from the backseat, slung it over his shoulders backpack-style, and hustled his way across the highway and through the woods in the direction of Barnett's house. About ten minutes later, Livingston chose his location across a well-kept pasture from Barnett's front door and sighted his shot. It appeared he would have no less than ten steps from the front door of the house to the driver's side door of Touch's Tahoe in which to take his shot. The only modestly complicating factor: the lack of incline forced Livingston to remail standing for his shot.

Touch exited Barnett's house fifteen minutes after Livingston established his position. Touch pausing at the front door to share a last word with Andrew Barnett enabled Livingston plenty of time to position the sheriff within the scope of the .300 Remington 7 rifle. Livingston progressed through his preshot routine: exhale, confirm sighting through the Schmidt and Bender scope, right index finger pressuring the trigger.

Chris Hauser obliterated Rafe Livingston at the last moment, just before Livingston squeezed off his shot. The momentum with which the chief tackled Livingston broke three ribs on the sniper's left side, puncturing his left lung. Hauser executed the perfect form tackle one would expect from a former All-State and third-team All-American safety. The hit pinned Livingston between the tree supporting his rifle and the Cooper chief of police's right shoulder. Hauser popped up from the tackle, quick as a cat, and prepared for hand-to-hand combat with Livingston. As Livingston struggled just to breathe, Hauser realized subduing Livingston required no further aggression. He threw the rifle aside and cuffed the man.

He waved frantically at Thomas and shouted, "Touch! Touch! Over here in the trees.".

Touch heard Hauser immediately, but he was understandably confused as to why the Cooper chief of police yelled at him from the trees across a pasture over 250 yards away from Andrew Barnett's house. As Touch took a second to adjust and then commenced sprinting across the pasture separating Barnett's house from the treed area, Hauser called for an ambulance and backup to meet him at Andrew Barnett's house.

As Hauser completed his backup call, Touch ran up. "Chris, what the hell's going on? What are you doing, and who's this?" Touch turned his head and saw the sniper rifle, and the situation made a little more sense to him.

"Touch, the FBI got a tip that someone had hired a hitman to take you out amid all of this drug bust business. I followed you out here as soon as I got the call, saw this guy's vehicle pulled off on the shoulder, and figured this was where it was going down. Thankfully, I got lucky and spotted him from about ten yards away. Looks like I had just enough time to pick my way over here without making too much noise before he squeezed off a shot at you. From the looks of that setup, this guy knows what he's doing—that's not a deer hunter's setup there. Anyway, I think I broke a couple of his ribs because he doesn't seem to be breathing too well anymore. I lit him up against that tree. Best tackle I've made in twenty years!"

"Whew, thanks for that, Chris! You got my back again."

Addressing Rafe Livingston as he helped the man to his feet, Touch said, "What's your name?"

"Rafe Livingston, Sheriff," the hitman answered as he gasped for breath.

"You want to explain what the hell's going on around here, or are you going to wait until we get you to the hospital? Doesn't look like it's going to matter much to us; you don't look like you're going anywhere too fast any time soon. No one else out here with you, is there?" Touch asked Livingston.

"You got my name, Sheriff," Livingston said. "That's all you'll get from me. I doubt it'll do you much good to have it."

Touch and Hauser helped Livingston get to his feet, and they looked at each other as they processed Livingston's last comment.

Each of them recognized Rafe Livingston from *Mi Tierra's* security tape. The little guy was ballsy; Touch gave him that.

Hauser had the larger jail and headcount, so Touch and Hauser agreed to house Livingston in the city jail. Shakopf remained at the county jail in the sheriff's office. Touch called Bonnie as soon as he started the Tahoe, asking if Shel Richardson remained in the sheriff's office.

"Bonnie, ask Shel Richardson to stay there until I get back to the office, please. I'll be about fifteen minutes. We've got a new development I want to make him aware of. Have one of the deputies put Mr. Shakopf in an interrogation room again as well."

"You got it, Touch. I just saw Richardson duck back into the break room for another cup of coffee—his fifth of the day, I think. Shakopf will be in room one when you get here."

Fifteen minutes, later Touch hustled through the sheriff's office to the break room and addressed Shel Richardson. "Mr. Richardson, a hitman by the name of Rafe Livingston just tried to assassinate me outside Andrew Barnett's house. Chief Hauser, who got wind of Livingston's presence from an FBI tip, managed to tackle Livingston before he got off a shot. Livingston's not saying anything, but the Dixie Mafia almost certainly is the reason he's here. If so, how did they know about the arrests?"

"One minute, Sheriff, please. That's a lot to take in given everything else that's already gone down today ... No, that makes no sense to me. Let's ask Shakopf and see where this takes us. Livingston appeared to be working alone, I take it?"

Touch mentioned the two Dixie Mafia players Timmy had told him and Hauser about Saturday night at the Roll'n. A minute later, the Richardson and Touch were in the interrogation room in front of Edmund Shakopf.

"Mr. Shakopf, Sheriff Thomas just informed me that a man named Rafe Livingston attempted to shoot him several minutes ago near Andrew Barnett's house. We speculate that the Dixie Mafia ordered the hit on Sheriff Thomas. Did you have any knowledge of this? Any prior conversations about Sheriff Thomas with anyone before or after your arrest?"

"No, sir. I in no way, shape, or form desired to bring any harm to Sheriff Thomas. I'm guessing that you two agree with me when I say that makes no sense given my actions last night and this morning. Otherwise, you'd not be asking me that question in such a reserved, unanimated manner. Touch, if I had wanted you out of the picture, it would have happened before Laceon and I came to speak with you, don't you think? Also, we'd never have mentioned David Barnett's death to you if we planned to eliminate you, would we?"

Touch replied, "Correct, Mr. Shakopf. We agree that it makes little sense that you'd attempt to have me removed at this point. It'd be a classic closing of the barn door after the horses escaped. Certainly, you would have had Livingston execute me the moment I opened the door to you and Laceon last night."

The three men allowed a moment of silence in the small room as they collected their thoughts and mentally walked through the other players that might benefit from removing Touch Thomas from the equation. None of the lower-level players possessed the contacts, knowledge, or motivation to set up anything like this. Laceon Shakopf made no sense; he benefited from the current arrangement more than anyone. No evidence showed that Davis Welch knew much about any of the details surrounding Shakopf's operation. Will Welch in no way exhibited the gumption necessary to order a hit on the sheriff even though keeping his involvement in the death of David Barnett could benefit him. That left Jerry Welch.

"Blood's thicker than water, even if that water's mixed with sixty years of friendship. Sweetening the deal for Laceon's immunity with his confession about David Barnett's death scared Jerry that Will would be behind bars forever. If the assassination of a county sheriff could be pinned on me, it would blow up any deal I might have been able to get for Laceon. Jerry's been jealous of Laceon since Will and

Laceon were in grade school. Granted, Laceon's no rocket scientist, but he's always had the upper hand on Will with everything. Jerry thought he'd be able to talk or buy his way out of prosecution for laundering my drug money. Given the inability of you guys to figure out what we were doing for decades, Jerry thought we'd never get caught. Initially, he didn't agree that turning in my suppliers and larger clients if we got caught in exchange for leniency was the proper strategy. Touch, I'm sorry, but I think he tried to double-cross me and convinced the Dixie Mafia, one of my main suppliers, to put a hit out on you. It's the only alignment of the facts that makes any sense to me."

Touch pulled out his phone and dialed Chris Hauser. "Chris, do me a favor and put Jerry Welch in an interview room ASAP. US Attorney Shel Richardson and I will be over in ten minutes to speak with him if that's okay. Also, can you pull his cellphone as well as Rafe Livingston's cellphone, please? I'll explain it all when Richardson and I get over there."

"Definitely, Touch," Hauser replied.

"Thanks, Chris. See you in ten." Touch hung up. "Sorry, Shel, but I recommend you spend another night with us in Cooper. I think we may be able to dig up some charges for the Dixie Mafia easier to prove and stickier than drug running."

"I agree, Sheriff."

"Tell you what, Shel. I'll sweeten the deal with supper at Big Bob's BBQ. It won't do anything positive for your waistline, but the rest of you will be thankful," Touch shared as the two me left the sheriff's office.

Richardson said, "I marvel at your ability to take all of the day's events in stride. What usually happens around here that allows you to manage such a volatile day and yet remain gracious enough to invite a visitor to supper?"

Ten minutes later, Richardson and Touch entered the City of Cooper Police Station just as the day shift officers rotated off the clock. It had been a long day for most of them. Hauser was to the left of the police station's lobby, and upon seeing Touch and Richardson enter, he grabbed their attention, motioned the two men toward the interview rooms, and handed over both Welch's and Livingston's cellphones to Touch.

"Thanks, Chris," Touch said as he took the phones from Hauser. "Mr. Richardson and I had a quick conversation with Edmund Shakopf. It sounds like Jerry Welch tried to undermine Edmund getting immunity for Laceon and contracted with the Dixie Mafia to kill me. Edmund doesn't think Jerry ever really was on board with his plan. Instead, Welch wanted to rely on never getting caught, then the legal system—or maybe just dying of old age before getting prosecuted. Who knows?" Touch let these ideas marinate with Hauser for a moment before continuing. "I'm thinking that we likely find a Dixie Mafia or Livingston's number on Welch's phone, or vice versa. While maybe not the most concrete evidence, just the threat, along with Livingston's apparent willingness to talk, will work in our favor getting Welch to squirm a little bit and open up. Attempting to assassinate an officer of the law would allow us to really squeeze Welch. I'd guess his reluctance to speak will fade into oblivion once we inform him we granted his son immunity, have Livingston in custody, and present him with Livingston's phone. What do you think, Shel?"

"Seems like a solid plan to me. Would you like me to put on my best rendition of a prosecuting attorney and see if I can't make this happen for you? I'm guessing that the power of my office may increase motivation for Mr. Welch. I can also directly allude to my potential willingness to negotiate with him if he starts to show a little softening around the edges regarding the validity of his prosecution. If he's really interested in his son being around for his grandkids, we should be able to exact some serious leverage on him to our benefit in identifying Dixie Mafia individuals to prosecute, as well as in identifying any accomplices he used to launder Shakopf's money."

"I say grip it and rip it, Mr. US Attorney," Chief Hauser affirmed.

Touch agreed. "That's precisely why I brought you along and wooed you with a barbecue supper, Shel. Go to it!"

Two hours later, Shel Richardson possessed two additional Dixie Mafia names on his list of implicated criminal kingpins, as well as a step-by-step plan Welch had conveyed to the Dixie Mafia to assassinate Touch. The former banker knew he'd spend the rest of his life in the court system or in jail. However, recognizing the value of the information Jerry Welch shared, and in exchange for his ongoing cooperation, Richardson agreed to accept the willful return of illegally received funds from Will Welch without prosecution. Will Welch also would be required to provide his written and sworn statement regarding the shooting death of David Barnett.

CHAPTER 45

Uncharacteristically, Touch Thomas took a two-week vacation several days after the final local cleanup of the Shakopf bust. He boarded an airplane at Nashville's Briley National Airport bound for Jamaica, found a beach resort, drank Red Stripe, sat on the beach and listened to the waves crash. By the time he returned, it appeared that Cooper had largely reverted to normal. A quick conversation with his good friend Chris Hauser confirmed that view. A steak dinner with Andrew Barnett, who looked ten years younger after learning what had happened to his son, saw the two men discussing Barnett's favorite stories about Touch's father, none of which involved the death of David.

Over the next three months, as fall and the football season progressed in Walter County, Touch welcomed the return to normal for the Walter County Sheriff's Office: a few driving-while-intoxicated arrests for boaters returning home from weekends on Lake Barkley, stolen farm implement investigations, trespassing claims, and an eviction every once in a while. The fear of a flood of drugs making its way into Cooper once Shakopf's operation went offline had thus far failed to materialize. It appeared that the FBI and Shel Richardson's office initiated multi-region investigations into the Dixie Mafia's drug-running connections as soon as Richardson returned to his office from Cooper. With corroborating evidence and willingness to testify from Edmund Shakopf and Jerry Welch, the FBI executed search and arrest warrants in Atlanta, Chicago, St. Louis, Memphis, and Nashville over the next month, bringing much of the drug-running and money-laundering infrastructure to its knees in the Midwest and southeast.

Tracking the methods and patterns Jerry Welch used to move Edmund Shakopf's money alerted the FBI, the Drug Enforcement Agency, and the Bureau of Alcohol, Tobacco, and Firearms to thousands of lookalike transactions that illegal drug and arms dealers employed to make their operations appear legitimate. The resulting disruptions to cash flows wreaked havoc on the physical trade of illegal goods. Funny things happen when criminals fail to get paid.

The downside of criminals not getting paid, however, materialized in a significant uptick in violence across much of the area. It also led to the dirty cops not getting paid as well, which incentivized them to commence taking down many of their former partners. That added to the violence in these areas. Dirty started to take out dirtier. None of this happened in Cooper, though, because the lack of cash flow removed any incentive for new players to enter the area. Louisville City Police, alerted by an anonymous 911 call from FBI Agent Carter Diaz's cellphone, found the man face down next to a duffel bag containing fifty thousand dollars, shot dead by a high-caliber rifle.

Janie Drummond, the *Cooper Courier* reporter who had instigated many of the events over the past few months, achieved one of her objectives. A portion of the money recovered from Shakopf and Welch found its way to funding construction of a new recovery, rehabilitation, and assimilation facility associated with the Walter County Hospital.

As Touch returned to the Tiger's Den for breakfast, Reva matched the smile on his face with one of her own. "The usual, Touch?"

Teaser chapters for the second book, *He Needs to Get Got*

***

CHAPTER 1

Red and blue lights strobed amid a bustle of activity as Walter County Sheriff Tanner "Touch" Thomas arrived at the accident scene. Even though he'd arrived at many similar scenes over the course of his forty-eight years, the dizzying effects of strobing lights always unsettled him. He gathered that was the point.

Sheriff Thomas knew what had happened before he arrived on the scene: Dixie Mafia goons had ambushed the US Marshal, Wayne Bogard, transporting Rafe Livingston. Livingston was a gun for hire on the mafia's payroll who had tried to assassinate Sheriff Thomas three months earlier as he and the FBI executed what likely was the largest drug bust in the history of Kentucky. The marshal had departed from Cooper, Kentucky, Thomas's hometown, bound for the FBI's regional office in Louisville about twenty minutes before being bushwhacked on the West Kentucky Parkway. Bogard suffered a broken collarbone, a gashed forehead, and some significant bumps and bruises. He'd be out of service for a few weeks but was none the worse for wear. Livingston, predictably, was nowhere to be found.

Whoever had executed Livingston's escape had at least a twenty-minute head start on Sheriff Thomas and his deputies. Given the degree of efficiency with which the Dixie Mafia, presumably, had executed Livingston's escape, Sheriff Thomas doubted much chance existed of recapturing the man. Not only could the culprits double back on the parkway and head west, but also they could continue east on the highway toward Elizabethtown or exit in only a mile onto State Highway 293 and take off to the north or south. This translated to an ever-widening search area of several hundred square miles that spanned five counties. Worse, the marshal never got a look at the car driven by whoever had freed Rafe Livingston.

After responding to a distress call from the marshal on the local law enforcement band, one of Thomas's deputies arrived first on the scene. An ambulance followed shortly thereafter with another deputy behind the ambulance by about ten minutes. Typically, Touch would have been sound asleep after midnight, when the incident took place, but the transport of Rafe Livingston proved personal for the sheriff. Knowing this, the Walter County Sheriff's Office night dispatcher phoned over to her Cooper City counterpart and had a city patrol stop by and rouse the sheriff from his bed.

Rafe Livingston had attempted to kill Sheriff Touch Thomas several weeks earlier at the direction of the Dixie Mafia. With the help of the US Attorney for the District of Kentucky and the FBI's Louisville regional office, Sheriff Thomas and his Cooper chief of police counterpart and friend, Chris Hauser, took down a drug-running operation, with almost twenty arrests spanning across West Kentucky and additional arrests in two surrounding states. The leader of that operation, Edmund Shakopf, had run it for over forty years. Shakopf, a Cooper native and one of the town's leading citizens, had operated a chain of gas stations and convenience stores. His stations had supported a bulk fuel transportation business that also covered as a drug conduit from the southern to the midwestern United States, from Atlanta and Memphis to Chicago and Detroit. His lifelong best friend, chief money launderer, and chairman of Walter County Bank, Jerry Welch, also ranked with Shakopf among Cooper's leading citizens.

The arrests of Shakopf and Welch, along with their sons Laceon and Will, respectively, and a nephew of Welch, understandably shocked the Cooper community. That shockwave had resonated relatively deeply and widely through the Dixie Mafia and its affiliated organizations as well. Shakopf's drug dealing predated the move of the Dixie Mafia into West Kentucky. As the drug trade evolved and the Dixie Mafia and Shakopf's operations butted against each other, the organizations recognized that the efficiencies offered by partnership outweighed the challenges presented by territory wars. In the early 1980s, the two groups had struck a deal that remained in place for the next forty years. The Dixie Mafia had supplied Shakopf's organization while Shakopf's long-haul fuel trucks moved mafia product from south to north.

The degree of institutional knowledge Shakopf gained over that period presented significant challenges to the ongoing viability of the Dixie Mafia. The ability of the mafia to continue skirting law enforcement after Touch and Hauser took down Shakopf's drug operation depended heavily on controlling the degree of information Edmund shared with the FBI and the US Attorney's office. At age eighty, Shakopf found himself in the twilight of life and caring little about himself. Rather, the man preferred to focus on immunity for his son and protection for his extended family in exchange for details on his drug-running operation and his partners, including the Dixie Mafia. To entice Sheriff Thomas into dealing with him, Shakopf also provided definitive information on a long-standing case that had plagued Walter County for decades: the shooting death of David Barnett. Barnett's father, Andrew Barnett, a well-known attorney across Kentucky, had been the best friend of Touch Thomas's father, Dean. Livingston had attempted to shoot Sheriff Thomas as he exited Andrew Barnett's house after sharing that David had died as the result of a terrible hunting accident at the hands of Laceon Shakopf and Will Welch over forty years ago.

Deploying Rafe Livingston to take out Walter County Sheriff Touch Thomas marked the Dixie Mafia's first move toward controlling the outpouring of incriminating data on its southeast US drug dealing and racketeering. Equally important, the detention of Rafe Livingston—entirely unforeseen on the part of Don Lipscomb, the head of the Dixie Mafia—exponentially complicated the Shakopf situation. While Shakopf retained a great deal of knowledge about the Dixie Mafia's drug dealing, Rafe Livingston had served as the Dixie Mafia's primary gun for hire over the past ten years or so. As such, Livingston could implicate Lipscomb and many of his lieutenants across the southeast for murder for hire, extortion, racketeering, blackmail, bribery, and a host of lesser offenses should he choose to do so.

In negotiating the deal to take out Sheriff Thomas, Livingston noted to Lipscomb that this operation likely would be his last, signaling a change in Livingston's mindset and potential complications for cleaning up the mess. The recovery of Rafe Livingston from his incarceration marked the first move in Lipscomb's efforts to clean up things. Thankfully, Livingston's military service and related awards offered the Dixie Mafia modest cover in procuring quality legal representation for the man without creating any discernible links between his attorney and the mafia. The circumstances under which Walter County sheriff's deputies apprehended Livingston, however, vastly confounded the situation: no logical explanation existed for Livingston, a Georgia resident, to be in a forested area opposite a well-known West Kentucky attorney's house with Walter County Sheriff Touch Thomas in the sights of his high-powered hunting rifle months outside of hunting season. Furthermore, Cooper chief of police Chris Hauser saw Rafe Livingston level his rifle at Sheriff Thomas, and he thwarted the assassination attempt with a vicious tackle that put Livingston in the hospital with broken ribs and a punctured lung.

Don Lipscomb had yet to figure out how best to control the fallout from the Shakopf situation. Likely, Shakopf had already spilled his guts to Shel Richardson, US Attorney for the District of Kentucky. Validating this conclusion, Cooper City Police released Laceon

Shakopf, Edmund Shakopf's son, shortly after the coordinated arrests of much of the family's dealer network. Laceon had assumed much of the day-to-day responsibility for the family's drug-running operations over the past few years. Of course, attorneys still needed to corroborate written statements with direct testimony in court, but the Shakopfs likely knew enough names, dates, places, and outcomes to connect much of the Dixie Mafia's organization to myriad illegal activities should they chose to do so. Thus, if the Shakopfs found themselves unable to testify, eventually the US Attorney's office would find someone willing to do so in exchange for immunity or a substantially reduced sentence. The fact that the feds chose not to commence arresting mafia associates by this point in the affair probably reflected the sheer magnitude of the case and not a lack of probable cause. In fact, when the mafia sprung Livingston, US Attorney Richardson was contemplating whether to start the arrest at the top, with Lipscomb, or at the bottom, with his grunts, to build the biggest and the best case.

The decision to extricate Livingston proved far easier than the Shakopf situation for Lipscomb, however. Livingston's directives from the Dixie Mafia often came straight from the top: Don Lipscomb himself. Cell phone records likely linked the two with the assassination attempt on Sheriff Thomas, among other notable politicians and business leaders across the southern United States. Despite his recent high-profile failure, history proved Livingston to be extremely adept at his job. As such, the man commanded a premium price that only the upper echelons of the Dixie Mafia could pay. Were Livingston to turn on Lipscomb, it offered prosecutors a direct line to the mafia leader and his closest associates.

Unlike his direct interactions with Rafe Livingston, Lipscomb always dealt with Edmund Shakopf at arm's length. The mafia boss employed at least one level, if not two or more, between himself and the Shakopfs. As such, Shakopf directly linking himself and his operations, or those of others, to Lipscomb would prove extremely difficult and maybe time-consuming, if not impossible. Hence Richardson's difficulties with where to commence his arrests.

Touch took a vacation after the whole Shakopf-Welch-Livingston ordeal—something he'd never done before. After polishing off a stellar military career relatively unscathed by the Iraqi Revolutionary Guard and the Taliban, the thought of being assassinated by another fellow serviceman, and basically in his backyard, weighed heavily on Sheriff Thomas. In addition, guilt related to some degree of failure plagued Touch because Shakopf and Welch had operated for decades unknown and unsuspected by not only Touch but also his father, who had served as Walter County sheriff for the entirety of Touch's childhood.

CHAPTER 2

The escape of Rafe Livingston flat-out pissed off Touch Thomas.

A pissed-off Touch Thomas proved to be a completely different person than Walter County Sheriff Touch Thomas. As Touch approached Wayne Bogard's wrecked black Tahoe, he could feel the hairs on the back of his neck and his forearms stand on end. The veins in Touch's neck pulsated. The sheriff removed his hat and rolled his neck. Then he shrugged his shoulders forward and flexed his biceps to the point of straining the hems of the sleeves of his Walter County Sheriff's Department polo shirt. He extended and contracted his fingers twice in and out of a fist. The last time anyone had gotten this far on the bad side of Touch Thomas was when Ricky Drummond, one of the Dixie Mafia's intimidators, had put his hands on Reva Dennis at the Tiger's Den café, Thomas favorite breakfast and lunch spot. Thankfully, Touch had managed to keep his cool, floor Drummond with a foot sweep, subdue him with a wrist lock, and drag him to his car by his hair—no blood and no mess.

Reva Dennis owned and operated the Tiger's Den, a breakfast and lunch spot in downtown Cooper adjacent to the sheriff's office. Reva had inherited the Tiger's Den from her father. Touch had known the woman all his life and retained a little more than a sweet spot for her. Pity the poor fool who raised a hand to Reva Dennis in Touch Thomas's presence, as Ricky Drummond had discovered.

Mike Menser, Sheriff Thomas's longest serving deputy, recognized Touch's body language as the sheriff approached. Menser had worked with Touch's father, Dean Thomas, in the sheriff's department as well. Both sheriffs shared the same traits when aggravated to an extreme. Having seen repeatedly what a pissed-off Sheriff Thomas was capable of doing, Menser shook his head and allowed a small, unseen smirk to appear on his lips. Menser silently said a short prayer for Rafe Livingston's soul because in Menser's experiences, it was now much closer to meeting its maker than it was an hour ago.

"Hey, Touch," Menser softly greeted the man. "Looks like Livingston may have gotten away free and clear. Thankfully, the marshal didn't get hurt too badly. It appears to be a very professional job: spikes dragged across the highway blew the front tires, with momentum carrying the car forward and blowing out the back tires as well. With the marshal losing control of his Tahoe, it careened to the south side of the highway and into the ditch. I'm guessing this was a prechosen position because the ditch to the side of the road's pretty deep and wide—no chance of the vehicle jumping it and continuing into the woods on the other side."

"Any sign of Livingston being injured?" Touch asked.

"Nope, no blood on the backseat at all. In fact, from the indentations in the back of the passenger side seat, I'm guessing Livingston more or less knew where the hijacking would occur. It looks like he managed to pull his knees up to his chest and brace himself for the impact. Worse yet, they had handcuff keys; the cuffs were left on the backseat."

"Shit. That means someone in the jail got word to him, and we missed it," Touch shared. "I was so busy patting myself on the back for all those drug busts and vacationing that I forgot to pay attention to this son of a bitch. I thought Shakopf held all the cards for pointing fingers at the Dixie Mafia, but they were more concerned about Rafe Livingston. Damnit!"

Touch Thomas had just cursed more in the last thirty seconds than Mike Menser had heard the man curse in the past thirty days. Touch was renowned for an unparalleled degree of self-control and discipline, so Deputy Menser confirmed for himself that Sheriff Thomas was indeed pissed off.

Recovering the situation, Touch continued. "I assume that the Kentucky State Police picked up the same call that we did? Any word on their deployments in the surrounding counties in search of Livingston and his accomplices?"

Donnie, the other Walter County deputy on the scene, joined the conversation. "No, sir, nothing out of KSP's camp since the call went out about forty minutes or so ago. Would you like me to get on the horn to them?"

"That'd be great, Donnie. I appreciate it," Touch replied.

Touch passed by the wrecked US Marshal's black Chevy Tahoe. It'd never see the road again: the driver's side wheel was flat on the ground underneath the front quarter panel, which now was about half the width it was an hour ago. All types of automotive fluids oozed onto the grass around the vehicle—radiator fluid, automatic transmission fluid, and brake fluid. Fortunately, there was no gasoline leak. It appeared that the momentum of the vehicle had ceased prior to collapsing the fuel system, leaving the gas line remaining intact. After rounding the rear driver's side quarter panel, which was undamaged, Touch approached the ambulance and the US Marshal laying on an inclined bed in its passenger hold.

"Marshal, I'm sorry this happened to you," Touch said by way of a greeting.

Still somewhat stunned, and apparently groggy from a probable concussion, the marshal replied, "Sheriff, I'm sorry I lost your guy. Going eighty, and by the time I saw the spikes across the highway, it was too late to do anything other than brace for impact. They must've been waiting off to the side of the westbound lanes of the highway. I can't remember seeing anything over there, though. Almost no traffic on the parkway this time of night."

Touch, fully recovering his wits, attempted to comfort Wayne Bogard. "Nothing you can do about spikes across the road at eighty miles an hour, Marshal. I'm just happy you're not any worse off than you appear to be. I'm guessing this was at least a two-car operation: a lookout at the sheriff's office to let another car on the parkway know what time you left town, and the escape vehicle. Possibly they even tailed you to gauge speed and act as backup in case the operation went sideways at some point. The odds were stacked against you."

With Wayne Bogard on his way to Walter County Hospital for further evaluation and overnight observation, Touch helped his deputies finish documenting and cleaning up the scene. As the flatbed tow truck with Bogard's damaged Tahoe on it pulled away, Touch and his deputies swept up the remaining debris, bagged it, and put it in the cargo area of one of the deputies' Tahoes.

Touch was the last to pull away from the scene, cross over to the westbound lanes of the West Kentucky Parkway, and head back toward Cooper For the first time in a couple of hours, he felt fatigued from his lack of sleep. Time quickly progressed to the wee hours of the morning with first daylight only a few hours away.

Despite his exhaustion, Touch developed a mental plan of attack. It had been years since he had planned and executed a seek-and-destroy mission. However, he ranked among the best the US military had ever produced at completing such assignments. The degree of training and talent required to fulfill the responsibilities of search and destroy never left some people, and Sheriff Touch Thomas was one of them. He'd had enough of Rafe Livingston and concluded that the man's escape provided sufficient motivation to see if he still had it. The man needed to get got.

"Take it easy," Touch Thomas counseled himself. "Fail to plan; plan to fail." He piloted his Tahoe back to his house. In his mind, self-discipline provided for most of the successes he had achieved in his life. Touch encountered few others through high school, college, and afterward who possessed his physical gifts, but he thought the discipline with which he applied those gifts defined what truly made him special. From a young age, Tanner Thomas understood that certain situations required selflessness for the team to advance. Rather than swing for the fences with a teammate on second and two outs in the seventh inning of a Little League game, Tanner Thomas inherently knew the best decision for the team was to choke up on the bat and slap a single to right field. Touch always favored wrestling, though, because it allowed him to be entirely focused on himself; he could let it all hang out. Even when he wrestled a heavier weight for the good of the team, Touch relished the opportunity to let himself go and see what he could achieve. The result proved to be the finest high school wrestler Kentucky had ever produced. Touch Thomas would go on to success on the national and international wrestling stages as well, competing for the US Military Academy. When he started talking to himself, though, he knew he was in jeopardy of losing discipline and, as a result, making mistakes.

Five minutes into his drive back toward Cooper from the accident site, Touch managed to calm himself. A psychologist he met with early in his US Army special operations training taught Touch a surefire method to recalibrate his mindset and center himself. Cease the desire to extrapolate a single incident into World War III. Maintain perspective. Accept what happened. Analyze the situation objectively. From that analysis, develop a step-by-step initial plan of action. Touch thought gathering background information on Rafe Livingston represented the proper first step.

CPSIA information can be obtained
at www.ICGtesting.com
Printed in the USA
BVHW041428250522
638039BV00001B/10